The
Money Tree

Helen Yeomans

GUARDS PUBLISHING

Published by Guards Publishing, an imprint of Yeomans Associates Ltd.
www.helenyeomans.com

This book is a work of fiction. Names, characters, places and incidents either are the product of the author's imagination or are used fictitiously. Any resemblance to actual persons living or dead, events or locales is entirely coincidental.

Febreze® is the registered trademark of Procter & Gamble.

Library and Archives Canada Cataloguing in Publication

Yeomans, Helen, 1949-, author
The money tree / by Helen Yeomans.

Issued in print and electronic formats.
ISBN 978-0-9693219-5-8 (pbk.).--ISBN 978-0-9693219-6-5 (epub)

I. Title.

PS8647.E65M65 2013   C813'.6   C2013-907661-1
**   C2013-907662-X**

Cover prepared by Pedernales Publishing, LLC

Printed in the United States of America

Table of Contents

Prologue

A few years from now

The money tree, *Juniperus lucre,* is a common sight in suburban gardens and hedges. It does not do well on roadsides or near airports, but in large landscaped areas—country gardens, urban parks and the like—it flourishes. Properly fertilized, the lush foliage is a pleasure to contemplate. The branched head makes the tree a natural candidate for decoration and on national holidays, money trees decked out as historical figures are a common sight.

Such practices are dangerous to the extent that they obscure the true nature of the species. But projects in various parts of the world, notably the Middle East and Asia, to grow and harvest a crop, are the object of serious international attention.

Acres of money trees can be found in Russia, China, Zimbabwe, Brazil and, most particularly, the United States. In North Dakota, a hundred-acre site is fenced and signposted: "In God we trust. In government, not so much." Visitors are encouraged to buy seedlings, and instructions for the care and feeding of this difficult, not to say temperamental, tree are available online.

It is hard to remember nowadays that the money tree might have remained forever a myth except for the skill and devotion of one man and his family. A chance meeting, a moment's curiosity, and the world was changed forever.

Chapter 1

Harvest Time

The present day

A tractor filled the entrance to the grove. Jane Frisby sat on the swiveled tractor seat, with the winch lever on one side and a megaphone on the other. She was motionless except for one finger, which tapped against the underside of the seat. She stared unseeing at the grove of trees, listening intently, a woman in her late thirties, of classic beauty with a brisk self-deprecating manner.

Music—"The Twelve Days of Christmas"— played softly in the September sun and small waves lapped against the pebble shore of the nearby cove. She ignored these sounds, waiting for another: the sound of a car.

The grove contained twenty evergreen trees planted in a circle. They were eight feet high with blue-green branches trained inward, and scale-like leaves, springy and profuse. The branches were bowed low with the weight of the woody berries, shaped like Brazil nuts, clustered along them. At the apex of each tree, two small semicircular branches formed an oval head.

A circular tarpaulin covered the ground inside the grove. George Frisby walked around the perimeter, stooping to check that the tarp was snug against the trunk of each tree. He finished up in the gap. "Nearly ready," he said. In his early forties, the horticulturalist had a bony, pleasant face and a high forehead.

Beyond the grove and the forest a car went by on the island road. Jane straightened as a girl ran up.

"All clear, Mum."

Highly intelligent, Daffy Frisby had hair the color of green grass, heavy eye makeup and a ring in one nostril. She had no tattoos because her parents refused to allow them until she could vote. Next year she would be nineteen and therefore able to vote, which she was beginning to care about, and wear tattoos, about which she was beginning to have mixed feelings.

Jane picked up the megaphone. They had only begun using it two years ago, and only after a good deal of discussion, but in the end, as is often the way, speed and efficiency won out over civility. "Ready, George?" She had an English accent and a pleasant voice.

"Do your stuff, love."

Daffy looked apprehensive as Jane addressed the trees. She spoke severely but did not raise the megaphone. "Now pay attention, you lot—"

The branches rustled and the trees' heads turned toward her.

"—because I don't want to have to say this twice." More rustling, and the plop-plop of a few nuts into the tarp. "I'm going to give you the word and when I do, I want you to," she raised the megaphone, "drop it!"

With a whoosh and a thump, the nuts dropped into the tarp. The branches rustled, rising, freed of their burden—all except for one tree. It remained laden.

"Oh Meshach," Daffy pleaded, "don't be like that."

"Meshach!"

The other trees sagged away from the sound as Meshach's nuts joined the rest. Jane lowered the megaphone.

"There now, you silly nits," she soothed, "that wasn't so bad, was it?"

The trees swayed toward her, besotted.

Jane toggled the winch switch, and the rope woven through the edges of the tarp slowly began to tighten. She climbed off the tractor and joined George and Daffy outside the grove, circling round the backs of the trees, looking for any loose nuts and tossing them into the tarp. They worked silently and quickly.

When the tarp had become a huge sack, Jane started the tractor and maneuvered through the orchard. George and Daffy followed, using rake and broomstick to help steer the sack in the right direction.

Emerging from the trees, the tractor picked up speed, the sack bouncing over the ground behind it. Now they were at their most vulnerable. As they approached the house, George and Daffy ran on ahead.

Small shrubs grew in a bed along the side of the house opposite the barn. George levered up a wooden divider set into the bed, which was actually one end of a shallow tray, three feet long. Daffy lifted the other end and they removed the shrubs, putting the tray out of the way of the tractor. They took out two more trays, and opened a trap door, revealing a wide hole into the basement. Jane brought the tractor alongside the house, stopping when the neck of the sack was abreast of the hole. They unhooked the tarp and loosened the neck while Jane backed and turned the tractor. She used the small front-end blade to push the sack over the hole and nuts poured into the opening and clattered onto the concrete basement floor, shedding a summer's accumulation of dust. It whooshed up through the opening and the Frisbys stood well back.

Once the shrubs had been replaced and everything made tidy, George and Daffy hopped on the back of the tractor and set off for the south orchard.

* * *

From the eastern point of the cove, Mike Frisby watched the rest of the family and listened for cars. The minutes ticked by. A small, thin boy of twelve with a watchful manner, he stood with Angus, a white and brown terrier, at the end of the road that ran the length of the island. Behind him to the north, other islands dotted the Strait of Juan de Fuca. To the west loomed Vancouver Island.

The whole farm was laid out before him: the cove with its stony shore and the runabout tied up at the wooden wharf; the grassy field sloping up to the apple orchard, and then more field bounded by woods. The house and barn lay on a ridge with an oak tree beyond, in the south field. There the land sloped down again, field giving way to orchards and finally forest.

At last he saw them hooking the tarp up to the tractor. They'd replaced the shrub bed next to the house, and Dad and Daffy climbed on the back. The tractor set off for the south grove and he let out his pent up breath and walked back to the fruit stand. The road curved away from the south grove, following the island's contours, and visitors were a lesser threat.

The island road ended in a concrete barrier and had been widened to allow vehicles to turn. The fruit stand was nestled in the trees near the point, and opposite, though it was only noticeable if you knew what to look for, the cliff split again, forming a second cove, albeit a very narrow one. Its entrance, silted over at low tide, was largely concealed by a fold of the cliff. There the Frisbys moored their yacht. In a way, Mike thought, it was like having a two-car garage.

He studied the counter with a critical eye: apples were piled in a woven basket lined with a cheerful red-checked cloth; two more apples were loose on the counter next to the basket, with a scale and a sign in an immature hand: $2.50/lb., and a small plate covered with plastic wrap, with slices of apple which, he noted, were beginning to discolor. Apples were little use to anyone. They cost too much to grow and you couldn't get anything for them. However, they had their place in the scheme of things. Next to the apple slices was another basket, this one holding large cookies. Each was individually wrapped and had a big purple and pink label shaped like a blackberry with white space for writing in the middle: Oatmeal raisin $2.50.

He heard a car in the distance and came to a decision. The apple slices went out the back of the fruit stand, where Angus made quick work of them. He sliced up another apple, as the tourists pulled up at the concrete barrier. They studied the view for several minutes, comparing the islands they could see with those on their map. Eventually they turned and approached the stand. Mike produced his best waifish smile.

"How you doin', son?" The male tourist was heavy and old.

"Ooh, what a sweet dog!" The female tourist bent down to pat Angus, who was falling all over himself to be friendly. "What is he, honey?"

"He's a guard dog."

The man guffawed, then noticed the price of the apples. "Say, that's a helluva a price, kid. They're a buck fifty down the road."

"Ours are better. Ours are organic."

"Oh, Stan, never mind." The female tourist beamed at him. "We'll take a pound. Two pounds." She looked along the counter. "And two cookies."

Michael weighed out two pounds, bagged them and handed them to the female tourist with the two cookies and a big smile. "Thank you, ma'am. Have a nice day."

The male tourist handed over a ten-dollar bill. "How about the exchange rate?"

"Oh, we're happy to take US dollars at par," said Mike naïvely.

Leaving a smile and a scowl, the tourists returned to their car and drove off. He leaned on the counter and watched as it disappeared round the bend. "A couple more soakees bite the dust," he said with satisfaction.

The small sign his mother had made was lying on the floor. "Galas $1.50/lb." He picked it up and put it tidily on the shelf beneath the counter.

The sound of the car was overlaid by the sound of the tractor. A few minutes more, a few minutes to dump the second load of nuts and they'd be safe again.

*   *   *

It was a painting of hills and sky, with cattle clustered in the foreground and an old oak tree, some tufted grasses on the left, a stone cottage in the distance. Jane found it restful and nostalgic; it reminded her of Northumberland, where she'd been born. She gazed at it a few moments longer, then wandered through the gallery looking at the other offerings. It was a showing of minor nineteenth-century English artists, what Antiques Roadshow would call second division. Jane didn't care. She wanted a painting for their bedroom, and she returned to the cattle picture after looking at everything else, and debated whether to buy it. As though he had read her mind, the gallery owner materialized at her elbow.

"Appealing, isn't it?" he murmured.

Jane smiled. "I like it. I honestly don't know a thing about paintings but I expect you hear that all the time."

The owner made pleasantly indeterminate sounds. The visitor was casually but expensively dressed. A serious prospect.

Jane made up her mind. "I'll take it."

He unhooked the painting and they walked to the desk at the front of the gallery while he complimented her on her choice.

The Frisbys always took a week's holiday in Vancouver after the harvest. They moored in False Creek and left Angus to guard the boat while they stayed at the Granville Island hotel. This past week they had toured Science World and the Maritime Museum; Jane had shopped and George visited the botanical gardens at the university. Daffy and

Mike had spent a whole day at a vampires, werewolves and zombies film festival, and they had all gone to ball games and eaten their fill of exotic and junk foods. Tomorrow they would head home.

The gallery owner gave her the total, and Jane opened her shoulder bag, took out her wallet, pulled out the bills and counted mentally as she laid them one by one on the desk. She hesitated at the ninth, her mind shouting an alarm. What was wrong with that eighth bill? *What?* Serial number? She hesitated a moment longer, thinking quickly, then lifted her head and smiled at the gallery owner. He smiled back. Hard not to.

"You know, I've just remembered we were going to the races later today. I'll pay by credit card." She returned the bills to her wallet and took out her credit card. A few minutes later, she emerged from the gallery with a shopping bag in one hand and her wallet safely back in the depths of her shoulder bag.

She felt exposed, as though she were standing in a spotlight. She stared at the sidewalk, composing herself, then summoned a pleasant expression and walked the few blocks to Solly's on West Seventh, where she had agreed to meet the others. She paid for a cup of coffee from the girl at the counter and took it over to join them at a table near the window. George and Daffy were studying a banknote on the table between them, a thousand-dollar bill, Jane noted as she sat down. Michael was working his way through an enormous cinnamon bun.

"Hello, love," said George.

Daffy looked at her mother. "What's wrong, Mum?"

"Nothing, darling." Jane smiled brightly and then dropped the pretense. "We're not using any more of our bills until I've checked them."

She took out her wallet, riffled through the bills, pulled out a hundred and placed it on the table.

"What's wrong with it?" Mike licked his fingers and leaned over.

"The serial number's different on the right." Daffy pored over the bill.

"I nearly gave it to him," Jane shook her head. "He must think I'm mad. I had to tell him we were going to the races."

George appraised the bill with a scientist's eye. Spoilage of one sort or another was an ongoing issue.

"That's the first time ever," said Mike.

"Mm." Jane was noncommittal. It was the first they knew of.

"You can see what it is, Dad," Daffy pointed to the serial number on the left. "It's not so much that the number is different, it just isn't fully developed on the right. See? 'B' on the left is 'P' on the right. The bottom part failed to form." They scrutinized the bill, looking for other anomalies.

Jane rummaged in her shoulder bag and produced a lighter. George glanced up.

"Do it outside, Jane. Don't call attention."

Jane stared at the lighter, wondering what she'd been thinking, then glanced around. No one was paying any attention.

"No harm done," George spoke soothingly. "We'll just have to be more careful, that's all."

"If the Feds found out they'd burn the house down and us too, probably." Daffy spoke matter-of-factly.

"Don't be extravagant, Daffy." Jane glanced at Mike as she sipped her tea. "They couldn't possibly do anything of the sort."

George looked quizzically at his daughter. "What happened to 'Be nice to the government, they're doing the best they can'?"

Jane laughed shortly. "That was three years ago, George. You don't listen."

An awkward silence fell, in which Jane continued to sip her tea while Daffy looked defiant. George searched his mind. Keeping up with Daffy took some doing. She'd been distressed over the financial meltdown a few years ago, he remembered that, and the unemployment rate. Ah yes, greedy bankers. And government officials. Oh lord, he remembered: terrorism. He glanced at his daughter thinking there'd be hell to pay when she turned nineteen, then met his wife's gaze. Jane raised an eyebrow.

"I remember," he replied, then changed the subject: "I don't care, love, you know that. Do you want to burn the nuts?"

Daffy giggled at Mike's expression and George ruffled his hair. "Sorry, son." He looked at Jane. "What do you think?"

Jane sighed. "We'll chalk it up to carelessness."

"Right!" George pulled out his wallet and picked up the thousand. "Shall we go to the races?"

Jane glanced at the thousand. "We're not having that conversation, George."

"I didn't say anything." He put the bill away.

"You were going to. Only drug dealers use thousands. We're not growing them."

She bought a dozen bagels at the counter, and they strolled back to False Creek in the warm sun, stowed their belongings, had lunch at the Granville Island market and went to the races. If the day was marred slightly for Jane, she made sure the others weren't aware of it. The following day, however, having slept on it, she issued a recall of all homegrown bills.

They had left False Creek early, sailing under the bridges into English Bay, watchful of the smaller boats and kayakers. The *Calypso Sue* was a cutter-rigged bluewater yacht. They passed the tankers anchored in the bay, where they put the sails up and continued under power due west until the Point Grey bell buoy was behind them. Out in the Strait of Georgia they cut the engine and sailed southwesterly on jib and mainsail. Mike and Angus sat forward of the mast on the cabin roof in their neon yellow life jackets. Jane had the wheel while George checked the tide and current tables for Active Pass, and Daffy read a book.

While they were eating lunch, with Mike at the wheel, Jane asked for all their banknotes.

"Growing money is one thing. Putting flawed bills into circulation amounts to counterfeiting. At least, that's how I see it."

George and Daffy were silent, digesting this, as she went on: "I want all the banknotes you have on you. That includes you, Michael," she called up through the cabin door.

"She's right, Dad." Daffy reached for her purse and pulled out her wallet. George did the same.

"I can't tell if this is ours or not."

"Give it to me anyway. Daffy? Any bills?"

"We can check them now, Jane."

Jane shook her head. "I'm going to 'scope them. Michael, stop messing and fiddling." She held out her hand and received two twenties.

"Is that necessary?"

"I don't know, George, but I'll feel better. Now you can both go on deck, if you don't mind. I'm going to search the boat."

The afternoon wore on in sun and silence. George and Mike played chess while Daffy took a turn at the wheel. The ferry crossed their path doing a comfortable fifteen knots en route to the mainland, with more than four hundred cars and two thousand bodies on board, and as they neared Active Pass, a powerboat approached and roared by, speeding toward Vancouver. Racing alongside it was a group of Dall's porpoises, baby orca look-alikes with their black and white markings. The sound receded, leaving only the ripple of water under the bow.

*   *   *

Jane finished arranging the first vase and turned to the second. She had a selection of dahlias cut from the garden and fern from the side of the road, and she stood in the dusky quiet of St Anselm's, the small stone Anglican church at the foot of the island, arranging the altar flowers for the Sunday service.

St Anselm's was a hundred and twenty-five years old, nothing by English standards but a good age for the west coast. Jane was not especially religious: she believed in God and right and wrong, and in George. But she had been born into privilege and community service was ingrained in her. She belonged to several nonprofits in Sidney, on the Big Island, where she had a small catering business. She was also a member of the Women's Auxiliary at St Kits, which maintained St Anselm's. In that way, she was able to volunteer to do the altar flowers, which helped to ease her conscience.

She finished the second vase and put one each at opposite sides of the altar. Then she used the remaining flowers for a third vase, which she put on the table at the church entrance.

She came out of the church through the small annex that doubled as a community center, and walked round to her car. The church stood on a knoll overlooking the harbor, the eastern arm of which was formed by the Rock, a half-mile-long appendage separated from the main island by a narrow channel. At low tide, islanders would take the path running down to the channel and wade across to the Rock for picnics or to fish off the southeastern shore.

A power boat rounded the southwestern point and with engine rumbling moved slowly into the harbor, and overhead a few seagulls wheeled and cried in the afternoon sun. Jane smiled for no particular reason, enjoying the sparkle of sun on water, reluctant to move.

Houses dotted the forested slope on the western arm of the harbor, where nearly half of the three hundred residents lived. Larger properties of five acres or more ran back from the shoreline up the west and east coasts. The Frisbys had the only dwelling at the north end.

Jane heard the whine of an electric scooter. Mrs. Bagnold was coming to visit her late husband. Doris Bagnold was ninety-one and lived next to the path leading to the Rock. Her house was small, old and picturesque, painted a vivid azure, with a dense garden all round. She was the island's oldest resident and most days, she drove along the road on her scooter to the graveyard at St Anselm's.

Ledyard Island had been named for a seaman on one of the exploration vessels that charted the coastline in the eighteen hundreds. When, a few years ago, a sacred burial ground was discovered to have existed next to the church graveyard, the island was renamed a long and unmemorable Salish name roughly meaning "Place of the Early Ones." Reaction was mostly unfavorable, but since the change was manifested only on the ferry schedule, most islanders ignored it. Following the renaming, a sign appeared on the graveyard gate stating that visits were by appointment only, and must be outside the hours of eleven and three p.m., when the spirits slept. "How do they know that?" asked Mike, but Jane had no idea. Mrs. Bagnold was one of those who liked the change in schedule: it gave shape and structure to her day. But she drew the line at making an appointment. "Tommy never kept an appointment in his life," she said. So she came along whenever she pleased (outside the hours of eleven till three) and now Jane waved to the old lady, sitting upright on her scooter, driving into the graveyard.

About to open the car door, Jane heard her name and turned. Her heart sank. Coming up the steps from the wharf, Ariadne Wu waved and hastened past the marine supply store toward her.

"I thought I would catch you," she said as she drew near. "Helga Johnston said you arrange flowers or something at the church. Are you religious? I didn't know."

Jane resolved to have a word with Helga and said nothing. Ariadne Wu was the most tactless individual she had ever met, a curious trait in a realtor. She had nevertheless been fabulously successful over the past thirty years in

Vancouver's property market boom. Now in her mid-fifties, she had bought a seaplane and a substantial property on the west side of the island, and she commuted to her Vancouver office.

"People say you are very good at organizing and you work on many committees." Ariadne smiled encouragingly.

Jane knew what was coming. "Far too many," she said. "I really don't spend enough time with my family."

Ariadne waved this away. "One more or less, what difference does it make?" Her eyes were fixed on Jane's face. "You should join the Channel Dredging committee. Mr. Dhasi and I could use your help."

If the channel between the island and the Rock had not been dredged once a year it would have filled in completely. This suited Ariadne and Mr. Dhasi, who had a substantial mixed farming operation and sold most of his produce on the Big Island. They wanted approval for a hundred-unit condo development on the southwest side of the Rock. Other islanders were averse to any more development, and the Channel Dredging committee was the field on which the warring factions met. Jane, who had an open mind on the subject, would have given a lot to join.

"I'm awfully sorry," she summoned a smile, "but I really haven't the time and I know nothing about dredging."

Ariadne laughed. "You wouldn't have to if we succeed." She held out a card and Jane took it reflexively. "Think it over, and give me a call if you change your mind." She began to turn, then paused. "Let me know if you ever decide to sell. I could get you a very good price for your place."

"Would you put a condo development on that, too?"

Ariadne shrugged. "You have to follow the market. People can't afford to buy here otherwise."

She gazed past Jane out to the harbor and the Rock. "The aquifer would support it, you know. With the additional contributions, we could increase the number of ferry sailings." She looked at Jane. "You could cater to some of those people without having to go to the Big Island, just like Mr. Dhasi. He wants a bigger local market for his produce." She paused, then added, "It all makes good sense."

Jane was beginning to agree with her. Then Ariadne ruined it.

"Of course, she would have to relocate." Her gaze had moved to the graveyard.

"Who?" Jane turned. Old Mrs. Bagnold was maneuvering her scooter round the graves, coming toward the entrance. "You're not serious."

Ariadne raised a calming hand. "She will be well taken care of. But the road down to the channel would have to be widened and it makes sense to remove her house. We would give her a choice of—"

"Please don't say any more." Jane paused to control her anger, and when she continued it was with a smile. "You must surely understand that she cannot be asked to move at her age. It might well kill her. She's lived in that house for, what—seventy years?"

Ariadne's expression became opaque. She gazed out at the harbor as though debating whether to say more. Then she nodded, sketched a wave and left, retracing her steps past the marine supply store, heading back to her boat.

*   *   *

George felt the same as Jane about doing his bit for the community. "I've joined the Solid Waste committee," he had announced one day a few months after their arrival.

"Well, you'll just have to unjoin it," said Jane briskly. Ledyard Island had few public facilities: the islanders had to pay for everything out of their own pockets, and no one wanted needless expense. The church annex was the only public place available to hold meetings, and since it was drafty and uncomfortable, most committees met in members' homes instead. Jane was quite sure any meeting George held would be a sociable affair, with beer and wanderings around the house and property, and awkward questions: "Say, George, that's a weird-looking tree. Are those Brazil nuts?"

The discussion had gone back and forth. "It's not just you," she had said at one point, "I'd like to help out, too." Since most residents wanted only to be left alone, volunteers for committee work were always welcome. The price of real estate had prevented more young families from moving to the island, so the population was gradually aging.

About five years ago, George had brought the subject up again. "They're calling for firefighters, Jane. I want to join and I've thought of a way we can get more involved all round." Frequently abstracted, he was vigorous and enthusiastic, and his family viewed him with something close to suspicion. They were sitting in the TV room at the time.

"Oh?" said Jane.

"We'll give everyone trees." He leaned forward. "I've worked out the nutrient cycle, and we're getting good harvests now. It should be fairly easy to show people how to care for them."

"Dad!" Daffy shook her head decisively. "You can't give away trees. It would lead to hyperinflation."

"What? What do you mean?"

Daffy had been sprawled in the small armchair and now she straightened up. "Get this," she made sure they were all listening. "In Germany in 1923 they needed wheelbarrows of money to buy anything. Wheelbarrows!" Daffy had run out of fiction and was reading history, and the story of the German hyperinflation following the First World War had both shocked and enthralled her. She screwed her face up, working through the implications. "Dad, if everyone had a money tree, so much money would flood the market that the dollar would become worthless."

She looked down at seven-year-old Mike, lying on his back on the floor. "Know how much an egg cost back then, Mikey? Just one single egg?"

He sat up and shook his head.

"Twenty-three billion marks." She spoke slowly and impressively, then added, "That was their money, marks."

George and Jane looked uncertainly at each other. Neither knew what to say.

"Money's interesting isn't it? I mean, everyone wants some, don't they? I'm going to read up on it, Dad, and if there's a way we can let people have trees, I'll find it."

The following day, Mike had expressed an interest in raising chickens.

*   *   *

George entered through the side door, next to the moveable shrubs, switched off the yard light and tapped the barometer as he did every night. Angus watched from his wicker basket, then lay down again as George went along to the den.

The north-facing front door of the house was seldom used, but it opened onto a wide foyer with a staircase up to the bedrooms. The living room and den lay left and right respectively.

Jane was bent over a stereoscopic microscope, her head framed in the light from her desk lamp.

The den held a battered sofa and armchair and two large, old-fashioned oak desks facing each other. They liked to sit there in the evenings, George doing his research, Jane paying the bills or reading committee-meeting minutes, or planning meals or agendas. There was a bookcase against the wall on George's side. On the wall behind Jane's desk was a framed map showing the Gulf Islands and the mainland: British Columbia and Alberta, Washington and Idaho.

George sat down opposite her at his own desk and opened a drawer, taking out a blue three-ringed binder. Like Jane, he had a laptop, but he used it mainly for research. He liked his binder for daily entries but after Jane impressed on him the need for discretion, it became a rather mundane record of daily temperature and weather readings. He kept important information in his head.

"Your halos are beautiful, darling. Yves would approve." She turned the bill and bent to view the reverse side.

"Mm?" George flipped the binder open to the journal section, noted the date and time and jotted his daily entry. Then he closed the book and leaned back, gazing at his wife. Earlier, a hundred-thousand dollars worth of twenties and hundreds had formed a six-inch stack next to her right hand. Now virtually all of them were stacked on her left.

"Find many duds?"

She finished scrutinizing a bill and leaned back in turn, stretching and yawning. "Not really." She glanced in the wastepaper basket. "Two, I think. And I'm probably being silly." She reached for another bill and bent over the twin eyepieces again.

Mike came in, wearing pajamas. "Can I have my money?"

Jane did not look up. "Where are your slippers?"

He came up to the desk as George pulled out his wallet and handed him a fifty. "That cover it?"

He took the bill with a grin. "Thanks, Dad." He peered in the wastepaper basket and stooped down, reaching for one of the rejected bills.

"Leave those alone, Michael."

"Daffy got you worried, son?"

"Michael!" Jane straightened up and glared at him.

"There's nothing wrong with them, for crying out loud!"

"Obviously there must be or I wouldn't throw them out."

He gave her a disillusioned look. "Give 'em to the food bank, they won't care. They're just a bunch of soakees."

"I've told you before not to use that expression. Now, go back to bed. Go on."

Michael straightened and George reached for him.

"Why are they soakees, Mike? Because they got soaked?"

He nodded.

"Listen, Mikey. Maybe they didn't. What if they just got sick or something?"

"Then they should stay home and not spread it around."

Jane snorted. "Save your breath, George." She leaned back, eyeing her son. "Has Daffy said anything more about becoming a terrorist?"

"No." His parents seemed to want more, so he added, "She's okay. She's just bent."

"Daffy's hormones may be out of whack," said Jane, "but her heart's in the right place. Which is more than I can say for some people."

She looked pointedly at Mike and bent again over the microscope. George hugged him. "Don't think it's hormones; it's the Internet." He gave him a swat on the rump. "Hop it."

Mike made his way upstairs to bed, the fifty tucked in the breast pocket of his pajamas, warming his heart. He climbed into bed thinking about tomorrow with a sense of pleasurable anticipation. Tomorrow he would pick up Mr. Lee's bottles. And the next day and the next. It was ninety days tomorrow, which meant (probably) ninety bottles. Twenty cents each, that meant . . . he turned on his side. Five bottles per Safeway bag, two bags per load. Two dollars. All his, not like the apple money, which was family money. So ninety times twenty cents . . . a dollar eighty? That couldn't be right. . . . He fell asleep on the recalculation.

* * *

Daffy sat at her computer, alternately tweeting, posting and chatting. One wall of her room was covered from floor to ceiling with books, an eclectic mixture ranging from Adam Smith to Danielle Steele, heavy to free-market economists: von Hayek, Friedman, Rothbard.

Daffy read everything she could lay her hands on. She had been eight when the Frisbys moved to Canada and she was kept back a year, over her parents' strenuous objections, because of her birth month and the fact that they had arrived in April, before the completion of the school year. She was a bright child and would have sailed through school with ease, even if she had been put a grade ahead. As it was, she turned to books to offset boredom. Boxes and boxes of childhood favorites were stored in the barn, including all her Harry Potters, all her L.M. Montgomerys, Tolkiens, Twilights, assorted Collinses, and hundreds of others. George had warned her she would have to become more selective, but the advent of e-readers had diminished the pressure for wall space.

She made a homework suggestion to a Facebook schoolmate, then turned to read her Twitter feeds on the effects of a new banking regulation. Daffy did not yet feel she had the credentials to contribute to such discussions, but she learned enormously from following them. She had found two or three young economists online, people who had responded to her questions and seemed happy to answer her follow-ups. She was chatting with one this evening, discussing the potential for hyperinflation in the world.

She studied a response, thought for a minute then typed:

OK, but I thought the way the system worked, the multiplier effect would lead to a rapid inflation once people start borrowing again. No?

The answer came:

Yes. But when? Dud banks aren't allowed to die. They just go on existing like zombies, not lending. And people are afraid to borrow. Whole system is stagnant.

So...how do we get rid of this crappy money and get good money?

Bomb Washington? hahahaha.

She mulled this over while monitoring the action on Twitter.

Chapter 2

The Smell of Money

Jack Halloran, Deputy Director of the Secret Service, sat on the edge of a table looking at a wall map of the United States. Locations were flagged on it with colored pins. Most of the pins were red. Halloran was a big man with a square face and a sharp mind.

Agent Lyle Hicks, tall, thin, in his late-30s and divorced, pointed at an orange pin in Texas. "This one was a horse in a town called Muleshoe."

"I know Muleshoe," nodded Halloran.

Hicks edited out the comment about one-horse towns and went on. "A guy got off his horse outside the bar, took out his wallet and fanned the bills. You know, checking how much cash he had?" Halloran nodded again, and Hicks resumed, "The horse reached out and ate them. Two chews and a swallow." At the other's expression, he added, "That's what the guy said."

Agent Sam Gumble, shorter, older and of a morose disposition, pointed at a black pin in Wyoming. "Campsite in Yellowstone. This happened back in June. Woman came out of the RV, found a bear at the picnic table. Honey jar on the table and she's expecting the bear to go for it." He eyed Halloran gloomily. The Deputy Director nodded: get on with it. "So anyway, the bear swipes at the honey jar. Sends it flying. There's a twenty underneath it. The bear eats the twenty."

"What was the twenty there for?"

"Husband left it. For groceries."

The two agents waited while Halloran studied the map.

"Random incidents," he summarized.

"All twenties and hundreds, as far as we can determine," said Hicks.

"Mostly dogs," finished Gumble. Dogs were the red pins.

"What's that green one?"

"That's the parrot, sir. San Diego."

"And the blue one? Up there?"

"Lab in Boston."

"What kind of lab?"

"Pharmaceutical. A monkey in an SBP lab. Two technicians had a bet on the Red Sox. The loser goes to hand over a hundred and this monkey on the table grabbed it out of his hand and ate the whole thing. They tried to get a piece of it. No luck."

"Theories?"

Hicks opened his mouth, but Gumble beat him to it. "I got one. Suppose you got a McDonalds, a distribution center where they parcel up the hamburger and send it out to the restaurants."

"Is that how they do it?"

"I'm just saying, this could account for it. So they got the previous day's take sitting near all this hamburger—"

Hicks suppressed a laugh.

"—and somehow the two get mixed up. So you got all this money with the smell of hamburger all over it."

Hicks laughed. He couldn't help it. Even Halloran produced a grin.

"So this money covered in hamburger gets spread out over the entire country? Gumble, you've got a rich imagination."

Gumble shook his head. "No imagination, sir. I'm just trying to think how this could happen."

"Any other theories?" Halloran raised an eyebrow at Hicks.

"What if the ink at one of the presses was tainted?"

"Tainted? How?"

Hicks shook his head. "I don't know. But it's the only thing I can think of. Either one of our presses. Or some crook's."

Gumble said, "We only need a piece of a bill. That's all we need to figure this out."

"Right." Halloran stood up. "We could go on like this till the cows come home and we'd still be playing catch-up. Time you two started being proactive."

"How's that, sir?"

"We can't find the printing press without a forensic analysis. For that we need a bill." He headed for the door. "Take a hundred thousand in twenties and hundreds to the pound. If you don't get a reaction, take another hundred thou. And another. Don't come back till you find me a bill that drives mutts nuts."

Chapter 3

Dear Abby

Sipping her tea, Jane stood at the kitchen sink gazing out at the drizzle. She liked to come downstairs each morning in her dressing gown, boil the kettle, warm the little brown teapot, make her tea and drink it while staring out the window over the kitchen sink. This was her routine, while around her Mike made his lunch and at the kitchen table, Daffy ate porridge and read the *Wall Street Journal* on her tablet, and George looked through the mail.

At some point would come the daily turmoil of gathering books, grabbing coats and lunches, and saying goodbye (Daffy kissed both parents, while Mike hugged George, and waved to Jane), then the children were gone and silence descended.

At no time during these proceedings did Jane speak, unless it was absolutely necessary. She preferred to give the tea time to permeate every cell, preparing her body for the coming day. "It's like a solar panel," she said once, out loud.

George looked up, startled. "What is?"

She'd turned away from the sink and gone back upstairs to shower and dress.

"Tea," he heard as she went up the stairs. "It stays with you all day."

On the Monday following their holiday, she finished her porridge and opened the local paper, which she liked to read with her coffee. George was absorbed in the latest issue of the *BC Fruit Grower*.

She turned to Dear Abby, one of her staple sources of news, commentary and advice. The second letter she read in growing consternation. "I don't like the sound of this." She finished the letter. "This won't do at all. George?" She looked round the paper at him.

"I'm listening."

"Listen." She paused, reading the letter again.

"Yes, dear?"

"Sorry. 'Dear Abby. I was at mom's last week when she gave her parrot a hundred dollar bill as a treat. Can you believe that? She never gives us kids hundred dollar bills as treats. The parrot loved it but I say it's the last straw.' Signed, Camel in San Diego."

She lowered the paper and they stared at each other. "Fabric softener won't do, George," she said at last.

He sighed. "I'm working on it." He reached behind him for a hefty book on the sideboard: *The Science of Smell*.

Jane looked annoyed. "You always say that. I know the smell problem isn't sexy and exciting, like growing thousands, but it's got to be solved."

*   *   *

Daffy stood under the eaves near the school's main entrance, tweeting on her phone. She saw Terry with a group of girls, one of whom was making a play for him. Good!

"Want to buy another gun, Daphne?"

The speaker was behind her but she knew who it was. She turned and scowled at him because he made her nervous. Connor had been had up on assault charges, and breaking and entering, and he liked to taunt her on a regular basis. Two weeks ago, he had mocked her green hair: "You one of those stupid eco-terrorists, Daphne?" And he always made a meal of her name.

"No, Connor, I do not want another gun, thank you," she answered distinctly. This time, it seemed, he was actually serious.

"I got a Ruger semiautomatic for sale. Give you a good price."

"I don't want another gun. Ever." She'd said that before but he never listened.

He eyed her hair, now orange, then looked over at Terry with the group of girls. "Break up with your boyfriend?"

"He is *not* my boyfriend! He never was!" She scowled again and stalked off.

Boys! Honestly, they were more trouble than they were worth. She had got this phrase from Mum and it expressed her feelings about the opposite sex very well.

She briefly considered the gun. She'd bought it two years ago because her frustration and anger with the banking industry and the government over the whole housing market economic collapse had made her think the only way to get through to these people was violently. Sixteen had not been a great year for her, she thought now, looking back on it.

She joined a group of female classmates near the school doors. Daffy had no close friends at school. She was automatically linked with Amanda Knowles because they were both brains, though they had little in common. In any case, Daffy was so ready and willing to help others in the class with difficult homework, and to do so cheerfully and without making them feel like dummies, that she was accepted with fairly good grace by the other girls.

Now she listened to complaints about yesterday's history assignment, ready to comment if asked, or stay silent. Other people interested Daffy, and she liked listening to them.

*   *   *

Still preoccupied with the Dear Abby letter, Jane stood in the mudroom preparing Angus's lunch. She opened a cupboard and reached for a cornflakes box filled with dud banknotes. She took out a hundred with a hairless Ben Franklin, tore it into small bits and sprinkled them on the bowl of food, then took the bowl outside and watched as Angus attacked it.

Homegrown money was like candy to Angus. They had discovered this years ago when he pounced on a bill that fell out of George's pocket and consumed it at once. Nor was it only Angus. They discovered that birds found their money just as exciting, and so did squirrels. On their next big-city outing George spent a day in the library followed by a visit to a bookshop, where he had purchased several promising volumes, including *The Science of Smell*. He had not made any progress on the problem since then. Jane resolved to keep nagging until he did. There were nearly ten years' worth of Frisby dollars in circulation, and if they were showing up in Dear Abby it was high time George came to grips with the problem.

Leaving Angus to his lunch, Jane tidied her hair, put on her coat and some lipstick, then fetching her shoulder bag, she crossed the yard to the greenhouse. George was leaning on the counter engrossed in the *Smell* book.

"I'm off, darling. Back at five."

"Mm." Eyes on the book, he reached out an arm, waggling his fingers. Jane came over and he looked up. "When are you doing the groves?"

"Tomorrow?"

He nodded and indicated a pail of fertilizer on the floor near her feet. "Give them that as well, will you?"

"Right you are. Bye."

He kissed her then looked at her. "We'll sort this out, love. Don't worry."

She smiled and left.

Next week the two of them would take off for a week-long cruise, leaving the children on their own. They'd tried this last year, judging that Michael was old enough and he and Daffy could manage, and it had been a wonderful break all round. Now, Jane concentrated on the day and week ahead as she drove the five miles to the ferry. She had a meeting this afternoon, and three lunches later in the week, and had planned her menus by the time Doris Bagnold's azure house came into view, on the corner where the island road turned nearly a right-angle, heading for the ferry terminal.

Aside from St Anselm's, the only other public places on the island were the recycling gazebo, next to the church, and the rust-red marine supply store, which was privately owned but had a bank of mailboxes on one side where islanders often met.

Just past the store the road forked, the island road continuing on the right. Jane took the left branch, a steep ramp down to the dock, and parked behind another vehicle. *All very well to say don't worry* . . . she stared unseeing at the ferry as it approached the dock.

* * *

A flash of bright red caught Daffy's eye, from the wire mesh wastebasket near the gym door. She walked over to look at it. A one-kilo plastic bottle lay in the bin. It had a garish red and green label, "High Velocity Muscle Building Whey Protein Drink."

"That's perfect," breathed Daffy. She'd been trying to find a suitable container for fertilizer. Hoping no one was looking she reached down and retrieved the bottle, shoving it in her backpack.

* * *

"Say Daff! Wanna catch a buzz?" Terry Parker sprawled along a metal bench in the cabin of the small ferry. A large, lazy youth, he was with Daffy the oldest of the twenty-five or so island kids. The cabin had metal walls and rattled like a cake tin from the engine vibration. Traditionally, the older kids sat at one end, younger at the other.

"No," said Daffy. "You want to be careful, Terry, or your gramps could lose his green card."

"I don't use his stuff," said Terry.

"Oh right. And the police will believe that."

She rolled her eyes and continued chatting with her neighbor. Daffy had tried pot once, with Terry, with disastrous results. She was interested in trying it again some-time, but definitely not with Terry and not until she was older.

Terry was the youngest of three children of Vern and Marge Parker, who had a fifty-acre farm on the western side of the island. Vern had some sheep and a few cows, a horse or two and some chickens. Marge worked at a department store on the Big Island. Their older son was a lawyer in Victoria and their daughter attended university there. Ron Parker, Vern's father, had been injured in a logging accident as a youth and lived in a cabin on the farm. He had a long grey beard, colorful suspenders much admired by Mike, and a green card, which entitled him to own and use sixty-two pot plants for the pain in his injured shoulder. He favored Texada Timewarp and was a common sight weaving along the island road morning and afternoon on his bike. The kids called him Permastone.

Terry pulled a face at Daffy and his eye fell on Mike, seated halfway between the little kids and the big ones. "What're you looking at, maggot face?"

"Nothing," said Mike and looked away. He had no friends except for Daffy because secrets were tricky things, best handled alone. He was okay with that: he had big plans and they kept him company.

When the ferry arrived, Daffy found Terry next to her as they wheeled their bikes up the incline.

"Connor give you any trouble this morning?"

Daffy said nothing until they had reached the top. Then she wheeled over to the side and stopped near the marine supply store.

"What am I going to do with you, Terry?"

His face lightened and she added, "That was a *totally* rhetorical question, you—," she wanted to say "dumbass" but Terry had feelings like everyone else, even if he had been a complete jerk since last summer. Now at least he was just trying to be nice, instead of making everyone think she was his property or something.

Trying pot had been on Daffy's to-do list for a couple of years. Last year she had accepted Terry's invitation and they'd gone to the Parkers' barn to try it out. It was a proper barn, not like the Frisbys', with stalls for the cattle and a hayloft, and Terry and Daffy had gone up to the loft. Lying in the straw she had taken a pull at the joint and passed it back. She wondered when it would begin to take effect. Looking up at the rafters, she said, perhaps unadvisedly, "Remember years ago, when we played doctor?" They'd been nine, and Daffy remembered the feel of his skinny arm locked around her neck. They'd been in gales of laughter, vying with each other to see who could deliver the slobberiest kiss. After two or three drags on the joint, she focused on the roof beams, waiting for the effect to kick in and paying little attention when Terry began to kiss her, and when he suddenly said "Okay, Daff?" she hesitated, *what's the rush* floating lazily through her mind followed by *why not*, and that was that. "Did you say no, Daff?" Mum had asked that evening, and Daffy had looked down at the carpet, trying to think. "Well, I was busy," she had blurted, and burst into tears. Mum comforting her, rocked her gently. When she heard about the joint, she said only, "Oh Daffy. One thing at a time, darling," and asked if Terry had used a condom. Daffy didn't lie exactly, because he had, although she didn't think it had been on properly. But she didn't want his dead body washing up on the Big Island, which would certainly have happened if he had not used a condom. If Mum hadn't killed him, Marge Parker would have. Mrs. Parker was totally different from Mum, but she had very clear ideas on what boys could and could not do, having honed her skills on Terry's older brother.

After that episode last summer, Terry had gone around with an infuriating grin on his face every time they were together, as if he owned her.

Now she looked at him and decided she had to be blunt. "Look Terry, we don't have anything in common. Nothing. Do we?"

He looked away and after a moment said, "We like farming."

Omigod, thought Daffy. "I'm a reader, Terry. That's my favorite thing. You're never interested in talking about books. You don't ever crack a book if you can help it. And—and I want to do things in the world."

"You mean, be a terrorist? You're not really going to do that, are you?"

Daffy regretted ever telling him. "Maybe. I don't know exactly what I'm going to do, but something." She went on the offensive. "What do you want to do, Terry?" She only gave him a moment because she knew the answer. "You want to take over the farm. That's fine, there's nothing wrong with that. But it's not for me."

"But we've always been friends."

"I know. And maybe we can go on being friends. But that's all." She turned away, then faced him again. "You were talking to Kayla, I saw you. She thinks you're the hottest guy in school, you know."

"Oh yeah?"

"Yeah. She told me." She considered, then added, "You two would be a good couple."

* * *

In the dim light, Mike looked at the pile of two-liter plastic bottles thrown any which way in the corner of the garage. He had knocked at the kitchen door and Mr. Lee had confirmed that it was okay to take them. Mike felt it was prudent to check because it was three months since they'd spoken, so he might have forgotten his promise. But no, he had remembered, and Mike was now the authorized plastic-bottle remover for Ledyard's most famous resident. Morgan Fiami Lee was a well-known artist descended from a Samoan who had landed on the island nearly a hundred and fifty years ago. He lived on wooded acreage overlooking the Strait of Juan de Fuca, next to the Eastens, another old family.

Mike had first met the artist last May, when he was biking up the road. Just before the crest, where you could coast for a bit, he'd heard a voice behind him.

"Hey! You there!"

He'd turned to see that a car had nosed out of a driveway. The driver beckoned. Mike wheeled round and went back down, staying a circumspect distance away. The guy had a swarthy look and big teeth. He could be trafficking in body parts, or an alien ready to suck out Mike's brains through his eye sockets.

"What's your name?"

Mike told him, and the man held out a hand. "Morgan Lee."

Mike wheeled closer and gingerly shook the hand.

"Want to earn some money?" Correctly reading Mike's expression, the driver went on, "I've got a pile of plastic bottles in the garage. You take them, you can have the recycling fee. Interested?"

"Yeah!"

They'd agreed Mike would come by tomorrow after school, and Lee had driven off to the ferry, while Mike sped homeward, flying down the hill and wondering how many bottles and what size.

"Morgan Fiami Lee?" Jane smiled at dinner, and didn't for once remind him to mind his manners. But in the summer, one of the artist's seascapes appeared in the living room over the fireplace and the whole family had taken a look at it. "It's lovely to be able to buy beautiful things, isn't it?" said Jane. Mike sat quietly while everyone admired the painting, but later, he went up to his room and lay on the bed and tried not to think about how Mum wasted the family money.

Now, looking at the latest batch of revenue lying in the corner of the garage, he pulled out his plastic bags and got to work. Safeway was the only place that had free plastic bags and his pockets were stuffed with them. He shoved them neatly out of the way in a cardboard box, all except for four. These he filled, five bottles in each bag, and a short time later he pedaled up the sloping drive to the island road. He unhooked the bags from his handlebars and shoved them under a salmonberry bush. They should be okay there until tomorrow morning, at which time he would retrieve them and take them to the Safeway near the school, exchanging them for four dollars.

*   *   *

Pail of nutrients in hand, Jane walked down the field with Angus to the north grove. They swished through the long wet grass in the orchard, Angus sniffing at one or two rotten apples, and entered the grove through the gap.

"Hello, you lot. I've brought you a pick-me-up."

Her voice was soothing and produced nothing more than a gentle rustle from the trees. Angus trotted across the grove and burrowed through the far side, disappearing into the woods with a whine as he scented squirrel.

Jane did not share George and Daffy's fascination with the money trees. In fact, she viewed them with something akin to suspicion. No one knew why her voice had such a pronounced effect on them, nor its exact nature. "They aren't sentient, love," George had assured her. Jane wasn't sure what that meant, but the trees could write, effectively—at least, they could create complex serial numbers out of letters and numbers—so she preferred to err on the side of caution. She assigned them a university-level education and behaved accordingly.

Walking around the grove, she threw handfuls of nutrients at the base of each tree, addressing them with the utmost courtesy but strictly. "Now it's been a good year on the whole, but I'm going to leave you with one very simple thought and I want you to reflect on it over the winter." She paused for a moment, choosing her words, then went on: "The right-hand serial number is not an afterthought. It is not an afterthought. It should be laid down at the same time as the left, so that they can develop together." She arrived back at the gap and stopped, facing the trees. "Let me put it another way: whatever you choose for the left serial number must appear in the right as well."

Angus pushed back into the grove and joined her.

"Now. If I can understand that, you certainly can."

She turned and walked out. "Come on, Angus. South grove, then lunch."

The trees and layout were identical in the south grove, and she delivered the same message. They walked slowly back to the house in the drizzle. Jane could hear the drip-drop of rain on leaves. She loved the island when the weather was like this, the sky lower, everywhere a near-monochrome of color with shreds of mist that drifted like tattered cotton wool over the trees and the cove. Today, the weather bothered her because the dripping interfered with her hearing. The Dear Abby letter had left her feeling on-edge, as though invaders might be lurking all around the farm.

Back at the house, she prepared Angus's lunch in the usual way, then took the bowl outside and watched as he attacked it. Years ago she'd given some shredded money to the grey squirrel that lived in the Garry oak, but it ate some and hoarded the rest, and they'd found bits drifting around the field. George put them back in the little knothole but evidently they had lost their smell and their allure. They had faded to nondescript paper fragments and Jane had stopped feeding the squirrel after that.

She sat on the doorstep watching Angus finish up. She loved the terrier, but for the first time she wished he were something more substantial, like a Doberman.

Back into the mudroom she came to a decision, empty-ing the cornflakes box into the sink. She lit the bills and washed the ashes down the drain, then sprayed round the sink walls. She took the box outside and burnt it as well.

Then she fetched the step ladder from the barn and carried it up to the oak tree. If the squirrel had stolen from Angus's bowl, unlikely though that seemed, incriminating bits of money might be floating around the property in the wind, ready to be pounced on by some interfering official.

She climbed up and, ignoring the chattering of the squirrel at this outrageous invasion, she investigated the hollow behind the knothole.

*   *   *

"Afternoon, George." Cam Shockley was the owner of the marine supply store.

"Keeping busy, Cam?" George put a winch handle and a couple of cleats on the counter and took out his wallet.

"Always something," said Cam, taking the twenty. The store did steady business from boats cruising the Gulf Islands. He handed back George's change. "Tell Jane hi. Haven't seen her for a while." As well as boat fittings, the store also sold canned and household goods.

George nodded and took his brass fittings back to the runabout, moored at the foot of the wharf steps, stowing them in one of the lockers.

Preoccupied with the smell issue, he glanced back up at the recycling gazebo. No one was sitting in it, so he retraced his steps and strolled over, sitting on the bench at the far end from the recyclables. At this time of year, recycling leaned heavily to end-of-summer gear: runners and beach balls and children's clothing from the hundreds of tourists and summer visitors. The island held several bed and breakfasts in the season, plus an inn on the southeastern side.

George gazed out at the harbor, watching others at work on their boats, and thought about smell. Vern Parker found him there half an hour later.

"Hey, George!" He leaned on the railing. "How you doing?"

"Hi, Vern, it's been a while," said George and asked after Marge and Ron.

"Same as always." Vern took hold of the wooden railing and tried to shake it. "Pretty good, eh? Must be seven or eight years since we put this up."

"It's ten," said George. "We came here ten years ago last April, and it was in the summer of that year."

"No kidding."

No one knew who had originally bought the gazebo but it appeared one day in sections stacked next to the recycling lean-to. After a few days it disappeared but a week later it was back. Once again, after a brief rest, it disappeared, and when it reappeared two weeks later, Vern decided enough was enough. George and Jane saw him wrestling with a section when they caught the ferry, and he was still there when they returned, three hours later. So Jane drove home, leaving George to introduce himself and offer his help.

Vern wanted to move the sections out of the way so that he could pour a concrete floor and bolt the gazebo to it. "Don't want to see it walk off again," he explained. So they moved the pieces around to the back of the church, put them together and took the measurements. It was oblong, nearly twenty feet long and they gazed at it and wondered why it had been rejected.

"It's those wrought-iron spokes in the railing," said George. "They don't seem right, do they?"

"Plus the size. You could hold a convention in there."

The following day they moved the recycling lean-to, constructed the forms for the floor, added some rebar and poured the cement. A few days later they erected the gazebo, using rope ties to hold it down, then moved all the recyclables into it and dismantled the lean-to. In the fall, when the concrete had fully dried, they bolted the frame to the floor. Now, ten years later, its cedar shingles and walls had a weathered, permanent look and the structure had become in good weather as much a community center as the annex. By custom, recyclables occupied the west side, and the benches on the east side were available for socializing. Vern and George had formed a friendship on the strength of that one project.

They talked about the weather and the harvest, and Vern was about to ask George a question about his apples but he saw Doris Bagnold heading for the graveyard on her scooter and glanced at his watch. He had things to do, he told George, and left in his truck.

George returned to the subject of smell. He'd had an idea while Vern was chatting, and now he considered it carefully. Whether it would work or not remained to be seen, but he walked thoughtfully along the wharf to the runabout and chugged gently up the western shore to the cove, deep in thought.

*   *   *

Wearing a coat over her pajamas, Daffy knelt on the floor of the greenhouse and ladled 6-8-6 from a sack under the workbench into the muscle bottle. A flashlight on the floor gave enough light that she could see to work.

She shivered and hefted the container, then continued to fill it, using a tin cup kept in the sack. Fertilizer, she mused, could be used to make bombs. She didn't know offhand whether 6-8-6 would do the trick, or whether you'd want something more bloom-oriented, like 19-30-30. She made a mental note to research the subject. *I don't think I could make a bomb*, she thought, *no matter how angry I was.* But it would be interesting to find out how it was done. Everything interested Daffy, and she discussed most of what she learned with one or other parent. To assuage her mother's concerns over online privacy, Daffy used the Tor browser and was careful about what she said. But online or off, she watched and listened, and learned.

She felt inside the rim of the muscle bottle and discovered the fertilizer was nearly up to the top. The lid was on the workbench and she groped for it in the darkness and screwed it on. Switching off the flashlight and holding it and the muscle bottle, she got to her feet. The house remained dark and silent as she came out of the greenhouse, and she was tempted to take the bottle up to her bedroom. Instead, she made her way over the packed earth of the yard to the barn. It had a door in the wall facing the house and she had made sure it was unlocked earlier that evening.

She opened it and used the flashlight to pick her way over to the boxes of books against the back wall. She put the muscle bottle in a small garbage bag. If Mike noticed her putting it in her backpack tomorrow, he would assume it was just books.

She retraced her steps, closed the barn door quietly and ran lightly over the yard to the side door of the house and inside.

Angus sat up as she locked the door. "Good boy, Angus," she whispered and the terrier lay down again. She tiptoed away, planning as she crossed the hall and climbed the stairs. Stop off tomorrow afternoon after school, she decided, and congratulated herself on a practical job well done.

Chapter 4

Offspring

When the afternoon ferry pulled in, Mike pelted off along the island road while Daffy wheeled her bike over to the marine supply store for the mail, as she did every day after school. A week had passed since she had spoken to Terry, and he hadn't been on the same ferry since. He seemed to be spending plenty of time with Kayla, to Daffy's relief.

The mail arrived on the six-thirty ferry every morning. When they'd first come to Ledyard, George would drive down for it before breakfast. He tried to interest Jane in taking on this task but she just gave him a look. When Daffy was old enough to bike the five miles there and back, he persuaded her to pick up the mail. She did it once, then appealed to her mother.

"Don't worry about it, darling. Pick it up after school and put it under the fruit bowl. He can have it the following morning." Dad had never seemed to notice the difference.

She put the two flyers and catalogue in the basket of her bike and began the ride home. She was lucky in her parents, she knew. For one thing, she actually had two of them, not like a lot of kids. They could be unreasonable, as in the matter of getting a tattoo, but they also had their good points. Mum could do anything, and even Dad had his lucid moments and was always supportive.

"Hi, Mrs. Bagnold," she called as the old lady came buzzing by in her scooter. Then she reached the end of the harbor road and turned north. The road began to rise imperceptibly as it skirted the side of Signal Hill.

*   *   *

Two bikes rested side by side on the crest of the road where it ran flat for a short distance before plummeting downhill to the north end. Ron "Permastone" Parker wore brown workpants and a blue shirt with big, bold plaid suspenders. Mike had feasted his eyes on these as he came up the road.

"Hold on there, kid."

"Hiya, Mr. Parker."

Mike had pulled in next to him. They were about two hundred feet above sea level and through a gap in the trees they could see the seagulls, calling and wheeling over the water.

"You working for the Eastens?" asked the old man.

Mike said nothing, just stared out at the view. The Eastens had the property next to Morgan Lee's.

"Reason I asked is, saw you last week with a bunch of bottles." He paused, trying to remember. "Saw you twice, I think."

Adults, thought Mike. You couldn't get away from them. They were worse than CCTV.

"Figured it must be the Eastens because Morgan only drinks scotch." In the silence, he added, "I ought to know. We drank enough of it together."

He glanced at his companion. "You don't want to talk, huh?"

Mike turned and gave old Permastone a Mona Lisa smile: knows everything, says nothing.

"You okay?" The old man unwrapped a Caramilk bar and held out a piece. Mike hesitated and he laughed. "It's not a bribe, kid." So Mike took it, and they munched together, watching the seagulls. Mike liked watching Mr. Parker's beard bob up and down. Sometimes it was tucked into his pants, like today, sometimes not.

"I was a seagull once," said Ron, "least, I thought I was. Came down with a hell of a crash, though."

Mike glanced sideways at him. He never seemed very stoned; he just had a kind of glassy look about him.

Far down the road, Daffy came into view, laboring toward them.

"Got to go, Mr. Parker. Thanks for the chocolate."

He turned his bike and pedaled along the crest. Behind, he heard Daffy greet the old man as she went past. He usually beat her up the hill because he was lighter and wiry, but halfway down the hill, she swept past and swooped down ahead of him. They both coasted at the bottom, skidding on the gravel as they turned into the driveway and pelted along to the garage. They arrived in a dead heat. Daffy went into the house while Mike played in the orchard with Angus and the soccer ball. Normally, Dad would join them, but he was away this week with Mum.

Mike came in the house and investigated the contents of the fridge. He went to the foot of the stairs and bellowed up to Daffy: "I'm cooking liver and onions, okay?" He grinned to himself.

She came out of her bedroom. "You know I hate that. Haven't we got any casserole left?"

"Oh. Yeah." he said solemnly. In the last year, he had discovered the fun in pulling Daffy's leg. She always fell for it. Now she stared down at him.

"You could be disappeared, you know."

"Yeah, right." He turned away, and went along to the kitchen to heat up the casserole and cook himself some liver and onions.

* * *

Jane clambered up the steep slope, taking care not to slip on the pine needles underfoot. She came through the trees onto a rocky outcropping and sat down in the sun to catch her breath and enjoy the view. She was sitting on an island smaller than the Rock at home, an island too small to have a name. Facing south, she could see Hornby and Lasqueti islands in the distance.

She drank from the water bottle on her belt, and got to her feet. George was taking the clockwise route round this island and they planned to meet on the eastern side and return over the top to the cove where the *Calypso Sue* was anchored. She continued along the rocks until they gave way to salmonberry bushes and more pines, working her way carefully round to the eastern, more sheltered side.

Their holiday was nearly over. They had begun by calling in at Vancouver. They'd rented a car and dropped off four envelopes with twenty-five thousand dollars each to food banks and charities, after which they had made a few purchases and returned to their hotel. That evening they'd gone dancing.

George and Jane loved ballroom dancing: waltzes, Latin dances, jive and modern. Any kind of dancing they loved. And they liked to dress for it. George wore a black silk shirt and trousers, and Jane a full-skirted silk dress. That evening, they went out to dinner and on to their favorite dance club.

"That woman stepped on my foot three times," said George later, in bed in their hotel room.

"Let's hope she's married to the man who stepped on mine. They're made for each other."

"He was holding you in a most improper way. I was tempted to sock him."

"I'd like to have seen that."

"Do you mind if I kiss you there?"

Jane smiled in the darkness and George kissed her there again.

The following day they had sailed out of Vancouver to explore the northern Gulf Islands, fishing and whale-spotting along the way.

The pines and firs were mixed with deciduous trees, alder, arbutus and birch, and Jane had an easier time of it as she worked her way along the eastern slope. She stopped again for a drink and sat on a rock looking across at Texada Island with the mainland beyond it, enjoying the warmth of the afternoon sun. She roused herself after a few minutes and glanced around, preparing to move on, thinking George must be nearly at the halfway point—and did a double take. A few feet away stood a money tree.

She stared at it in annoyance. "Can't I get away from you lot?"

The blue-green branches twitched and something fell off. She reminded herself to moderate her voice, sighed and made her way over to the tree, crouching in front of it. About four feet tall, it was not nearly as lush as the trees at home. It had fewer branches and the leaves were sparse. Nevertheless, it was a money tree, with nuts clustered like juniper berries along the branches and one on the ground underneath. "There, there, little muggins," she said soothingly, and the branches rustled and lifted. Then she heard the scrape of cleats on rock. She eyed the tree and hardened her voice.

"Boo!"

The nuts dropped off.

"That you, love?"

"Over here," she called. "We've got company."

George came into the clearing, his face red from exertion. "Not one of my better ideas. It's an awful climb." He followed Jane's gaze and his eyes lit up. "Look at that."

He crouched down next to her, delight written all over his face, reached out and examined a branch. "Looks healthy, doesn't it?" He noticed the nuts on the ground and glanced at his wife. "Was that your doing?"

"I have the power," she said glumly.

"Cheer up, love. The trees'll still be listening to you long after the kids stop."

He took off his backpack and swigged some water. Then he picked up a nut and looked around for a rock. "How about putting those into the backpack."

Jane gathered up the nuts with a sigh. The content of their conversation would now be fixed for the remainder of the holiday. She heard George banging a rock as she picked the few nuts remaining on the tree. He came back and sat down next to her, carefully removing the shell from the cracked nut. Inside was a tightly wrapped kernel and he examined it closely, looking for an edge.

"Here, let me," said Jane, more practiced than he was at this part of the process. She gave the kernel a hard twist to loosen its folds, and managed to find an edge to unfurl. Patiently, she worked it loose. "It's much harder when they're damp, George."

"I can see. It isn't ready to be opened. I'm just curious."

Eventually, the kernel was revealed to be a one-dollar bill with a transparent plastic strip on the left, running through the coat of arms, and a portrait of the older Queen Elizabeth on the right. George pored over it. "Fascinating. Fascinating."

They scrutinized both sides carefully.

"It's absolutely perfect," said George.

*   *   *

Daffy and Mike were eating fish and chips in a Sidney café. Jane allowed them one night on the town while she was away and they'd made it tonight because the *Calypso Sue* would be back tomorrow. They'd gone to see the new slasher movie after school, and Mike was reliving it as he ate his dinner. Daffy hated slasher movies but she liked to be in the know, so she had spent most of the hour and forty minutes looking at the floor and clutching Mike's arm.

However, she had nailed the soundtrack, which would enable her to be an informed listener tomorrow.

The café had old-fashioned vinyl booths down one side, next to windows looking out at the harbor, and a counter with stools along the other. A couple of older men sat at the far end of the counter drinking coffee and chatting up the waitress.

"Remember when that spear thing came up through the floor? Ugh!" Mike wriggled and shifted uneasily. "That guy looked like a hotdog on a stick."

"Shut up, Mike."

Behind her brother, she could see the top of a head in the next booth. Mike suddenly drew up his legs and levered himself to his feet, standing on the seat.

"What if it came up right here!" Horror distorted his face, and relish.

A bellow from the waitress: "Get your feet off that seat!"

Mike dropped down, the head in the next booth turned sharply, and Daffy got to her feet and apologized to the waitress. She frowned at Mike. "Stay here and sit still."

Next door was a young Asian man of twenty or twenty-one. One leg was drawn up with a foot on the seat, his smart phone resting on his knee. As Daffy appeared, the leg quickly disappeared.

"I'm not the waitress," she assured him and he grinned. He had been texting with one hand, she saw, and eating poutine—fries, gravy and cheese curds—with the other. "I just was sorry if we disturbed you. My brother's being a twelve-year-old." She studied him. "Weren't you at that movie?"

"Yeah." Judging by his expression, he hadn't thought much of it.

Mike slid out of the booth and joined Daffy, studying the man. "You live on Ledyard, don't you?"

He nodded. "I'm building a house there."

He seemed ready to chat, so they brought their fish and chips over and sat opposite him. His name was Satoshi Yamata. He was American and his parents lived in Los Angeles. They discovered he was a cryptography geek. He had created a social media site, and had sold it recently for five hundred million. "That's not much compared to some of the others, but—"

"It's huge." Mike spoke involuntarily.

"Satoshi. . . ." Daffy was thoughtful while Mike worshipped from afar. She went on, "Satoshi, the man who created Bitcoin?"

Satoshi grinned, a little awkwardly. "No, but I wish I had. That's beautiful code. You're thinking of Satoshi Nakamoto." He made a face and added, "I didn't think anyone here would know about him. My name's really Ken."

Eyed disapprovingly by the waitress, Daffy and Mike chose desserts from the glass display case at the front of the café. When they returned to the booth, Satoshi/Ken wanted to know what Daffy did.

"I'm finishing up school," she said. "My parents want me to go to LSE to study economics, but. . . ." her voice trailed off.

He nodded understandingly. "School's a waste of time. You going to be an economist?"

"Probably. Money really interests me." She hesitated. "I don't see Bitcoin surviving long, do you? The government'll shut it down for sure if it gets too widespread."

Satoshi/Ken shook his head. "It'll grow too fast. Cryptography's the key to freedom."

They discussed Bitcoin over dessert. Daffy argued that it had no value and no tangible form and therefore could not strictly speaking be called a money. Satoshi/Ken disagreed. "You can make payments easily and anonymously anywhere in the world, with low or no transaction costs. There's the value." He eyed her. "I suppose you think money should be whatever the government says it is."

"Are you kidding?" Daffy stopped eating, put down her spoon and looked directly at him. "Money should be whatever people choose to use."

In that case, he said, an awful lot of people seemed to think Bitcoin was money.

The waitress moved along the row of booths, replenishing salt, pepper and sugar, and they became aware of how late it was. They biked back just in time to catch the last ferry. Daffy and Satoshi/Ken, who had by now told them to call him Ken, argued about Bitcoin all the way over to the island.

That night Daffy fell sick. Afterward, she wondered if it was some bug from the desserts in the display case, but at eleven-thirty she suddenly felt dizzy, then violently nauseous. She managed to reach the toilet in time to lose her dinner, then stayed there as wave after wave of nausea washed over her. Eventually she felt sufficiently recovered to make her way to bed, but barely managed to undress before the onset of another attack. An hour later she climbed into bed, with the bucket from under the sink handy on the floor beside her. She spent the night alternately dozing and vomiting until Mike's knocking woke her at seven-thirty.

He brought her a glass of water as she asked, and emptied the bucket with only a little complaint. "Maybe Ken slipped something into your Coke because you knew he was a phony." He frowned and decided as he went downstairs and off to school that Ken should be watched. Daffy turned on her side and fell asleep again.

She awoke alert in the middle of the afternoon. She felt much better but something had woken her and she sat up wondering what. Too early for Mike. The silence was broken by a man's voice and the hair on the back of her neck rose. It was not Dad's voice, she knew immediately.

Her skin felt clammy again, this time from fright. She threw off the bedclothes, grabbed her housecoat and put it on, then rummaged in the closet. In one corner of the top shelf, under a mound of sweaters, she withdrew an army revolver, vintage World War II.

Much practice had enabled her to chart all the squeaks on the landing and stairs, and now she crept silently downstairs, holding the gun in both hands as they did on TV. She could hear someone in the kitchen and outrage rushed through her body, driving out the fear. How dare anyone break into her home? She suddenly remembered the gun had a safety catch and she thought it was still on. She tried to decide whether to stop and find the safety now, or keep going and do it later, when she had him in her sights. Were you supposed to do that, she wondered? Line up the shot and then remove the safety? People on TV were so decisive—did these thoughts not occur to them?

She reached the main entrance hall floor and turned toward the kitchen. There were two ways in, one along the hall near Angus's basket, and the other straight ahead of her, bringing her in by the breakfast nook and near the TV room. She heard a familiar squeak: he was leaning on the counter, probably with his back to the TV room. That decided her and she moved cautiously straight ahead. Out of the corner of her eye she saw Angus sit up in his basket.

She reached the entrance. He was leaning on the counter, writing on the pad Mum used for making lists.

Daffy stood there indecisively, gun pointed at his back. He straightened up.

"Hold it!"

He whirled around, a pen in one hand.

"Put your hands up!"

"I'm so sorry. Please forgive me, I had no idea—"

"Put your hands in the air!"

His hands flew up, the pen dropping to the floor. They stared at each other.

"Look, please excuse me. My name's David Randall. I knew George Frisby—would he be your father?—years ago. I was just writing a note." He began to move, to reach for the pad.

"Don't you move! You broke in." She stopped and sighted along the barrel.

"Oh, Christ. I promise you I mean no harm." He became still.

Daffy frowned. He was tall, about six feet, with brown hair and regular features. He had on what Mike called tidy clothes: slacks, a shirt and a windbreaker.

"Look. How would it be if I wait in the car?"

She regarded him suspiciously. "Which ferry did you catch?"

"The twelve o'clock."

"What have you been doing since then?"

"I knocked and when no one answered I went along to the point out there? Near a wooden stand? I was hoping your dad would come back before the next ferry." He glanced at the wall clock. "Which I'd really like to catch."

Neither of them heard the side door open.

"Look—"

"Daff?" Mike came into the kitchen, Angus behind him, and took in the scene. The guy was a stranger, the second in two days. Daffy was a fright. She had on her ratty pink housecoat over an orange Lions football jersey. Her hair was red and all over the place and her face looked like liquorice allsorts where her eye makeup had spread.

"Is there a car out there?"

"Yeah." He dropped his backpack and reached for Jane's marble rolling pin, which sat in a wooden cradle next to the canister set.

"Look, as I said to—"

"Mike, see if you can read that note. He said he's a friend of Dad's."

"David Randall. I knew your father years ago, when you lived in England."

Keeping an eye on the intruder, Mike reached for the pad on the counter next to the fruit bowl. "Hello, George!" he read. "Remember me from the Amazon expedition? Sorry to miss you but I'll be at this number for a few—"

He relayed this to Daffy and added, "We can put him in the steam room." Randall began to protest.

"It's not for long," said Mike. "They'll be home soon." He badly wanted to bash the guy over the head but he'd have to stand on a chair to do it. He gestured with the rolling pin toward the entrance where Daffy stood. The decision had been taken out of her hands and the relief showed on her face. She began to back up into the entrance hall.

"You listen to me," said Mike. "If you try anything funny, I'll take out your kneecap." He brandished the rolling pin. "Count on it."

Randall walked reluctantly after Daffy. There was a door under the staircase and she threw it open, revealing stairs leading downward. Keeping both weapons on the intruder at all times, the short procession wended its way down the stairs, Mike resisting the urge to apply the rolling pin to a head that was temptingly accessible when he stood behind it on the stairs. Randall must have sensed that, because he made no further argument.

Once he was in the steam room and a chair had been jammed under the door handle, the two Frisbys returned to the main floor, where Mike lodged another chair under the basement door handle. Still carrying the gun, Daffy went upstairs without a word, and had a hot bath, then washed her hair. She appeared about an hour later looking normal, as Mike was pouring tea into a mug for the intruder. He placed the mug on a tray with milk, sugar and a plate of cookies, and Daffy realized she was starving and rummaged in the fridge for some cheese and a piece of bread. Then she retrieved the gun and followed Mike, who carried the tray downstairs. They gave the prisoner his tea and cookies without incident and returned to the main floor.

"You okay now, Daff?" She had been preoccupied ever since they'd disposed of the intruder.

"Yeah. Will you be okay?" She looked at him without really seeing him, and walked out of the house with the gun, down the field to the cove, where she climbed down into the runabout, took it out to the middle of the cove and stopped. Mike watched from a front window, as she drew up her legs and rested her chin on her knees. He turned away. She was thinking. Daffy did a lot of that.

*   *   *

Sitting on the washing machine, Mike faced a retractable folding wall of simulated wood paneling, a wall that divided the basement along its length. To his left were the stairs, to his right, two dryers and the steam room. Two paintings hung on the retractable wall. The one directly opposite him was of an eighteenth-century gentleman with a burgundy coat and big hair.

"Grampa was an earl, see? And granny got sick of only having girls so she took a hike after Mum was born."

"You mean she left? Permanently?" The voice came from inside the steam room, where the prisoner languished.

"Yeah. So Mum got through twelve nannies in ten years. You might be wondering why I'm telling you this."

"I don't mind. Passes the time."

"Because I'm against you. And Mum will be too. And we're tough sons of bitches, the both of us."

Message delivered.

"I remember. Frank Finlay to Roger Moore. *The Wild Geese*. Good movie, that."

Mike frowned. "Just so you know. We aren't like Dad."

"I think I met Lady Jane years ago. When they lived in Falmouth."

He transferred his gaze to the other picture on the retractable wall, the Mona Lisa.

If anyone had asked Michael to draw Almighty God, he would have used Mona as his model. He had discovered the print when he was seven, in a second-hand shop in Victoria, and had run in a panic to find his mother. "She knows everything, Mum! Look at her!" In a gusty whisper, cupping his hand around her ear, he'd added, "She knows where the nuts are." Jane had smiled and looked at the print and replied, "I believe you're right, darling. But I don't think she'd tell."

Mike wasn't so sure, so they had bought the painting and hung it downstairs, where the only person she could tell was the eighth Earl of Craggan, a gift from her grandfather to Daffy, who had expressed a liking for the painting.

Mona didn't worry him so much these days, and now he looked at her and tried to duplicate the smile. He picked up a small hand mirror taken from the upstairs bathroom. Old Permastone's reaction made him realize that inscrutable smiles were not easily accomplished, so now he practiced, comparing the results in the mirror with Mona's expression.

Several minutes of total silence elapsed, and then the prisoner spoke:

"Mind if I ask a question?"

"Go ahead."

"Are you growing money here?"

Mike jumped down off the washer and went upstairs.

*   *   *

George and Jane arrived shortly before six. "Mike? Where are you, Mike?"

Mike had been opening a can of pop and thinking about dinner. "Hi Dad, hi Mum."

"Darling! Thank goodness." Jane came in with armfuls of clothes. "Whose car is that?"

George came through from the mudroom. "What's Daffy doing in the cove?"

Mike had an audience and he made the most of it. "There's a guy in the steam room. He wants to know if we're growing money."

They stared, nonplussed.

"Is he with the government?" Jane had been expecting this day.

"He said he knows you, Dad. He broke in." Mike was matter of fact. "And Daffy held a gun on him."

"What?"

"So then I came home and found them and we put him in the steam room until you got here. I gave him a cup of tea, Mum. And Daffy got dressed and—"

"Dressed?" George and Jane exchanged frantic looks and separated. He headed for the basement while she ran out the side door and down the field. Mike investigated the mudroom. Good. Salmon for supper.

*   *   *

"My poor Daff!" Jane regarded her daughter with concern.

"It's okay, Mum. I'm feeling better." Daffy smiled reassuringly. "I think it may have been the dessert. It was in one of those glass display cases, you know? The ones you always say are unsanitary."

She fell silent and the boat rocked gently. The runabout had a wheel rather than a tiller, and they sat side by side in its padded seats. The gun was on the armrest between them.

One of Jane's guiding rules was "Don't say a word, just listen." She had been ready to abandon this rule when she climbed into the boat and saw the gun; nevertheless, she managed to refrain from comment. Daffy looked pale and drawn and it seemed safe to ask how she felt, and Jane heard how she'd been up all night and had stayed home from school.

Daffy broke the silence. "So anyway, when I heard someone downstairs, I was glad I had the gun and I thought it would be good practice to use it."

"Where did you get it?" The question came out of its own accord, and Jane heard all about Connor at school and what a creepy pest he was.

Daffy fell silent again, and rested her chin on her hands. "I've been thinking," she said at last. "People just don't understand, Mum. The government has this monopoly on money, and people don't even question it."

"No, darling." Jane wondered whether to drop the gun overboard.

"They don't realize how much harm those guys can do. A lot of people don't even understand what money is. There's a real need there, Mum. Somebody has to get the message out."

Jane glanced at her daughter, a look holding pride as well as love.

Daffy was silent for a long minute. "You know, I could see that bullet going into his head and all the stuff coming out? It made me sick." Another, shorter silence. "I don't think I'm cut out to be a terrorist."

"No, darling?"

Daffy turned and looked suspiciously at her mother. Then she smiled. Framed by the shrieking red hair and the heavy makeup, it was a smile of startling sweetness.

*   *   *

George worked for Schmidt Brothers Pharmaceutical when he and Jane were first married. They lived in Falmouth and he worked at the experimental station, and was included one summer on SBP's expedition to the Amazon. David Randall came along because his parents, professors at Exeter University, didn't want him underfoot during their summer sabbatical. He attached himself to George, who made no objection because the boy was no trouble. George discovered the money tree during the expedition, a small evergreen seedling, a Cupressaceae of some sort, with two curved branches forming the head. He noticed it was sensitive to sound, but other than that it seemed to have no particular value and aroused no interest in the other members of the expedition, and he forgot about it. Curiously, he found it again, three months after he returned home, growing in the back garden.

"Maybe it knew that was its destiny," said Daffy. She never tired of hearing how the tree came to live with them. Unlike her mother, she was well aware that while it might respond to sounds the money tree was not capable of reason. However, she had read twenty-five Harlequin romances one rainy weekend, and some of it had stuck.

George liberated David from the steam room and memories of that expedition came back to him as he gazed at the young man, an adult version of the thin, self-effacing, quiet boy. They shook hands and George apologized for any inconvenience. "We're not used to visitors, David. The kids meant no harm."

"It was my own fault," David glanced at his watch.

"You'll stay for dinner, of course. And we'll put you up for the night as well." He wouldn't hear any argument. "It's the least we can do. Now, I'm dying to hear how you found us and what you've been doing, but I'm sure Jane and the kids would like to hear as well, so let's leave that until dinner." He led David upstairs to the mudroom and they chatted about the islands and the weather while he cleaned the salmon and cut it into steaks.

David was introduced to Jane, whose hand he shook rather gingerly, while apologizing once more for his intrusion. She was courteous but reserved. Daffy, the horror he had thought he would never forget, turned out to be quite different now that she was cleaned up and dressed, and they shook hands with no hard feelings. "I don't think I could have actually shot you," she said.

"Not with the safety on," said Mike, and Jane wanted to know how he knew it had been on. Mike shrugged: he just knew. Jane's lips tightened and to prevent a flare-up, George took him with David out to the barbecue, while Daffy set the table and Jane rustled up some rice and vegetables to go with the salmon.

* * *

"What brought you out here, David?" Dinner was over and they were sitting in the large living room with its windows overlooking the orchard and cove. It held two chintz armchairs and a loveseat (occupied by Daffy and Mike), a pair of Edwardian upholstered tub armchairs and one or two antique tables scattered about. David sat near the fireplace.

"Two things, really. I happened to meet Pedro one day, and soon after that I was let go."

George leaned back and put his feet up on a footstool with a bright Turkish pattern. "You were working for SBP?"

"That's right. I'd always stayed in touch with the fellows at the Falmouth station and they helped me get a job there. Then I was transferred to Dusseldorf and that's where I saw Pedro. He didn't know who I was at first, but when I mentioned you he remembered me as the kid."

Pedro Medeiros had been one of the botanists on the SBP expedition. "He'd been transferred to Dusseldorf to care for this super-hush tree they'd found. It was the first I'd heard of it, but he said they were spending a fortune on security. I got the impression he wasn't supposed to be talking to me, so we didn't linger. Then just as we were saying goodbye, his eyes sort of widened. I think it was at that point he genuinely did remember me, and maybe that's what brought the rest back to him because he stared at me and said—whispered, really—'George found the tree! You remember? The money tree,' then he stopped. I think he'd have said more but someone was coming along the hall. He'd looked quite lively up until that point, but his face suddenly went completely blank. I stared at him, but he just nodded and walked off. I turned to watch him and found some suit from the front office behind me, so I just turned away and went back to work."

Daffy drew her feet up and wrapped her arms round her knees in excitement.

"Very cloak and dagger," said Jane.

"It was," David agreed. "Pedro had said it was a new species, a cypress of some sort, and they'd named it after Werner Schmidt, the president. *Cupressus werner.*"

Daffy had a poor opinion of that. "Tell him your name, Dad."

George took his time. "If anything, I think it's closer to Juniperus than Cupressus, though they're both of the same family. Be that as it may, I call it *Pseudojuniperus lucre*." He looked apologetic. "It's a bit of a mouthful, but only DNA testing will resolve the matter."

"How did you find us?" Jane was ready to move on.

"I knew George was Canadian. He told me once—do you remember, George?—that your father had recently died and left you this property. You said you and your wife might retire here."

George nodded slowly, remembering.

"Pedro said an odd thing. Odd at first, I mean. He said they weren't satisfied with the Brazilian output, so he was sent to Dusseldorf to try something different." He looked at George and then at Daffy. "I was thinking over the conversation that evening, and I wondered if they were trying to grow money, and if they'd only been able to grow Brazilian *reals*." He gave a small laugh. "It all seemed wildly improbable, you know?" George nodded. "Then a couple of days later I was given three weeks pay in lieu of notice."

Jane studied him. "What reason did they give?"

"Oh—outsourcing, cutting back, the usual stuff." He glanced at her. "I can't say I was all that sorry. I've never much cared for SBP, but I didn't have the gumption to get out. They just made the decision for me."

"When did this happen?"

"Months ago. Back at the end of May. I went home to England and stayed with my parents, or in their house, because they spent most of the summer at a symposium in

Odessa. I took a trip to Scotland and another to Majorca and I really don't think I was followed. Just to be sure, I left late one night and went to Prestwick in Scotland, and flew out from there. I had a bit of money saved up and thought I'd look you up then carry on and visit Singapore and Australia before looking for work."

Silence fell, while the others mulled over his words. Eventually, David spoke. "I take it you grow dollars, do you?"

"And apples," said Jane.

*   *   *

"I don't like it." Mike was agitated. "Two strangers in two days? Something's wrong."

"It's just life, darling. We have to adapt, that's all." Jane shook out the sheet and Mike took hold of one end. They fitted it onto the mattress in the guest bedroom.

"For two whole weeks?"

Jane sat down on the edge of the bed and patted the mattress next to her. Mike joined her and she turned to face him. "Dad said why don't we ask him to stay for a few days, and I thought, well, what's the good of that? If he's a baddie, he'll be off before we know it." She paused while Mike evaluated that. He nodded and she continued.

"So I suggested two weeks. If we ask Tara to do a background check on him, she'll need a week at least. Then we'll know where we are."

Mike looked at her. "Good thinking, Mum." His expression relaxed. "And if it turns out he's a bad guy, we'll dump him in the cove."

"Let's cross that one when we come to it." She paused, and added, "You know, Dad's pretty confident that David is on the up and up, and I don't think we can ignore that, do you?"

Mike thought about that and eventually agreed. Dad had pretty good instincts about people stuff. They stood up and smoothed the sheet on the mattress, then finished making up the bed.

"Who's the other stranger?" asked Jane.

Mike told her all about their meeting with Ken Yamata, who had called himself Satoshi. Jane had already heard of the young multimillionaire who was building a house on the south slope of Signal Hill, and she seemed unperturbed about his name change and quite confident that he had not poisoned Daffy.

The guest room occupied the whole eastern end of the upper floor. It was a spacious room overlooking the barn and drive, with an ensuite bathroom. They finished making up the bed and Jane opened the window. BC Hydro offered rebates to homeowners who upgraded their homes for greater energy savings, and she had thought for some time about installing double-glazed windows. She was ambivalent only because it meant workmen, who could ask awkward questions. So the guest room, like the other upstairs rooms, had wooden windows that opened by sliding upward. They often stuck and they were always noisy. She braced herself and hauled, and with a squeal the window came up a few inches. Mike pushed from below and they got it up high enough to let in plenty of fresh air. Then they returned to the living room.

"It's really sad, Mum," Daffy said. George had gone out with David to get his bags.

"What is, darling?"

"His parents always wanted to get rid of him in the summers. That's why he went on the SBP expedition. He was an only child and they had plans of their own. And now he hardly ever sees them. It's so sad."

Daffy evidently had no qualms about David staying, Jane was relieved to find.

"It must be awful not having any family," Daffy mused. She looked at Mike. "He probably thinks of Dad as his dad."

Mike stared at her, wondering if she had really lost it. She added, "You were great today, Mikey. You should have seen him, Mum. 'One false move and I'll take off your kneecap.' That's what he said. It was so cool."

They heard George and David going up the stairs, and a few minutes later George returned alone. Creaks came from overhead as David moved about in the guest room.

Daffy spoke first. "Did you buy the printer's ink, Dad?"

George nodded. "It's in the barn." He sat down. "This will be excellent, don't you think, Jane? The kids can practice their social skills. He can help us with the nuts and the smell—he's already expressed an interest—and we'll teach him how to raise money trees."

Jane looked surprised. "You're not going to tell him everything, are you?"

"Sure. We'll all tell him." He looked at his son. "He can be your first franchise, how about that?"

Mike brightened. Jane frowned.

Chapter 5

The Legend

At the desk in his office, Deputy Director Jack Halloran listened to the visitor seated opposite. Clarence Pringle was a botanist with a specialty in Central and South American flora. Currently an associate research professor at George Washington University, he had agreed to call in after work that day, and had spent the past three hours being mined for information.

Pringle had spent many months in the Amazon on numerous expeditions, most recently this past summer. Halloran had encouraged him to speak of the plants he had found. The professor had gone on at tedious length about Amazon lilies and fire vines and *Hevea brasiliensis,* which turned out to be the rubber tree. That gave the Deputy Director an entry, and he asked what other useful plants came to mind. So then they talked about the kapok tree and *Bertholettia excelsa,* the Brazil nut, about which Pringle became expansive, and then *Pseudobombax munguba,* a species of silk-cotton tree. Halloran asked him a lot of questions about munguba, including what it looked like and whether it produced nuts.

Pringle wound down eventually, and after a pause said, "This has been interesting, sir, and I hope the information has been helpful." He began to rise.

"Don't go just yet, Professor."

Grown not manufactured. Halloran was still adjusting to the shock of reading those words in the forensic report, and they had persisted in floating before his eyes in the hours and days that followed. *Grown not manufactured.* He'd called in the forensics chief, Jaio McCaffrey, a woman of 45 of mixed Scottish-Chinese descent, confirmed her findings, sworn her to silence (unnecessarily, as she pointed out: "I can think, too, Jack") and proceeded with the utmost caution. A series of high-level meetings had concluded with the obvious: they could do nothing without identifying the plant responsible.

Halloran had another huddle with Jaio, who had suggested Professor Pringle. She had called on his expertise recently in the identification of an exotic poison, and learned he had been on numerous expeditions to the Amazon rain forest. Halloran invited him in and proceeded to pump the professor. Now they seemed to be at an impasse.

Halloran could not bring himself to lead his witness. Even thinking about a plant that could grow US dollars nauseated him. Either the professor knew of the plant or he did not. Halloran would not himself add another to the growing list of individuals who possessed this incendiary information. He leaned back in his chair and waited.

Pringle began to look uncomfortable. The silence lengthened and became almost unbearable. It was broken finally by the academic. "You're the Secret Service. You deal with counterfeit money."

"That's right."

"You're looking for the money tree, aren't you?"

"The money tree?" Halloran leaned forward. "What would that be?"

Pringle eyed him then began to speak. He had never seen a money tree, he said; he had only heard rumors. Halloran made no comment.

"I believe them," said the professor stoutly. "I've heard too many rumors from too many people. The tree exists, I'm sure of it."

"Any idea what it looks like?"

Pringle shrugged. "Green or possibly blue-green in color. Scale-like leaves. I'd say it's a member of the Cupressaceae family." Seeing Halloran's blank stare he added, "A cypress or sequoia, possibly a juniper."

Halloran turned to his computer and searched for cypress trees. The varieties seemed endless. He tried sequoias, and found mostly redwoods. The juniper family also offered great variety, but at least some of them were blue-green in color. "Like that?" he asked the professor of one picture.

Pringle hesitated, then shrugged. "I've heard the actual money tree has a sort of head, formed by the branches. Two Brazilians found one, or so the rumor goes, and flew it out. It was dead when they reached the coast."

"Any idea why?"

"They flew at about two thousand feet. The cabin wasn't heated. I would say the change in temperature was traumatic." He shook his head. "So stupid. They turned round and went back in, but whether they found another specimen, I don't know."

"Do you know anything else about these Brazilians? Their names, or occupations?"

Pringle shook his head.

"How do you know this tree of theirs grew money? Does it hang from the tree? Money, I mean?"

"No, no." Pringle leaned forward and launched into a description of male and female cones and the production of pollen and seeds. "Now, in the female cone you find the woody seed. It looks something like a Brazil nut, or so I was told. The Brazilians found a one-*real* note inside the nut. Can you believe that?" He suddenly looked quite lively. "Think of the sophistication of this organism! I heard the banknote was fully and completely formed in all its detail, identical to a genuine note."

He looked at the Deputy Director. "Is it true? Have you seen this tree?"

Halloran took his time about replying. "No, but I've seen what else it produces." From a drawer in his desk he took out a crudely torn hundred-dollar bill. He passed it across the desk to Pringle, who seized it, fingered it, smelled it. About a third of the bill was missing.

"How do you know it comes from a money tree?"

"We did a forensic analysis, professor. That bill was grown, not manufactured."

"Why is it torn?"

"A dog ate it," said Halloran briefly.

"This is astounding. Absolutely astounding. Where did you get it? Where is it being grown?"

Halloran was silent while Pringle waited breathlessly for the answer. The Deputy Director finally looked straight at him and appeared to reach a decision. He, too, leaned forward.

"Like you," he spoke softly, "we get to hear things in this agency. But we need more than rumors. We need cold, hard facts." His palm slapped down on the desk and the professor jumped.

"Professor Pringle, would you be prepared to help your country?"

"Help how?" The botanist had dealt with government bureaucrats before. He might be naïve but he was not stupid.

"The US government wants to mount an expedition to the Amazon. A small expedition. We'd like you to lead it. You'd have every comfort, every piece of equipment money can buy. We'd like an American to find that tree and—," he turned to study the picture on the computer screen, then turned back, "—and we'd like an American to have the honor of naming it. *Juniperus pringle*, sir. How does that sound to you?"

Pringle demurred. "It may not be a true juniper." But the idea had its appeal. He drew himself upright. "I am a leading authority on tropical cash crops. If, as you say, this magnificent species has survived, I will find it and the world shall know about it!"

Halloran made no comment, but pressed a button inside a drawer of his desk and got to his feet. He had settled the details with the academic by the time two agents entered the room. Pringle looked dazed. Halloran grasped his hand. "I'm counting on you, Professor, and so is your country. Keep in touch."

The agents escorted the scientist out, closing the door. Halloran turned to the computer and printed a selection of junipers, different in appearance but all blue-green in color. He shook his head in frustration, turned back to the phone, pressed a button and spoke briefly. Gumble and Hicks entered and he waved at them to sit opposite him.

It had taken nearly a million dollars before they got a reaction on a bill, and that had happened three days ago, when a hound at the pound had pounced on the tray of bills, barely a snout ahead of a spaniel. Gumble and Hicks had planned for this moment, but it nearly caught them by surprise. Both were wearing thick leather gloves and they sprang for the hound, Gumble grabbing its head, while Hicks threw the spaniel to one side and grabbed the body. Gumble got his hands between the dog's jaws and held them open, shaking them until the remains of the bill dropped to the ground, where Hicks retrieved it. "I'd have opened its throat if I had to," he'd said later. They'd been sitting in the pound's play area for too many weeks and neither was in a mood to play nice.

Halloran fingered the bill. As Pringle had described, it was perfect in every respect. He felt sick. "This was good work, gentlemen." He returned it to his desk drawer. "Now you're going to find the printing press."

He reached for the pictures and arrayed them before the two agents. They leaned forward, puzzled, staring at the pictures. He waited patiently. They'd need time to adjust to the fact that they would be chasing a tree, not a crook working on a basement copier.

Their heads came up and both agents stared at him. Hicks was the first to speak. "I don't get it, sir. What are we looking for?"

Halloran leaned forward and with a felt-tip drew two oval spurs on each tree, branches in the form of a head.

Chapter 6

Settling In

When George opened the guest room door, he found David sitting fully dressed in an armchair. "Sleep well? Come and have some breakfast and I'll give you the grand tour."

David followed him along the landing. "Would you mind if I went for a swim in the morning?"

"Not at all. That's your thing, is it, swimming?" They chatted as they went downstairs, meeting a pleasing aroma of bacon and eggs and coffee as they entered the kitchen. It was a dull, overcast morning, but the sky was lighter to the south.

David said good morning to Jane, and sat down next to George with Mike on his left. Daffy sat opposite, eating her breakfast and reading the *Wall Street Journal* on her tablet. Mike finished his breakfast and took his plate to the sink just as Jane, dressed and made up, sat down at the other end with the coffee pot.

"I want you to take the car over to the Big Island, Daff, and leave it in the car park. Take your bike in the back."

"Okay, Mum."

She was reading again. "You're an early riser," said David.

"Daffy picks up the papers and mail from the ferry," said George.

"At five-thirty?"

He had their attention. Daffy turned off the tablet and got to her feet.

"Daff?" George was puzzled.

Mike was putting his jacket on. "She's got a thing going with Terry Parker."

"Good lord, Daff, again?" asked Jane, "What do you see in him?"

Daffy loaded her backpack. Mike went on:

"She should have had sex with three point four guys by now and she's running way behind."

"Oh!"

David caught a glimpse of the girl's outraged face.

"Shut up, Michael," said Jane and looked at David: "Coffee?"

He passed his cup. "Thank you."

"Is this true, Daffy?" George looked perturbed.

Daffy grabbed her coat. "It's three point two, Dad. 'Bye."

The side door slammed and silence fell.

"Will you have bacon and eggs? Or toast? Or both?"

*   *   *

Wide enough for four vehicles, the barn had a concrete floor and an open-rafter peaked roof. The car was parked next to the tractor, with bikes leaning against one wall and George's workbench running along the other. Daffy wheeled her bike to the trunk of the car, where Mike waited.

"Bug off, you little wart." She lifted her bike in.

"Maybe you should have just said about your seedlings. I really hated to lie." He managed to look pious.

Daffy stared at him as he loaded his bike on top of hers. "How long have you known?"

"I saw them down by the creek last summer. Nice cold frame. Then a couple of times you didn't come home after school so I figured you were moving them."

Daffy nodded. "It's taken forever. I found a place on Signal Hill. No one'll find them up there."

She closed the trunk and they went to open the barn doors. These were two Z-reinforced wooden doors, held closed with a simple lever latch. Daffy lifted the latch and they each pushed one of the doors open.

"How many you got?"

"A hundred, all from Meshach. I raised them from cuttings. They look great, Mike."

They climbed in the car and drove out to the road. Firs, balsam and arbutus rose above the tangled undergrowth of Oregon grape and salal. Up and along the flank of Signal Hill they went, then back down toward the harbor and the small ferry.

*   *   *

Jane had asked Daffy to take the car because she wanted to stay close to David Randall when he returned his rental car. The two of them caught the midmorning ferry over to the Big Island. They picked up the Frisbys' car and she followed him to the car rental. Afterward, they drove to a clothing store. Jane stopped once, to mail a letter to their lawyers in London, asking for a background check and giving all the details she knew of their guest. Then they picked up thick work socks, work boots and work gloves, along with work pants and a shirt or two. Jane insisted on paying for these things.

"You have no idea what George has in store for you," she said with a smile. "We'd feel terrible if you didn't allow us to buy these few things. You'll be a huge help to him."

David had stopped protesting. After they'd paid for the items and returned to the car, he said, "George was awfully good to me when I was a kid. It stayed with me, you know." He glanced over to see if she understood and Jane nodded. He went on, "And I must say, this tree is beginning to fascinate me."

The morning's overcast had disappeared and the sun danced on the waves as the ferry ploughed its way back to Ledyard. David had no wife or girlfriend, she learned, and seemed very much as George had described, a quiet, self-contained, pleasant fellow. They talked about the island and Jane gave him something of its history, confirmed that no one knew what they were growing up at the north end, and acknowledged that growing money was an isolating occupation.

"Do you have, um, ethical concerns?" And when Jane made no reply, he added "I'm sorry, it's none of my business."

She spoke at last. "There's no actual law against growing money. I like to focus on the good we can do with it."

*   *   *

"Would any music work, or do the numbers make a difference?" David crouched in front of a tree in the north grove. At the base of it sat a waterproof CD player. George had removed the CD and was explaining the music: pop songs with numbers in them, like Rock Around the Clock, This Old Man, Knick Knack Paddy Whack.

"That's the question, David," he handed the CD to him. "We tested one grove against the other last year and the results were inconclusive." He was full of enthusiasm, delighted to have a fresh audience for his favorite subject. "Next year I want to run number songs against orchestral instead of pop—Mozart, maybe—and see how they do."

Both men got to their feet as Daffy and Mike arrived, bursting into the grove, their eyes searching David's face.

"Hello, kids. Mike, don't forget to take the players in." George indicated the CD player.

"Did you tell him about Meshach, Dad?" Daffy tried to gauge David's interest level.

"Meshach? As in Shadrach, Meshach and the other chap?"

"Abednego. Mum says you can't go wrong if you stick to the Bible. Personally, I think there's too much religion in the world these days, don't you?" David made no comment and she introduced him to other trees in the grove. "That's Washington and Disraeli and Sir John A Macdonald. And Dasher and Dancer—Mike named them."

"Donald," said Mike. "But it doesn't matter."

"Dasher and Donald?"

George examined the underside of one of Meshach's leaves. "This specimen has a far higher decibel tolerance, David."

"We've got one of his babies in the greenhouse, did you see?" asked Daffy. "The one with the orange tag? If we can develop a tougher strain, they could be grown in urban areas."

George put his arm round her. "My daughter the optimist. Let's go and have a look at the south grove, David."

As they walked up through the orchard, David mentally reviewed what he had learned so far. They grew twenties and hundreds, though he had yet to see a bill. George had shown him the starter fluid in the mudroom, an aquamarine nutrient cocktail that was mixed with a bill of the denomination you wanted to grow.

"You tear up your bill into smaller pieces, put them in the blender with five hundred milliliters of fluid, blend for about five seconds, then pour over the root ball, fill in the hole and Bob's your uncle."

"I wonder if Pedro's crowd have figured that out," said David.

George went on to explain that they had equal numbers of each denomination in both groves.

Angus pushed a soccer ball through the orchard and Mike and George went after it, while David watched absently.

"Do you think people should have the right to issue money?" asked Daffy.

"I certainly do."

"There's ample historical precedent."

He smiled. "I'd like to meet her."

Daffy was impervious to distraction when following a train of thought. "What I mean is, it's been done before. Scottish banks were issuing their own money in the eighteenth century. Isn't that cool? The country of Adam Smith?"

Downfield Mike managed to get a foot on the ball and kicked it uphill, pelting after it with Angus. George followed them.

"You'd want to regulate it, though," said David.

"How, exactly?"

"You wouldn't want everyone growing money, would you?"

"Growing money?" Daffy stared at him. "I'm talking about decent money, honest money, not legislated dreck." Disappointed, she stalked off toward the greenhouse. Upfield, George broke off and joined her.

Mike kicked the ball downfield, and he and David traded possession for a while, until Angus nosed it away. They walked up to the house, David preoccupied.

"How much do you make here?" he asked. Forty trees, twenties and hundreds, say a hundred nuts per tree . . . or was that too few?

"Do you like money?" Mike asked politely.

"I love it, actually. I'm just beginning to realize how much. Excuse me." David headed for the greenhouse.

Outside the greenhouse door, six young money trees in pots were catching some rays. He walked inside. On the counter sat a tray of money tree seedlings alongside trays of cuttings for various flowers and vegetables. Down the center was a workbench with a sink and next to it, a large mixing bowl filled with black liquid. Underneath the bench, along with bags of fertilizer, was an assortment of trays and clay pots. Here, George and Daffy were tagging summer bulbs dug out of the beds along the driveway and around the house.

"What did you say the yield was, George?"

George looked up. "We get a long ton from the south grove, slightly less from the north. But there's spoilage, of course."

David never heard Jane come in, but he happened to be looking at the seedlings when she spoke.

"I've told you before about using my mixing bowls," she said, and all of them, except for the one bearing an orange tag, wilted before his eyes.

"Jane!" George spoke in an undertone, but urgently.

"Sorry, sorry, sorry." She bent over the tray and spoke tenderly to its occupants, her expression alone betraying annoyance. "There, there. Darling precious angels, Mummy isn't angry at you. No, she isn't." They cheered up almost at once. She glimpsed David's expression. "You must think I'm mad," she said awkwardly.

"Can't be helped, love." George addressed David. "They're highly susceptible to Jane's voice, for some reason."

"A sort of audiotropic response?"

"What's this in my mixing bowl?" Jane was still annoyed, but quietly.

"Printer's ink. I want to see if it separates."

"You can see if it separates in an icecream bucket."

She went out, followed by George, and David joined Daffy, who was crooning over the seedlings. "Aren't they cute? Don't mind Dad. He only ever thinks about tonnage and yield. We made about three billion last year."

"Billion? Billion?" His voice, he saw, had some slight effect on the seedlings, and Daffy maneuvered him farther away.

"That's the value in rubles, which tells you how bad the ruble was, doesn't it?" She looked up at him. "Mind you, that was in 1994. They had hyperinflation in Russia and it reached 2500 percent per year. It was before I was born, but I feel so sorry for the Russians, don't you? Their life-savings got wiped out."

George returned with an icecream bucket. "Audiotropic is a good way of putting it, David. That reaction of theirs to Jane's voice is the reason I get her to read the alphanumeric system to them. We can't be sure, but I have a suspicion it helps."

David felt he had had enough for the time being. "What alphabet, Cyrillic?"

* * *

Jane had cleared the decks for the next two weeks, arranging for her appointments to be catered by a colleague who was also something of a competitor. They had an agreement not to poach on each other's turf but while Jane knew she was putting temptation in Brianna's way she wanted to keep an eye on developments at the farm. Now she busied herself in the kitchen, testing a new dessert.

The side door slammed and Mike came in. "It's a new world order, Mum." He looked unsettled.

"Is it, darling? Try this and tell me what you think."

He sat down at the counter and she passed over a bowl with a helping of what looked like whipped cream.

"He's telling him everything." He took a mouthful. "Almost everything. He wants me and Daff to tell him stuff, too." He tried another mouthful and finished it off. "This is the end of the world as we know it." He pushed away the bowl and headed for the door.

"What do you think?" She heard him leaping up the stairs. "One to ten," she called.

"Um, nine." He reached the top. "Maybe eight. It's got a funny taste."

"Damn," said Jane.

David was the second guinea pig, a few minutes later. She studied him while he was tasting it. '"How are you getting on?"

"Um . . . it's awfully temperamental, isn't it? The tree?"

"Mm." It would be disloyal to say more.

"I was going to say this is delicious, but it's got a bit of an aftertaste. What is it?"

"Chocolate tiramisu mousse cake. Filling for." She sighed. "I have a client who loves to entertain but hates putting on weight. The aftertaste is stevia. Natural sweetener."

"Pity." He hesitated, then said, "If you're thinking of serving it for dinner, don't stop on my account."

"Right." Jane was abstracted, clicking through Daffy's tablet for more dessert ideas.

David wandered off. He visited the living room again; nothing to see there. He stared at the seascape over the mantle, his mind elsewhere. He crossed the hall and entered the den. Mike sat in the armchair reading a book. David started to withdraw.

"You're welcome to look around," said Mike politely.

David shoved his hands in his pockets as he walked over to the window, and discovered he still had the CD. He looked out the window, then down at the label. Just a collection of number songs, George had said. Twenty-Six Miles, Sixteen Tons, Fifty Ways to Leave Your Lover.

There was a large wall map behind one of the two desks, and he walked past the boy to look at it. "You like reading, do you?"

"Sometimes."

Bizarre kid.

The map showed the western part of the continent, and the Gulf Islands and Vancouver Island. The dotted border threaded its way in what seemed a fairly random fashion between the islands. "I suppose the border's quite close."

"The forty-ninth is north of us."

"The what?"

"The forty-ninth parallel. Longest undefended border in the world." Mike looked up from his book. "The border between us and the Yanks. Except that this end it gets all squirrely. Probably because of Victoria."

David stared at the map, something niggling at the back of his mind. He traced latitude forty-nine degrees and realized it did indeed form the border between Canada and the United States, except at this end. Ledyard was too small to appear on the map. *Probably because of Victoria. ...* "You mean, if the border went straight across, Victoria would be in the United States?"

"Yeah."

He had a sudden hunch. He turned abruptly to face the boy. "You grow US dollars, not Canadian. Don't you?"

Mike shrugged. "Whatever. The trees do their own thing."

Another useless answer. David began to turn away and Mike took pity on him.

"Yeah. Dad tried growing Canadian, but they made a mess of it and he realized they wanted to grow US money. So we dug them all up and replanted with American." His gaze dropped back to his book.

David looked more closely. It was oversized, not quite large enough to be called a coffee-table book. He could make out part of the title: *Franchise 500.* He regarded the boy with fresh eyes. "Donald . . . Duck?"

"Trump." Mike lowered the book.

"It's Michael, isn't it?"

"Mike."

David smiled. "You must be the family financier. I wonder if you'd mind telling me what you make here?"

Mike considered. "We've got forty trees. You wouldn't be getting that many."

"I just want some idea of the amounts involved."

Mike eyed him for a while. "We average around a million. 'Course, we don't have to pay a franchise fee."

"I see. And how much might that be?"

Mike decided he'd said enough for one day. He stood up, took his book and walked to the door.

"We could discuss it sometime, if you're interested."

*   *   *

Daffy led the way up the slope of Signal Hill. Angus followed her, pushing his way through a salmonberry bush then scampering up a moss-covered boulder to range on ahead.

"You okay, Mike?" She looked back down the slope. The climb was harder if you were short, but Mike wasn't about to ask for help. He hauled himself up a steep section with the aid of a contorted arbutus.

"Fine," he said briefly and scrambled up the slope. Daffy turned and resumed the climb, eventually pushing her way through scrubby bushes into a clearing with needles thick on the ground and firs and cedars scattered throughout. Mike joined her.

"What do you think? Nice, huh?"

Dotted at random under the trees were dozens and dozens of money tree seedlings, twelve to fifteen inches in height. The earth had been humped protectively over the base of each seedling, and covered with needles. They looked natural in the setting. Mike was impressed.

Daffy felt around between two boulders and brought out the muscle jar. She began to throw handfuls of fertilizer over the seedlings.

"They're awful little, Daff. Dad wouldn't plant them out this small, would he?"

"Dad coddles them. I'm going to prove it, too. They've already survived a winter in the cold frame. He'd say that's impossible." She sat down, in the grip of a thought. "But I wish I could get Mum up here to talk to them."

"Does she still do that?"

"Of course. Dad drags her into the greenhouse once a week or so."

Angus nosed round the clearing as Daffy continued to spread fertilizer and Mike did some calculating. Twenty trees per franchise. He was looking at a potential five profit centers. "Say, Daff. If you give me some trees for the franchises, I'll tell you how to get Mum up here without her knowing."

Daffy looked wary. "How many trees?"

"We can work that out later. Whaddya say?"

Daffy thought for a while, then came to a decision. "How?"

"Okay. You take her into the greenhouse and tell her you're going to tape her. Tell her that way she won't have to do it again, and Dad can play it whenever he likes. Better give him a copy of it, in case they actually talk to each other. Then you bring your copy up here. Okay?"

Daffy stared at him in amazement. "Why didn't I think of that?" He grinned. "Mike, you tell her. She'll be as pleased as anything."

"Gimme a break. If I tell her, she'll say it's a lousy idea. If you tell her, she'll let you off bathrooms for a month."

*   *   *

A farm offers plenty of opportunity for work even in the off season, and George had a backlog of disagreeable chores requiring two able-bodied men.

The wharf decking and pilings needed repair. Several of the pilings were beginning to rot and replacing them required someone to spend a good part of each day in the water. David was a natural choice for this, being acclimated by virtue of the daily dip he took before breakfast. They made several trips to the Big Island, using the runabout to bring back planking and other supplies. Repairing the wharf took a week, and fixing the path down to the creek, where the yacht was moored, took another week. Most of the time they worked in a light but persistent drizzle.

While they worked, David learned how to grow money. He was instructed in nutritional requirements and soil amendments. He learned the value of a kelp bath in providing potassium and repelling insects. "We spray it on in the spring. The trees smell fishy for a few days, but it doesn't last." Seaweed was collected in an oil drum by the barn and allowed to decompose for a couple of months. On the whole, David was glad he would be gone by then.

They spent a day pruning the base of each money tree and doing soil tests in the groves. "Our soil here is acidic, so before the trees were planted I added a mixture of mushroom manure and potassium. This has to be done prior to planting, you understand. We'll do a soil test at your location and prepare your soil accordingly."

It had become accepted that David would grow money. He was free to read the Blue Book, but found little in it beyond mundane day-to-day records of temperature, nutrient cycles and the like. One of his jobs every morning was to put out the six saplings in their individual pots. They were to be planted next spring on the western arm of the cove. "It's isolated; no one goes there," said George. Tens and fifties were planned for the saplings, and possibly one thousand-dollar tree. "Jane won't let us circulate thousands, but I want to see how the tree handles the larger denominations."

David was glancing through the *BC Fruit Grower* in the den one evening when Daffy came in and flopped down on the sofa opposite.

"Do demonstrations ever work?"

He lowered the magazine and considered.

"I've always thought the biggest drawback was the lack of toilet facilities. That's why I never join one."

Daffy looked skeptical. "You don't look like a demonstrator. Mum?"

Jane sat at her desk paying bills. "Mm?"

"Why demonstrate?" asked David. "What's on your mind?"

Daffy heaved a sigh. "I've been wondering how to attract attention at the G20 Summit."

David crossed one leg over the other and heard a rundown on demonstrations at past summits and Daffy's ideas for the next one.

Jane finished with the bills and picked up the letter from the lawyers. After a comprehensive background check, they had found nothing out of the ordinary about David Randall, his parents, associates or friends. He appeared to have led a blameless life, which suited Jane very well. He had fit into the family almost without a ripple. Michael had stopped flattening himself against the wall every time David went by, and now played soccer with him after school and called him Dave. Daffy had discovered a fresh audience for her theories, a slightly better informed one at that. Jane glanced over at the two of them arguing, and opened a drawer to file the letter. "David seems to be fitting in," she said to George later that night. "Why don't we ask him to stay on for a month or so?" Preoccupied, George had hardly heard her.

*   *   *

The dryer completed its cycle and George, who had been sitting on a chair between Mona and the Earl, came over. He opened the door and pulled out a handful of rags. They looked tie-dyed, streaked with black.

"Oh lord," he said. He held them to his nose and inhaled the smell. Nothing to speak of. He bent and felt around in the dryer, removing a small mesh bag with a cloth inside it. The cloth was almost completely black.

The smell issue remained intractable. The printer's ink had sat for ten days in an ice cream bucket without showing any sign of separating. "Another idea down the drain," he'd said ruefully, then later had thought of testing it as a type of fabric softener. Now the inside of the dryer was a mess and when Jane came downstairs with a basketful of dirty clothes she found him staring at it ruefully, rubbing his chin.

"What are you doing?" Past experience made her suspicious. "Let me see." She bent down, looked at the interior of the dryer then accusingly at George.

"I know." He shook his head in disbelief.

"Is that printer's ink? What were you thinking, George?"

"I honestly don't know, love. I remember thinking we might be able to use it like an anti-static," he said.

Jane straightened. "Of all the pea-brained ideas—," she looked around. "Where's David? I should have thought he'd have more sense."

"He's, I don't know, doing something." It was a point of honor with George: he should be able to solve this problem without the aid of a rank amateur. He reached for the spray cleaner on a rack behind the washer, and began to scrub the inside of the dryer. Jane watched for a minute then told him to go away.

"I'll do this, George. If indeed anything can be done, which I doubt."

George continued to scrub. She went upstairs and explored the contents of the back cupboard in the mudroom. Filling a bucket with SOS pads, industrial-strength cleaner, spray bleach and cleaning rags she returned to the basement. Crossing the hall, she stopped and stared.

Dressed in his one and only suit, with a book tucked under his arm, Mike came sedately down the stairs.

"What on earth are you doing?"

"Taking a meeting." He reached the den door, opened it, entered, and closed it behind him.

She shook her head, unamused, and continued down to the basement, meeting George on the stairs.

"From now on, the house *and its contents* are off limits, George. Is that clear?"

"Yes, love."

"Talk to David about it. Two heads," she continued down the stairs, "have to be better than one," and prepared to attack the dryer.

Holding the rags to his nose again, George sniffed, frowning abstractedly.

*   *   *

The meeting was not going well. Sitting at his mother's desk, Mike had proposed a franchise fee and David, seated opposite, had dismissed it. "Fifty percent? That's extortion."

"It's less than Taco Bell." Mike opened the franchise book. "They charge five and a half percent a week. That's over two hundred and fifty percent a year."

"No it isn't. It's five point five taken weekly instead of annually. I'll pay you five point five."

Mike's voice rose. "I'm offering you a monopoly. No other franchiser does that. None."

"Why a monopoly?"

Mike eyed him moodily. This was not going as he had planned. "Because of hyperinflation. Daffy says only one grower per country. Think about it. You can have any country you want except the U.S. Like the UK or Germany—anywhere you want."

David was momentarily diverted. "What would it grow on the continent? Euros?"

"We don't know," Mike admitted.

"Germany—there's a thought. I could set up right in SBP's backyard." The thought amused him. "Can I choose my denominations?"

"A bit, yeah," said Mike. "Like, Mum won't let Dad grow thousands because they're rare. Like that. You'll get the biggest bills allowed. Thirty percent. That's my absolute bottom offer."

"Unacceptable." David opened the Blue Book. "I'm doing the work and taking all the risk. I'll get substantial spoilage, if your experience here is anything to go by, which means double the work for half the output. On top of all that, you want thirty percent? Not happening."

A lengthy silence ensued. The prospect of passing up even a percentage point of profit, no matter that it was a hypothetical, future-indefinite profit, pained Mike horribly. He did not want to be the first to speak, because that would be to lose ground, but finally he said, "A franchise is founded on mutual trust. Finding people you can trust is tough. Because once they know what to do, they could just disappear and we'd never get our fee."

David considered this. "You can prevent that by packaging the nutrients. Supply them pre-mixed in individual packages, dated for each application."

Mike was unable to hide his interest at this practical solution to a problem that had bedeviled him for months. David held his gaze.

"I could perhaps come up a shade," he said, reluctantly, and the negotiations continued, torturous and painful.

*   *   *

George took a bill out of his wallet and placed it in the middle of the table. It was the Canadian dollar bill from the tree on the small island.

Mike was the first to grasp what he was seeing. "Wow!" He sprang out of his chair and pored over the bill, Daffy with him.

"Where's the tree, Dad?"

Jane told them about the island.

"Just one nut?" asked Daffy, and George said there was a bag in the barn waiting to be opened.

David watched curiously. "Would you process them with the others?"

"No point," said Mike. "No such thing as a Canadian dollar bill."

Daffy finished examining the bill and handed it to him. David studied it. "So this was grown without a template?"

George nodded. "A one is the default harvest in any currency. It's somewhat faded because we opened it early, before the colors had had time to set."

Mike was enthusiastic. "We can replant it next spring, right, Dad? With a hundred?"

George agreed and asked for volunteers to open the rest of the nuts. "I'm curious to find out the spoilage rate, who's going to help? There aren't more than about thirty to do."

Only David volunteered.

"We're like chocolate-factory workers," said Jane apologetically as Mike and Daffy began clearing dishes.

"I can only imagine," said David.

George took him out to the barn, produced the bag of nuts and a hammer, showed him how to twist the kernel to unfold the bill, and left him to it. David sat on a stool at the workbench and laboriously opened nut after nut, reflecting that this could get old quite quickly, unless you were processing hundred-pound notes. Mike took pity on him and came out to help, and after an hour they totted up the reckoning: out of thirty bills only three appeared to have anything wrong with them. Mike seized on this fact as an excuse to renegotiate their franchise agreement. David wanted to wait: "I agree it should be revised if my spoilage is as low as this. Let's see how I get on."

Mike reluctantly agreed and they gathered up the bills to show George. Angus trotted over as they were crossing the yard.

"Watch this, Dave." Mike held out a bill and Angus leapt at it, devouring it on the spot.

"That's why we have to fix the smell," said Mike.

Chapter 7

The Febreze Factor

Pruning the fruit trees was the biggest of the autumn jobs, using the small chain saw and assorted hand saws. One afternoon, George unburdened himself to David on the subject of smell. They'd finished cutting down a couple of diseased trees and David was lopping off branches while George piled them for pickup by the tractor. The trunk would be cut up and the logs used for the living room fire.

"Processing happens after Christmas, David, after the nuts have cured. That's when we experiment with ways to remove the odor. You'll see—or you would if you were here." He dragged another branch over to the small trailer hitched to the tractor and dropped it on top, completing the load. After driving it up to add to the pile in the north field, he returned with the empty trailer for more.

"I've tried using liquid fabric softener. Tried baking soda, vinegar, even kelp once, but all it did was smell up the dryer." The year before last they had stored the harvested nuts on activated charcoal in the basement. "Jane wasn't crazy about that and I can't say I blame her. It was a nightmare to clean up." Nor had it helped.

David mulled over the problem while lopping off branches. When George unbent and told him about the latest dryer incident, he was careful to say nothing.

"I know," said George, as though he'd spoken. "Don't know what I was thinking. It's quite remarkable how common sense goes out the window when you're testing a theory."

"What made you think of printer's ink in the first place?"

George took some time to answer. Eventually he said it seemed logical that since the trees were duplicating a printed bill they would know what to do with ink if they had it.

They worked in silence for a while. "Ever tried Febreze?"

"The air freshener? Interesting stuff, that," said George. "Know anything about it?"

When David shook his head, he went on, "The active ingredient is beta-cyclodextrin. It's a donut-shaped enzyme. Likes water on its outer surface but repels it in the donut hole. That's where smell molecules attach themselves and when they do, it changes their nature, so that they no longer give off a smell."

"So, did it work?"

"It showed promise. But we didn't like the smell—it leaves its own smell, you see. I wonder, though. . . ." He paused, thinking. "You can buy beta-cyclodextrin in powder form."

"Might be worth a try," said David.

* * *

Daffy and Mike biked along the central valley road. Fields spread out on either side: spinach and chard, beets. Here was a field of Brussels sprouts, nearly ready to harvest. And further on, winter squash and pumpkins. They drew abreast of a truck parked on the roadside, and waved to Raaj Dhasi, the oldest son. Behind him, other Dhasis were bent over in the field harvesting melons, machetes flashing as they severed the stalks and carried the melons to nearby carts. Big, outgoing Raaj gave them a smile as they passed, then headed into the field. Mr. and Mrs. Dhasi had both been working at the fruit and veggie stand at the entrance to the valley, off the main island road.

The central valley was almost entirely occupied by the Dhasi farm. Beyond it, they drew nearer to the slope of Signal Hill, and as the road began to rise, the fields gave way to woods. Farther out, they had seen Ken's house, nearly halfway up the slope, and now they labored up the narrow, winding road until they arrived, breathless. The house had been built in a natural clearing, and it extended out over the hillside on massive supporting beams. It was huge. They stared in silence.

"Maybe the Dhasis are moving in," said Mike at last, and Daffy giggled. The extended Dhasi family lived in a pokey house in the middle of a field on their farm.

Ken's house was unfinished, with glass in the windows but exposed insulation. They looked up and saw him at a window. He waved and they leaned their bikes against trees and joined him. He showed them all over the two levels, including the six bedrooms and six bathrooms and a huge games room. The house had been wired and the games room was loaded with electrical outlets. They noticed a sleeping bag and air mattress here as well and Ken admitted he had already moved in. "It's so quiet I can get a lot done."

Daffy asked what he was working on. Mike frowned at that, but Ken didn't seem to mind. "A cloaking device."

Both Frisbys said at once, "Like the Romulans?"

"Not quite. A web cloaking device."

Daffy was disappointed. "Like Tor, you mean?"

"Sure. But more." That was all he would say.

He led them to the kitchen where crates of soft drinks were stacked against a wall, along with more crates containing potato chips. "Just got the appliances," he said, opening the fridge and inviting them to help themselves. Mike managed to give Daffy a look and she said something vague about exploring and headed back to the living room, soft drink in hand. Before Ken could follow, Mike asked, "Do you like money?"

Ever since the conclusion of his negotiations with David, Mike's head had been filled with thoughts of more franchisees. David's presence and the successful agreement made the whole concept a reality, and his suggestions on nutrient packaging removed what had until then been the biggest stumbling block: the problem of controlling a franchisee once you had him.

Mike had never taken much interest in the actual growing side of the business: he left that to Dad and Daffy. He knew the money trees could be tiresome and temperamental, yet he had overlooked this in his calculations. He had simply feared that once he signed a franchisee, that person would disappear and start growing a fortune. But of course he wouldn't, not if the Frisbys' own experience was any guide. Of course Mike would have to supply instructions and carefully prepacked nutrients and guidance. It was a perfect set up for a franchise.

That left his mind free to consider the kind of person he wanted to attract. He had concluded that attitude was the first priority, people who, like him, got a warm feeling when they picked up a penny on the street. Those kind of people could be taken to the next level. He had run this past Daffy, who said Ken had so much money he probably wasn't interested in more. Mike disregarded this foolish statement. In any case, if Ken wasn't interested he might know someone who was. So he had asked his key question, "Do you like money?", and now he watched carefully.

Ken's indifference wasn't feigned. He shrugged. "Sure, it's okay."

Mike took a moment to regroup. "Know anyone who really likes it?"

The American laughed. "Yeah: all my cousins and all my friends." Mike seemed to want more, so he added, "My Dad takes care of my money, and I told him to give them whatever they want." He thought for a moment. "Y'know, I don't think he does." He pushed himself off the counter and they started for the living room. "Even the neighbors want in on the deal. People are funny, aren't they?"

Mike looked at him seriously. Being a franchisor was obviously a learning curve, but it was equally obvious that Ken was far removed from the franchisee profile. No point even asking if he knew of anyone in Japan.

On the way home, he wondered about the Dhasi family. They worked hard, and Mum said Mr. Dhasi was a good businessman, so he probably appreciated money. Most important, he came from India, where everyone was poor. So he must know someone who would love to have a money tree. The big question was, how to approach him? Giving away the Frisbys' location was not to be considered, not until a potential franchisee had been reviewed and approved. He parked his bike against the barn wall and after kicking the ball around with Angus went in the house.

A plate of brownies sat on the counter and Jane was making pastry. "Mrs. Bagnold's looking for someone to do chores on Saturday mornings."

Mike had already heard this, from the boy who used to have the job.

"She pays ten dollars. I said I'd ask you."

He pulled out the counter stool and perched on it, eating a Brownie and thinking. "Trouble is, she's awful picky."

"Awful*ly* picky."

"Yeah. It's supposed to be two hours' work but Cory said it's always three."

Rolling out the pastry, Jane considered this. "Would you do a better job than Cory? Is he disorganized?" She glanced at her son. "In other words, was he doing twice what you'd do right the first time?" She flipped the pastry and floured the top, giving him a smile.

Mum had a point. And nobody wanted to pass up ten bucks, but if the old Bag, as Cory called her, was going to kill off his entire Saturday morning . . . on the other hand, maybe Cory was a soakee. He decided to interview Mrs. Bagnold before making a decision.

* * *

It was generally recognized that George Frisby grew the best apples on the island, although when Vern Parker stopped the Island co-op truck and had a look at George's boxes, he couldn't see any appreciable difference between Frisby and Parker apples. But George charged, and got,

$2.50 a pound on his direct sales, a dollar more than anyone else, so his apples had to be better. Either that, or Jane was selling up a storm. Vern aired these thoughts during the news hour and Ron said he wouldn't mind paying an extra buck just to look at Jane. Marge gave her husband a sidelong look and said "Hello?" Marge Parker was a heavy woman—in another era she might have been called "motherly"—who worked at The Bay in Sidney, in women's clothing. She was much in demand among the high school girls, especially the motherless ones with little or no clothes sense who didn't know enough to ask for advice and whom Marge nudged in the right direction with gentle tact and encouragement.

The subject of Frisby apples was dropped, but one April day, Ron biked farther than usual up the island road, and when he came to the top of the long hill he really thought he'd become a seagull and was going to waft away on the wind. He whooshed down the hill and coasted round the bend and along the flat with a great smile on his face and his beard waving behind him, then he crashed into the concrete barrier at the end of the road, and bent the frame of his front wheel. He had to walk home, and it was then that he heard the music. He came home humming "Fifty ways to leave your lover," until Marge finally told him to shut up. Vern drove him up to pick up the bike and they listened for the music but heard nothing. Vern assumed he'd imagined it.

That fall, when yet another tourist stopped at the Parker fruit stand and mentioned the higher prices at the north end, Vern resolved to ask George about it. One day in late

October he got his chance, when George invited him for a beer later in the day at the gazebo.

Cam had phoned to say a parcel had arrived, and George and David decided to bring the runabout down to the harbor. It was an Indian summer day, warm and sunny, and after dropping the package, the beta-cyclodextrin George had ordered, in the boat they walked over to the gazebo with a six-pack of beer. The Furry Forest Friends Society was wrapping up its meeting and Vern arrived just as the members left. After introductions, the three men settled down in the east end of the gazebo, watching the harbor activity as they chatted, each with a beer, David between the other two.

After listening to a rundown of everything George and David had accomplished in the past few weeks, Vern brought the subject round to the price of apples.

"Say, George, I got a couple of CD players. Thought I'd put them out in the orchard next spring. Play some music. I was going to try some Thriller album, New Kids on the Block. Maybe Madonna. Nothing too radical, you understand." He glanced at George, who nodded.

"Anyhow, I'm just wondering if I should try classical?"

George was enthusiastic. "Funny you should say that, Vern, because—," he caught himself and collected his thoughts, and went on, "—ah, I've been thinking the same thing."

"You have?" Vern was delighted. George had letters after his name and could be considered a professional.

"I'm going to try both next year in different places and compare them."

Vern slapped his knee. "I'm sure glad to hear it. Margie put me on to the classical, said it's good for developing kids' brains." He gave David a grin. "Apples don't have brains, but I thought it might make the trees happier, eh? Grow a better product."

"Anything that reduces stress in the plant, I always say, must be beneficial." George had made this point at length to David not long ago, with regard to spoilage, and he faced the younger man's gaze without blinking.

"Do you find you get a better quality of apple?" Vern looked earnest. "Don't want any trade secrets, George, but your apples don't look any different from mine."

George opened his mouth, but Vern went on: "It's just, I wondered why you're charging a buck a pound more, is all." He took a long swallow of his beer. David glanced at George, whose mouth remained open.

"I've been hearing a lot about George's nutrient mixes," he said to Vern. "That's probably the reason."

Vern nodded. "Fertilizer's expensive. Price of apples is terrible, George probably told you. I'm thinking of yarding out my trees, growing nuts instead."

"How interesting," said David, without batting an eye.

After the six-pack had been finished and Vern had contributed another beer each, they broke up. George and David returned to the boat and chugged peacefully up the western shore. In the late afternoon under a bright sky, the channel was blue-black, the trees a somber dark green. David studied the houses along the shore. As on the eastern side, they were widely spaced, some modern and quite large, with luxury cruisers and seaplanes tied up at their wharves.

George was silent until they drew abreast of a farm-house and could see a distant figure, pail in hand, heading for a barn. The figure raised an arm and George waved back.

"Vern," he said. "You pay a price for growing money, David. Your kids won't be able to have sleepovers, your wife won't be able to mix in community life, and nor will you." He paused and then added, "And you can't be honest with your friends."

David was enjoying the late-afternoon sun. "You could have told him it was Mike who was horsing around with the price. Couldn't you?"

"Oh that. Yes, I meant the other."

"That's not good, of course," said David. "But as for the rest, you have a close-knit family. That must be worth a lot."

*   *   *

A week later, after Jane had left to cater a lunch, George and David took over the kitchen. They brought in ten pounds of onions and a spray bottle full of beta-cyclodextrin, and chopped onions until their eyes ran.

"Can we stop?" George wasn't used to this type of work.

David estimated they had cut up half of them. "Should be enough."

George groped for the bottle. "I hope to God this works," he said, wiping his eyes. He sprayed the room generously, with particular attention to the pile of chopped onions. They would be left out on the counter until dinnertime.

David opened the fridge. "Do you know what Jane has planned for this leftover roast lamb?"

"Good lord, no. Why?"

"Fallback plan. If the spray doesn't work we'll need a policy of appeasement. Want to ask her?"

Out in the yard, George called Jane on his phone and passed it over after the preliminaries.

"I noticed we've got a good bit of that roast lamb left over," said David. "Would you like me to make curry for dinner?"

"Why?" The voice was laden with suspicion. "Have you two been doing something in the house?"

David made a face at George then spoke into the phone. "Look. No pain, no gain, right? You wanted George to find a solution for the smell. So, we may have found one. I just thought it'd be nice if you didn't have to cook."

"Is the house still habitable?"

David hesitated. "Barely." He grimaced at George.

A laugh came through along with the go ahead.

That evening, Jane sat down to a dinner she had not cooked, in a kitchen which still smelled of onions, but only faintly.

George was not enthusiastic, mainly because of the lingering odor. "Pity you chose curry, David. Scrambled eggs or something would have been better."

"Really, George!" Jane's look was wasted on him. "It's delicious, David," she said firmly, seconded by Mike and Daffy.

George was oblivious. "We should have kept those onions. We'll do some more tomorrow."

"In the barn, if you don't mind."

David had a thought. "Heat might improve the results, mightn't it? You said you use the dryer during processing."

George considered. "What do you think, Daff?"

Daffy shrugged. "I don't know, Dad." She ate another forkful of curry. "This is awfully good, David. Just the way I like it. Mum's is too hot."

George looked discontentedly out the window. "The way I see it," he said, "we have three chances to introduce an anti-smell agent. We can put an additive in the ground before we plant, or in the nutrients, or we can introduce something during processing. But our goal ideally is not to mask the smell but to remove it."

David thought about this. "You mean, we might treat the bills then six months later the smell would be back?"

"Exactly."

$*$ $*$ $*$

David hefted a silver dollar. "You wouldn't want a pocket full of these, would you?" He put it back on the kitchen counter. "What's it worth today?"

"About sixteen dollars," said Mike. He had used the proceeds of his bottle returns to buy another one, and now he began to fill a Teflon muffin tin, putting one dollar in each of the twelve cups.

David leaned on the counter across from him, watching as he finished filling the tray and took it over to the stove, putting it down next to a double-boiler. He removed the top saucepan and carefully poured liquid chocolate onto each dollar, just enough to cover it.

David pulled out a handful of coins from his pocket. He had quarters and Canadian one- and two-dollar coins. He lined them up next to one of the silver dollars. It was half again as big. Just an ordinary silver dollar showing signs of wear and tear. Even so, it made the contemporary coins look cheap and tawdry. He picked it up: creamy silver to the touch, with a young Queen Elizabeth on one side and the date, 1964, on the other. "What's with the two men in a boat?"

Mike had finished with the tray and left it on the counter to cool, returning the saucepan to the double-boiler. He was now working on a tray from the freezer, carefully loosening the chocolate-covered coins from their Teflon surroundings, using a small knife with a very thin blade. He frowned at David. "That's a canoe, you moron. And those are voyageurs, they explored this country, they opened it up to the settlers and trapped furs and sold 'em to the Hudson's Bay Company."

"Ah! Nicholas Garry."

"Who's that?" Mike was concentrating on removing each coin from its cup.

"He was a deputy-governor of the Hudson's Bay Company and he's who your oak tree is named for." He nodded out the window at the oak in the south field. "*Quercus garryana*."

Chin propped on hand, David watched as he fitted each chocolate coin into an After Eight mints box. When he'd finished the box was full and he closed the lid carefully. Later, after he'd processed all his coins, they took the boxes out to the freezer, and removed most of its contents. The After Eight boxes joined several others at the bottom of the freezer.

"He's always been a hoarder, haven't you, son?" said George during dinner.

"It's a waste of good chocolate," said Jane. "You could just as well keep them in a box under your bed."

"No—," Mike was irate. Daffy intervened.

"I told him that when times get really bad the authorities like to confiscate gold and silver. That's what they do."

"You said there wouldn't be a hyperinflation for years and years."

Daffy rolled her eyes. "Mum. It's not up to me."

* * *

On Halloween they held a bonfire of the pruned apple-tree branches, and roasted wieners and marshmallows. They lit one end of the pile, and added more branches as the evening wore on. Jane tended the fire with David, while George, Daffy and Mike did the cooking.

"I love apples, don't you?" said Jane, "They're so sociable. And useful and good for you. Michael and I run the fruit stand, you know. It's like having a shop, gossiping and weighing apples and making change. I love it."

David shoved a branch further into the flames and watched as a shower of sparks rose up into the night.

Chapter 8

Canadian Connection

One of the biggest drawbacks to being responsible for the world's benchmark currency was that America's trading partners had to be kept informed of any changes in or threats to the dollar. Not only were all currencies valued in terms of the greenback, but US dollars were in active use in black markets, in drug deals, in bazaars and on street corners the world over.

The frontline troops in the battle against counterfeiting are citizens on the street. In the case of the dollar, that was the principal reason its look and feel had changed little over the years, although many subtle security measures had been added. It was essential that people be able to spot a counterfeit, whether they were Afghan shepherds or Zairean street vendors.

Following a high-level meeting two days earlier, the Secretary of the Treasury had notified senior banking officials of the potentially devastating blow to the world monetary system represented by the money tree. Halloran was in the process of informing senior law enforcement in key countries because this was an official investigation and he needed their help. Any stories of money being eaten by animals should be checked out immediately and details forwarded to Washington.

He was interrupted by Jaio McCaffrey, the forensics chief, who brought a visitor.

"Yves," Halloran shook the older man's hand. "Good to see you. What brings you to town?"

Yves Simard was Chief Scientist in the Counterfeit division of the RCMP, based in Ottawa. In his late fifties, he was a grey-haired, ascetic individual who had over the years amassed formidable data and experience on counterfeiting. Because the greenback was widely circulated throughout Canada alongside domestic dollars, his knowledge of US dollar counterfeiting was second only to that of the Secret Service.

They sat down. "Yves has an incident to report," said Jaio.

"After your call yesterday, I reviewed our files," said Simard. He'd found a two-year-old report about a horse eating a bill at the Calgary Stampede. An RCMP constable was attending with his family when it happened, and overheard some chat about it from spectators. "He found the rancher who owned the horse and confirmed it. The horse had reached out and taken a twenty-dollar bill from an American tourist. It had eaten the bill, and the rancher ended up compensating the tourist."

Halloran nodded. "That's the way it's happened here. Mostly dogs but not always."

"It's a subtle smell," said Jaio. "Perceptible to animals but not humans." She glanced at Halloran. "I've filled Yves in on everything, Jack." She had shown him her slides of the torn bill, and told him about the interview with Professor Pringle.

Halloran nodded. "I've been reviewing what we learned from Pringle." he said. "We think it grows Brazilian *reals*. We know it grows US dollars. The question is, how?"

Jaio sighed. "Maybe the question should be, where?"

Yves nodded. "And if it will grow dollars, will it grow Euros or pounds or yen? Or Canadian dollars, for that matter?"

"We can't rule any of that out," said Halloran. "It's a living nightmare, that's what it is."

The only constructive action he had been able to take was to alert Brinks and other currency-handling companies that the Secret Service had heard a rumor of tainted drug money entering the system in large quantities. He recommended their guards use dogs when making pickups. Brinks was happy to oblige, but that had been weeks ago. The waiting was killing them all.

Chapter 9

Storm

The runabout was moored on the eastern shore of the island, and David and Daffy were digging for clams. The tide was out, the day overcast. The beach was a mixture of gravel and sand, dotted beyond the high-tide line with large boulders and isolated logs.

They were using short-handled rakes to expose the clams, dropping them into buckets filled with water. Jane liked to leave them in salt water overnight, to flush out the sand in their systems. Tomorrow night they would feast on linguini with clam sauce, which was why clam-digging was one of David's favorite occupations. He raked and collected with gusto and no longer had half his clams thrown back by Daffy because they were too small.

They moved further along the beach toward the runabout and raked some more. Daffy's strokes slowed down and then stopped, and she spoke. "I've been thinking . . ." she said, just as David straightened up and threw another clam in his bucket; and she was about to continue when she saw his expression.

"Forget it." She picked up her pail, and carried it to the boat.

"Sorry," said David. "Tell me." He couldn't resist adding, "'Another Wacky Theory' by Daffy Frisby."

She heaved her bucket over the side, and deposited it carefully on the floorboards. "It burns me to think I actually lay in bed one night and *cried* because you're all alone." She climbed in and sat down, chin on hand, scowling at a seagull.

"I'm not alone, Daffy," he said patiently. "I have friends and girlfriends."

"Oh right. Y'know, one of these days you'll really fall in love and I just wish I could be there—"

She saw an involuntary glance in her direction. "What?"

David turned away and began raking some more. Daffy climbed out of the boat and came over.

"What?" she asked again.

He stopped and straightened. Glanced briefly at her. Heaved a sigh and shook his head. "Promise you won't tell? You'll have to swear."

"I swear," said Daffy avidly. "Tell me."

"Especially not Jane."

"Oh, sick! You're in love with Mum."

"Not in the least," replied David. "But I'm deeply— passionately—in love with George. Head over heels—"

Daffy aimed a kick at him and he dodged it, laughing, and went on digging for clams. Daffy climbed back in the boat and sat down.

"How did your parents arrive at such a perfect name for you, Daff?" he said at last. "Does every first-born Frisby have a daft gene? Or did you grow into the name? Was that it?"

Daffy was trying to decide how long to wait before forgiving him, so it was a full fifteen seconds before she replied. "In the first place, smartass, my theories aren't dumb just because you say so. In the second, I was named for my grandmothers." She smiled at some memory and went on, the words tumbling out. "That was Dad's idea and Mum only agreed if Daphne came first because that was Granny Frisby's name. She really hates Granny Carruthers. And in the third place—"

"Gracious, what sordid revelations."

"Shut up. In the third place, Mum fell in love with Dad the day I was born and I'm really really glad I was there, even though I didn't have much to do with it." She paused, then added, "Although I guess I did, in a way."

"What took her so long?"

Daffy shrugged. "Mum loves us a lot but she isn't all huggy-feely like Dad. She says it's like riding a bike. If you don't learn when you're a kid, you're never any good at it."

David dug up his last clam and carried his bucket over, putting it next to Daffy's. Then he pushed the boat out and climbed over the side, and they headed back up the eastern shore.

The wind was stronger as they came to the point and turned toward the cove. Daffy had been staring off at the distant islands, and she came back to the present.

"Are you saying I should change my name? I've been working on this idea for ages and it's pretty fundamental. 'A Theory of Money and Violence' by Daphne Frisby. I mean, is there a credibility problem here? David?"

David was fighting the wind and currents so he waited until they were well round the point before answering.

"Oh I don't know," he said at last. "Being an ex–would-be terrorist gives you a certain authority, I think." He could see

Daffy was not amused. "All right, let's have it. In twenty-five words or less."

Daffy stared at him, doing a fast edit. "Unstable money means people can't plan their lives. They don't know what their kids' education will cost, or how much they'll need to retire. Unstable money adds stress to society and that leads to increased violence."

They neared the dock.

"I don't know about unstable money but we have rotten economies where people can't get good-paying jobs. I should have thought that would be more likely to cause violence. In fact, I think it has, don't you?"

Daffy grabbed the dock and hooked the rope over the bollard. "Interesting point, David. That's all part of it." She climbed out and turned to take one of the buckets from him. "This is more of an hypothesis than a theory because I have to do a lot more research. I'm trying to define levels of violence, you see, and correlate them with—," she stopped, staring at the dock, thinking deeply. "I can see I'll have to broaden—," she looked up and saw him holding up the other bucket. "Sorry."

She took it from him, set it down with the other and went on. "I want to develop a unified theory for economics, similar to what Einstein did for physics, do you see?"

"I think Mike's ahead of you."

"Be serious," she said but he was busy hanging orange floats over the side of the boat, to protect it from the wooden dock structure. He threw Daffy the stern rope and she tied it round the second bollard. He climbed onto the dock.

"See, it's a gradual thing, not overnight. Money affects everything, David. So when the government manipulates it, they're manipulating everything."

They each took a bucket and started up the shingle to the field.

"So what do you want to do? Go back to the gold standard?"

"I don't know."

"You can't be advocating Bitcoin." David didn't like digital currencies because they had nothing tangible behind them.

"Oh God! You're so conservative! Why not?"

"Because it has no real world reference. The money tree wouldn't know what to grow and it'd have a nervous breakdown. And that, young Daff, would never do."

She stopped dead and looked at him. "Are you happy in your little closed-off world, David?" She put her pail down. "Don't you ever want to try new things?" She marched off to the house.

Pail in each hand, David followed at a gentle pace. He glanced up at the farmhouse as he came through the orchard. He would miss this place. He was returning to the UK next week to find a place to live, a place where he could raise a few money trees of his own in peace and quiet.

*   *   *

Daffy sat at the computer reading her favorite blogger, an investment and financial analyst who had been following the markets for thirty years.

Trust takes years to build. It can be lost in an instant and once lost is difficult if not impossible to rebuild. The loss of trust in banks generally and in the big investment banks in particular has been well documented. Far more worrisome these days is the loss of trust—of respect, even—for the fractional-reserve system and the central banks that run it. European central bankers have made no secret of the fact that in a crisis, depositor funds are up for grabs. Japan has been mired in an institutional depression for years and its central bank shows no sign of finding a way out.

Unemployment everywhere is high and savers everywhere are being cheated of the interest earnings they deserve for their thrift. As for the linchpin economy, the US recovery is anemic and the Fed's "qualitative easing," the mammoth purchase of bonds that swelled the Fed coffers to fully 20 percent of government securities, has been a complete fiasco.

* * *

Mike biked up the island road with a ten-dollar bill in his shirt pocket, pay for two hours' work for Mrs. Bagnold. Last weekend he'd had to put in a half-hour extra, but that was mainly because of not knowing where she kept things. This time, he'd finished in two hours, though he'd had to push to do it.

He'd gone to see her ten days ago after school, with a clipboard on which he'd noted all the chores she wanted done on Saturdays. He'd surveyed her small, tangled back garden, and the small, crowded house, and evaluated her list, and informed her he could manage the job in two hours and would be happy to take it on. The following afternoon, he had dropped off a list of all the jobs with his signature underneath. "Did I miss anything, Mrs. Bagnold?" She had read through the list and appraised him over the top of her glasses. "You did not." She reached for a pen. "You don't have to sign it, " he'd said, "I just did it so we'd have an understanding." "But of course I must sign it," she had said, and meeting Jane on Sunday, after the first session, she had waved her over. "That's a most unusual young man, your Michael. He'll go far." Jane had smiled and thanked her. *In what direction,* she had wondered.

Mike saw a familiar figure in the distance, and pedaled faster.

Ron Parker hummed to himself as he cruised along the island road. Texada Timewarp gave him a better buzz and a more gentle descent than any other strain he'd tried.

"Hiya, Mr. Parker." Mike drew abreast of the old man, who nodded pleasantly.

"Kid." The wind had a November edge to it and he was glad of his sweater.

"Can I ask you something?"

Ron lost the tune but not his mood. "Sure," he said amiably. They continued biking in tandem until Mike spoke.

"Can we stop? I mean, to talk?"

They pulled in to the side of the road.

"So what can I do you for?"

"Mr. Parker, do you know anyone who likes money? I mean, really likes money?"

The old man looked up at the sky. It was becoming noticeably darker. "Doesn't everyone?"

"No," said Mike seriously. "A lot of people say they like it, but they wouldn't really break into a sweat to get it. I mean, if you gave them ten dollars they'd go and spend it, but it wouldn't really matter to them." Ron held up a hand and he stopped talking.

"I get it. You're talking about Ariadne Wu."

"Does she like money?" Mike had heard his parents discussing the realtor.

"Is the Pope Catholic?"

Mike waited for more.

"Listen, kid. She lives for money. She loves it. She won't part with a penny. Cheap? You wouldn't believe." He pulled out a Caramilk and peeled back the foil wrapper, breaking off a row for Mike and one for himself. They chewed companionably and he went on. "Couple years ago, she tried to build a fence inside our property line. Tried to tell Vern the line was marked wrong. Give me a break. That property was surveyed and marked in my dad's time. She comes busting in here and starts messing with the stakes?" He broke off another row of chocolate. "Vern found out her surveyor was fresh out of surveyor school, and told her to tell him to check his azimuths. Whatever. Then he sent her a bill for half the lawyer's fee for an hour's consulting. Still waiting on that one. Cow."

"Gee. I'm sorry, Mr. Parker."

"Not your fault, kid." Ron waved the Caramilk bar like an admonitory finger. "Don't you go messing with Ariadne. She'll push you around from here to Sunday. Or eat you alive." He glanced upward again. "Time to get on home. Storm's coming."

Mike biked thoughtfully homeward. Ariadne Wu sounded perfect, a person with a proper appreciation of the value of a dollar. Even better, she was Chinese. Mike was prepared to forego Canadian harvests if he had to, but if Ariadne could be persuaded to raise trees in China instead, that would be perfect. If she wanted to do both, they'd have to haggle. He pulled into the driveway. Another good thing about her: she worked in Vancouver, so she must have an office there. He could write first, without giving too much away. He mulled this over as he patted Angus and entered the house. Two jobs, then: hone his negotiating skills, and draft a letter. He decided to hold off on the Dhasi family for now.

The fall weather broke decisively that afternoon, and a storm raged. The wind roared round the house. Tree branches tumbled up the north field and thumped against the barn, and water gushed down the drainpipes.

The Frisbys and their guest sat snug and warm in the living room after the linguini feast, and played canasta. David was not familiar with the game, but found it fairly easy to learn. Since Jane wasn't playing, they formed partners, George and Daffy against David and Mike. It was really no contest, as David soon discovered. Mike had a memory for the discard pile and a genius for ending a game at the worst possible time for the other team.

"Okay if I go out?"

The others groaned.

"Fine by me," said David.

"I don't believe it." George leaned back in his chair and they all watched as Mike completed three canastas already on the table and added a concealed one in eights.

"I *knew* you wanted eights, you stinker," Daffy cuffed her brother as Jane came in with a bowl of popcorn.

"Put another log on, David," said George. The rain pelted against the windows.

"We won," said Mike, unnecessarily. "Three in a row."

"Give them the prize, Daff. They're partners in this crime."

The prize was a one-hundred trillion dollar Zimbabwean banknote. Mike passed it over to David.

"What's this for?"

"You get to carry it round all day tomorrow." Mike watched him enviously.

David laughed and handed it back. "Can't say Zimbabwe's high on my list of places to see."

"Nor me," agreed Jane, then shrieked as George grabbed her and pulled her on to his knee with a leering "Want to play a round?"

"Just ignore them," said Daffy. "Aunt Cristobel sent us that. She sent one to all the sisters, not just Mum. It was just for fun."

David took a handful of popcorn. "They were talking of doing that in the States, weren't they? Creating a coin to pay the debt or something?"

"Yeah. It was just a gag," said Daffy. "They don't need a coin, they just have to agree to do it. It's only a keystroke, really."

Jane heard that. "What do you mean, Daff?"

"It's just a bookkeeping entry, Mum. They don't have to print the money or anything. Just make an entry in some electronic ledger and bingo, another trillion hits the books."

Jane stared at her in silence. "That's just wrong," she said at last. "Isn't it, George?" He shrugged. "Well, it seems wrong to me."

"That's all very well," said David, "but debt is part of what government's about. I mean, the dollar's backed by the full faith and credit of the US government. Isn't it? Same as the pound."

"That's true," said Daffy. She got down on her stomach and rested her chin on her hands, staring at the fire's flames. "But I'm reading a book right now that says money ought to increase in value, not decrease. It makes sense if you think about it. All the productivity gains. All the hard work of ordinary people, plus the plants and equipment plus innovation. . . ." Her legs crossed, swayed above her back. "Just suppose. Just suppose you could know that your pounds or dollars would be worth more when you retire than they are now. That your savings would not only earn interest but would actually appreciate in value, so that a dollar in twenty years would buy more stuff than it does today." She glanced up at him. "That's what makes government waste so sickening. They squander that potential wealth by piling up debt so that the dollar isn't worth more every year, it's worth less."

David looked at Jane. "Why don't you come and play? Take my place."

"She doesn't like cards," said Mike. "She can't play. She's as thick as—"

"Michael," warned George.

"I'm just saying what Mum always says!"

"It's not hard," said David. "I could give you a hand."

Jane shook her head. "I'm no good at cards, David, and I hate playing. Except for Snap," she laughed. "I'm very good at that."

Daffy was still musing. "Bitcoin should appreciate in value, if it lasts long enough."

"Bitcoin, Daff?" George sat up. "What's that?"

"It's a digital money, Dad. It started a few years ago."

"Started how?"

"The code was announced on some cryptography forum by the guy who created it, Satoshi Nakamoto. He kicked things off by paying himself 50 Bitcoins."

"Yes, but . . . what did he receive? Fifty what?"

"Each Bitcoin is a bit of digital code with two addresses, one public and one private."

They stared at her. "Look, it's a peer-to-peer network. Like Skype. So anyone can join in and anyone can look at the code. You can buy more and more things with it, and use it in restaurants and pubs. Or you can become a Bitcoin miner. That way—"

"Wait a minute." David looked annoyed. "Miner? Come on, Daff."

"Listen, I don't understand all of it myself, but we'll talk to Ken if you're really interested. The idea was to make Bitcoins hard to create, like gold's hard to find. So the code requires miners to solve a problem. If they can do it in the time available, the first solver earns a bunch of coins."

"Like how many?" Mike sat up.

"What kind of problem?" George was curious.

"Time available?"

Daffy threw her hands up, and addressed Mike first. "It used to be fifty. Now it's twenty-five. Twenty-five new Bitcoins are created every ten minutes or so. The number's supposed to go down every four years. When they get to 21 million coins in circulation, it stops."

"That's not many coins, Daffy." David was dismissive. "In a global economy? Twenty-one million?"

"Yeah, but a Bitcoin is divisible to eight places. That's, like, quadrillions of units. The idea is, if Bitcoins become viable, they appreciate in value. So you might spend .01 of a Bitcoin on a cup of coffee, or .001."

George wanted to know what kind of problem you had to solve.

"See, that's partly why Ken says its such beautiful code. If the problem is too easy, too many miners reach the answer too quickly. So it's self-adjusting. And it also allows for more and more powerful computers, because everyone started climbing on the bandwagon to mine coins, so nowadays the problems are so difficult you need a very expensive, fast computer to solve them." She sat up and crossed her legs, facing the others. "Basically, each block of transactions includes some random data, part of which is relevant to the number you're looking for."

"I'm looking for a number?"

"You're looking for two. See, here's a simple example. Think of a number."

"Twenty one!" Mike still had his mind on card games.

"Okay. Now what two numbers do you have to add together to make twenty one?"

"Ten. And eleven."

David glanced at him. "Or nine and twelve."

"Eight and thirteen," said George.

"Even I can do this," said Jane. "Seven and fourteen."

"Okay, okay. That's easy. Now: suppose the number's . . . 35,623?" Her eyes sparkled. "Tell me what two numbers to add together."

"Crikey," said Jane and David laughed shortly.

"Bitcoin mining is like that, only way more complicated. It's based on something called a hashcash proof of work. Your answer is in the form of a block that includes a verification of all the transactions that happened in that brief period. You have to find the right number, your answer has to start with four zeros and include the hash of the block before, and you have to do this in under ten minutes."

"Whoa," said George.

"I know. And if your answer is wrong, the network just rejects it. It's really cool, because every transaction is recorded, every one since the beginning, and they all form this blockchain, which anyone can look at, which is like a public record of all Bitcoin transactions." She added, "It's a lot different from using a credit card. And you can't get a refund with Bitcoin."

They mulled over these details. Then David said, "So twenty-five new Bitcoins are created every ten minutes or so?"

"Right."

"And given to the first computer that comes up with the correct answer?"

"That's right. It's got so competitive now, that people join mining consortiums just to be part of the process." She thought, then added, "Which is one measure of how it's grown, I suppose."

"What's a hash, darling?"

"Don't ask me, Mum," said Daffy cheerfully. "But you know what? Ken's in love with hashes." She added, "They're part of cryptography, I think."

George said, "That must be why transactions can't be reversed. Because they're all part of the record. The blockchain, you call it."

"That's right, Dad. And that, and the fact that there's no central banker, no one controlling Bitcoin, is why it's easier to trust. You can just read the code if you want. Bitcoin's governed by math not by central bankers."

"So, wait a minute," David sat up. "If I buy something with Bitcoins, do I have to wait while the transaction is verified?"

"Ten minutes or so."

"What if I just want a cup of coffee?"

"Good question. I guess you just stand there in line until it's verified, then they give you your coffee."

Jane looked askance. "I'd rather use Michael's silver dollars."

"Hear, hear," said David.

"What if you wanted to travel round the world or buy a house? You couldn't carry enough silver or gold to do it. You can duplicate your Bitcoin holdings on a flash drive and carry it with you or store it somewhere safe. See, it's simple to use, just like sending an email, and completely anonymous."

"What does that matter?" David looked at Mike. "One whacking great electromagnetic pulse could wipe out the lot."

"Yeah!" Mike raised his electromagnetic pulse gun. "You're wiped out, Dave!"

The evening degenerated into floor wrestling among the males.

Chapter 10

Religious Differences

On the bright, sunny Sunday morning after the storm, Daffy biked off to visit her seedlings. Jane and Mike went to church. She had made a rule years ago that both children would attend church until they were sixteen, after which they could do as they pleased. Mike expressed his view of this policy as the car moved off.

"I've got a busy agenda, too, did you ever stop to think of that? It's not fair."

Angus sat by the side of the driveway, his ear cocked, listening.

They came upon Daffy wheeling her bike, red-faced, halfway up the hill. Mike turned to watch her, his head pressed against the window, his expression doleful. Jane honked as they passed, then they were up to the top and along the flat.

Mike had little time for most Christian doctrine. He was okay with "honor thy parents" and he quite liked people like Daniel and David, and Matthew the tax collector. Others he wasn't so crazy about, and his least favorite was Jesus, whom he despised. "He doesn't do anything. He just goes around telling other people what to do."

After the service, Jane chatted with Helga Johnston, a member of the Channel Dredging committee. It was Helga who had mentioned Jane's name to Ariadne Wu and she was unapologetic about it. "I thought she might persuade you to join. And I don't believe you'd vote with her once you know all the facts." She looked past Jane, who turned to find the Sunday School teacher, a devout young girl of seventeen, hovering.

"Mrs. Frisby," she said anxiously, then words failed her. She held out a sheet of paper, on which were displayed large donut letters of green and black felt tip. "Jesus is a dweeb," read Jane.

Helga repressed a smile.

"Maybe he's too old for Sunday School," said the girl. Beyond her, Michael stared glumly along the road.

Jane thanked her, shoved the paper in a pocket, wound down her conversation with Helga, collected Michael and drove homeward. When they reached the flat section of road before the long hill, she pulled in and stopped.

Along the side of the road the Oregon grape was a carpet of green and red. The boughs of the firs and cedars sparkled with raindrops, the sea was a bright blue and puffs of white cloud dotted the sky. It was a day to gladden the heart of any but the car's two occupants. They were oblivious.

Jane turned toward Michael, wondering what to do about him. She had never had these kinds of battles with Daffy, these energy-sapping engagements that ruined her day.

She decided to start with the price of apples.

"Dad heard you were you charging two-fifty for the apples. Is that true?"

Michael was staring at his knees. The question caught him by surprise. "Yeah."

"Did anyone pay that price?"

"Yeah, lots of people." He looked defiant.

Jane had had time to think about this. "Look, Michael, I don't mind what you charge. If you can get two-fifty, good luck to you." She paused, considering.

He lifted his head at this unexpected reaction, and looked at her in surprise.

She added, "I have to wonder if you'd end up with happy customers, but that's another conversation." She looked at him. "However, I do not like you doing it behind my back. That's deceitful."

"If I told you, you'd just say no, so why bother?"

She disregarded this and took out the sheet of paper. "What's this in aid of, Michael?"

"I told you. I'm sick of church."

"I don't care, dear. I went to church when I was your age. So will you, until you show me that you've learned how to behave."

* * *

Daffy labored up through the sodden undergrowth, slipping on rocks and grabbing at shrubs to pull herself forward. She reached the clearing and stopped for a moment to catch her breath. The San Juans lay like a blue-green smudge, the color of her hair, on the distant horizon.

The clearing was covered in branches and debris and at first she could not see any seedlings. Then she glimpsed the familiar small heads.

"Hi, little guys, Daffy's here."

She picked her way over to a large fir branch and lifted it carefully. Underneath lay three flattened money trees. Pulling off her backpack, she removed a small cassette player, knelt down and switched it on, placing it roughly equidistant from the three seedlings.

Mike's idea of getting Jane to tape her money tree classes had proved unexpectedly difficult for Daffy. For one thing it was low on Jane's list of priorities; for another, she generally had these personal development sessions with the seedlings in the afternoon, while Daffy was still at school. In the end, Daffy had again stressed the benefits of taping, and left the cassette deck on the workbench, ready for use. The result, when she finally heard it, was more than she had expected, and Daffy was delighted. Not only was there a full half-hour on alphabet and numbers, Jane had added an alphanumeric section directly related to the creation of serial numbers and with particular emphasis on capital letters. But the final section was the best, in Daffy's view, perfect for disasters and events such as the storm.

She fast-forwarded and switched on the cassette. Jane's voice was heard, preceded by a gusty sigh: "All right, you lot. Let's wind up with a song." Daffy turned up the volume ever so slightly. A jaunty nursery song danced through the clearing:

The sun has got his hat on, he's coming out today—

She watched the flattened seedlings closely. Definite signs of life. She cleared away twigs and debris as Jane's voice continued:

The sun has got his hat on and he's coming out to play....

The nearest seedling raised its head. Another one lifted itself up on an elbow, so to speak. Daffy left them and began to clear debris away from other storm victims.

*   *   *

Jane stood at the kitchen counter filling a shopping bag with baked goods in small decorative cake or cookie tins. There were two tins of cherry cake, two of Nanaimo bars, and several containers of cookies, either oatmeal or chocolate chip. As a member of the St. Kit's women's auxiliary, she volunteered one Sunday each month to visit shut-ins on the Big Island, chat with them and leave them some goodies. It wasn't difficult work: most of the old folks were pleasant enough company, just lonely.

Mike sat at the kitchen table. She had told him to find a pad and pencil and now he stared glumly at the oak tree in the sunshine and waited for orders.

Angus sat halfway between the two of them, looking from one to the other.

"Jesus was the Son of God," said Jane, adding a couple of paperbacks to the shopping bag.

"Big deal. So am I." He returned his mother's look. "Well, I am. We're all supposed to be the children of God, right?"

Jane gestured at him. "Write. Jesus was the son of God and a very good man."

Mike wrote it down. "So's Dad." His mother looked severe. "Isn't he?"

"Stop interrupting, Michael, and do as I say!" She added some quilting squares for one of the shut-ins. "Next line. The meek shall inherit the earth."

He rolled his eyes. "Yeah, right."

Angus whined unhappily.

"Okay. Are we done?"

"No," said Jane. "Neither a soaker . . ."

He stared at her. She gestured again and his head bent over the paper. She added some sandwiches and two bottles of water to the bag. Mike looked up and she went on, ". . . nor a soakee . . . be."

"B?"

"Be. B E. Neither a soaker nor a soakee be." She paused, savoring this phrase, pleased.

"Mum. You have to be one or the other."

"I don't think so."

"I'm telling you! You have to be—"

"Now listen to me. You will write each of those lines out one hundred times. Is that clear?"

He slumped over the paper, and Angus whined and lay down.

"Is that clear?"

"Yes! But I invented soakers and soakees and I'm telling you! You can't be neither!"

"Well, Michael, I disagree with you. There is a civilized middle ground. And when you've written out those lines, you will go to your room and reflect on what it might be. And you will stay there until I get home. Is that clear?"

Mike shot to his feet. "That's not fair! It's not fair! This is the only day I get to do anything!"

"You should have thought of that before. Now get on with it." She picked up the carrier bag and walked out.

*   *   *

At lunchtime, Mike returned to the kitchen with Angus at his heels. He carried a thick stack of paper that he thumped onto the counter, squaring the pile and admiring it. The top sheet was handwritten: MUM.

"That'll fix her," he said.

The house was silent. Opening the fridge door, he rummaged for fillings and made himself a sandwich. Angus whined, and Mike went into the mud room and filled his bowl and changed his water. Then he sat on the floor next to him and they ate their respective lunches, deep in thought.

Mike had done considerable research into franchising. He'd explored multilevel marketing as a business model and soon realized it was completely inappropriate for his purposes because recruits were expected to recruit, and the product was secondary. He spent quite a while exploring affiliate marketing online, and would have liked to build a Google ad campaign. If he could have guaranteed his anonymity he would have set up a website offering people the opportunity to grow money, built traffic with an ad campaign, and sold advertising through Google adSense and affiliate marketing. It was painfully easy to see how lucrative this might have been, except for the fact that anonymity doesn't exist on the Internet.

An eBay business looked like a wonderful opportunity, and there were times when Mike wished he were grown up so he could pursue that avenue on his own, without parental interference. And maybe he would one day, but right now he was tasked with selling the money tree, and the only way to do that was with franchises. Which brought him back to the introductory letter. How did you reach out to a potential franchisee?

This morning he had googled "home business opportunities" and here he struck gold. He found all kinds of letters extolling opportunities in catering, cleaning, pet grooming and assorted exotic plants. Many of the letters were extremely long-winded, but he got that concept. You grabbed the guy with a good, greed-based opener, then you pulled him into your make-believe world of Maseratis and yachts and vacations, then when he was well and truly hooked, you gave him the lowdown on fees and costs and, in Mike's case, secrecy.

Studying these offerings, pulling out a sentence here, a concept there, he had managed to cobble together a letter of his own. But the angle still eluded him, the logical thread that pulled the viewer inexorably to the kicker at the conclusion: the initial investment and costs. He finished his lunch and made his way back upstairs, Angus at his heels, to try again.

*   *   *

George and Daffy were busy at the workbench in the barn when Jane and David arrived home mid-afternoon. Jane had had a successful day visiting all her shut-ins and delivering her bits and pieces. David had booked his flight home, explored the shops, gone for a long walk and eaten a leisurely lunch in the café by the harbor. When he saw the car pull in, he paid his bill and walked down to the terminal.

Jane had greeted him cheerfully as he put a carrier bag in the rear and got in beside her. "Had a nice time? What's that?"

"Thought I'd do dinner since it's my last night."

"How lovely."

They pulled into the garage and joined the others. George's workbench took up half of one wall and consisted of a wide bench with cupboards and shelves above and drawers below. He glanced up briefly, pleased to see them, then continued to pour printer's ink into a flask suspended over a lighted Bunsen burner.

"What's all this?" David looked at the apparatus then at George. "I thought we'd given up on the ink?"

George shook his head. "Change of plan."

Beta-cyclodextrin had never fully satisfied him as a solution. The most it seemed to offer was a temporary patch. He'd continued to worry away at the problem, and had even spent a night sitting downstairs considering ways to impregnate the bills with pepper. At five in the morning he realized this was just as bad as doing nothing: animals would still have a strong reaction to the bills, just a negative rather than positive one.

George felt in his bones that there had to be some organic solution to the smell problem. Two days ago he came full circle: since the money tree was essentially an imitative plant, it might have an affinity for printer's ink. This reasoning had led him to try it in the first place, and now he returned to it.

The ink itself was obviously not a solution, being viscous and, as he had discovered in the dryer, difficult to remove once it adhered to anything. A transparent printer's ink did not exist, which left only one other option that George could think of: a distillation of the ink. Accordingly, he had rummaged around in the workbench cupboards and assembled the Bunsen burner, a length of rubber tubing, and some stands and flasks. He'd attached these items, with the flask suspended over the burner, and the tubing running from a stopper in the flask, along the counter, through a tray of ice and into a jar. Now a thin stream of clear liquid was trickling from the tube into the glass jar.

He replaced it with an empty one and brought the jar over to David and Jane, who had been watching in fascination.

"What's this?" asked Jane.

Daffy was writing on a label at the workbench.

George said, "I call it—ahem!—'Essence of printer's ink'." Daffy applied the label to a full bottle, and turned with a flourish to display it.

"Will it work?"

"Find out at Christmas," said George. He added, to their amusement, "But I'm—quietly confident."

"Darling, aren't you clever!" said Jane, giving him a kiss. "I must get Michael. He'll be thrilled."

Daffy stared at her. "What do you mean? I thought he was with you."

She followed Jane to the house. David joined George at the workbench.

"Why wait till Christmas? I know the nuts aren't seasoned but we could still test it, couldn't we?"

George picked up the can of ink. "I thought of it, but the fact is, the bills need moisture and heat to take up the odor. That's my theory, anyway. We'll have to introduce it into the processing cycle." He poured more ink into the flask over the burner. "Next year, we'll add it to the starter fluid. See if that does the trick."

*　*　*

Jane leafed through the stack of printed pages on the kitchen counter. Page after page of single sentences, widely spaced, six to a page. First "Jesus was the son of God and a very good man," page after page. Then more pages with "The meek shall inherit the earth." Finally, "Neither a soaker nor a soakee be." Daffy stood at her elbow, awed.

Jane continued to turn pages until she reached the end. The last page was different. In very large bold capitals it read, "SOAKERS OF THE WORLD UNITE."

Jane's lips tightened as she stared at this. Daffy put a hand on her arm but she shook it off, gathered up the pages abruptly and went out.

Dozing on the carpet in Mike's room, Angus sat up, his ears pricked. Mike, working at the computer, heard the sharp rap on his door and swiveled round cheerfully.

"Hi, Mum." He saw the pages in her hand. "A thousand times each. Pretty nice, huh?"

"No, Michael, it is not pretty nice. I asked you to write each line—"

"Nobody writes any more, Mum. It's inefficient."

"It wasn't intended to be efficient! It was intended to drum some inkling of decent conduct into your depraved, ignorant skull! How *dare* you try and fob me off—"

Angus slithered out the door as she threw the pages at Mike's feet. The last page was visible and he grimaced; he'd forgotten that.

"And just what is the meaning of that? As if I needed to ask."

"Well, I was pretty mad, you know!"

"And I'm pretty mad, too. I'm sick to death of you and your cheap money-grubbing attitude. I'm sick of the sight of you! So you can stay here until dinnertime. And don't bother showing your face for that unless you've written those lines out properly."

She left, closing the door sharply. Michael's voice reached her on the stairs.

"You make me *sick!*"

It also reached Daffy, listening unhappily in the kitchen with David.

"*That paper cost ten bucks!*"

A thump . . . and a tinny crash, and she knew his printer had fallen off its metal stand.

David was amused. "Wicked witch one, Scrooge nil."

Daffy glared at him. "Stick it in your ear, David." She ran outside.

Sitting on his bed, Mike scowled at the printer table. He felt like kicking it again, but changed his mind. His mother would just make him pay for a new one. He'd found this one in the dumpster next to the ferry and it suited him perfectly. It was the wrong size for the room and the space available, and if you moved it the wheels came off; but the price was right. So after a while he got up and righted the table, straightened the bent leg and put the wheels back on. After he'd restored it and the printer to their rightful location, he went and sat on the window seat, looking out at the afternoon sun.

Mike's room was unnaturally tidy. Unlike Daffy he did not have walls and walls of books, just one smallish bookcase with a few books and some bits of Lego. He had a chest of drawers and a poster of Donald Trump on one wall. He'd sold most of the toys he'd outgrown but a few remained and were stored along with various games underneath the window seat.

The bedroom overlooked the south orchard with the big oak tree in the left of his vision. He watched his parents walking downfield. Dad put an arm round Mum's shoulders. Mike shook his head.

"Don't touch her, Dad. She's poison."

He looked down to find he was holding the letter that had been sitting on the printer. It represented his latest attempt at a franchisee letter, and it was done in the best Publisher's Clearinghouse manner, a style for which Mike felt a natural affinity.

Good news, ARIADNE WU! You have been selected as a potential FRANCHISEE for the most exclusive FRANCHISE in the GALAXY.
YES, ARIADNE! You too can join a select, privilege group of people. You too can learn how to GROW YUAN. Genuine real yuan!

And so on, down the page. He had a solid couple of paragraphs in the Maserati vein, and after some thought had added another on how, instead of actually spending your money, you could put it in the bank and spend your evenings looking at your bank book (his personal preference). Some of the letters he'd read online described in detail the processes involved in making the promised fortune, so he had added some words on that as well, based on remarks from Dad and Daffy about nutrients, and assuring the reader he would receive copious instruction and support. It was a solid letter, he felt: attractive and appealing to the right person.

He looked outside. His parents were approaching the south grove. "She's going to be so sorry one day."

His gaze fell on the letter again. Should he sign it Michael Chen (or Wong or Sung)? He frowned over this for a while, then made up his mind and typed "Michael Smith, Franchisor."

A few minutes later, as he was running the letter through the spell checker once more, he heard Dad calling from outside. He went over to the window seat.

"Michael! Come on out of there. I've posted bail for you."

Mike waved and returned to the computer to finish up. He put on his coat, zipping it up with his arm next to his side, securing an envelope. He listened: his mother was coming upstairs and he waited until he heard their bedroom door close at the end of the hall, then he clattered downstairs, rummaged through a drawer in the den for a stamp then slipped outside, found his bike and headed off to the ferry. There was a box for outgoing mail at the marine supply store.

*   *   *

George had not had an easy time securing Mike's release. Jane had been furious and he'd let her vent as they walked through the orchard to the grove. Once there she had to lower her voice because of the trees. George took the opportunity to examine one or two branches. The first sign of anything amiss with a money tree was a yellowing of the leaves.

When Jane had finished describing Michael's behavior, he said nothing for a minute or two. "Did he ever tell you about his deal with David?" he asked finally, and that set her off again.

"No, and I wish you'd stop encouraging him. We told Daffy she couldn't be a terrorist until she graduated, and the same went for Michael and his bloody franchises."

"Daffy came to her senses because we let her try. Why not do the same with Mike?"

Jane said nothing, so he reverted to his first question. "He said he was pleased with his deal. So I asked him: who soaked whom?" He glanced at her with a smile. "He had to think for a minute, then he said David's a soakee because we get fifteen percent of his income for doing nothing."

"You see how his mind works? He has no concept of decent behavior—"

"His heart wasn't in it, love. Give him time, he'll come round."

He gazed at the grove of trees, luxuriant, verdant, peaceful, wishing Jane could take the same pleasure in them, knowing she did not. He came to a decision and turned to her. "I've been thinking about the trees. If this solution doesn't get rid of the smell, I want to forget about growing money." Her face began to lighten and he added, "I want to grow trees for landscaping. All around the orchards."

"What?"

"They're beautiful trees, Jane. They'd fetch a good price. I think landscapers would be glad to use them in gardens."

"Would I have to talk to them?"

He considered. "Maybe take the megaphone out once a week and bellow at them. Just to toughen them up."

He took her hand and they began to walk back up through the orchard of pruned apple trees.

"He should be outside, not stuck indoors on such a nice day."

Jane had felt guilty about that. "Yes, all right." She added, "Children have to be trained, George. Just like your trees."

"All right, but you can't train a money tree to grow apples."

She turned away, but he took her arm. "You try to make him into something he's not. No child likes that. You'd get a lot further if you were more accepting."

Jane erupted. "What is it you want me to accept, George? Jesus is a dweeb? Or soakers of the world unite?" She stepped away from him. "Honestly, I could shake you sometimes."

She stalked off angrily up past the oak tree toward the side door.

George experienced a sudden burst of anger himself. "See that it doesn't drag on, that's all!" he yelled, then approaching Mike's window, "Mike! Michael! Come on out of there." The white face appeared at the window, and Mike gave a brief wave then disappeared. George shook his head worriedly.

*   *   *

David peered into the twin eyepieces of the stereoscope, studying the hundred-dollar bill. A stereoscope simulated a three-dimensional effect by providing two views of the same object, each from a slightly different angle. The printing processes that went into the makeup of a banknote—intaglio, offset printing and letterpress—presented quite different appearances under the stereoscope. He studied the numeral in the top right corner.

"It's all fuzzy round the number, like a halo. Is that good?"

George sat at his desk opposite David. "It's one effect of the letterpress process, according to Yves."

David looked up, replaced the bill with another hundred. He studied it carefully, both sides, then looked up. "I can't see anything different. It's amazing." He added, "Are you sure this one isn't grown as well?"

"Angus wasn't interested in it," George reminded him. The dog had lunged for the other bill, displaying no interest in this one.

Daffy came in with a book, saw David and turned to leave. He had no idea how upsetting family quarrels could be and she knew she ought to feel sorry for him, but she wasn't in the mood. George seized his moment. "Come and give David a hand, love. I want to finish cleaning up." He got up and left before she could argue.

She flopped full length on the sofa and began to read. David took another look at the money-tree bill. After a while: "Is Eve an authority on other currencies, or just the dollar?"

"I don't know."

"I hear she's a friend of Jane's. What sort of age is she?"

Daffy sat up with elaborate unconcern and glanced over casually, but he was buried in the stereoscope. She lay down again, this time facing David. "Gosh, I'm not exactly sure. She's such a knock-out you never think about her age." She hid behind her open book because she was not very good at this sort of thing.

"George said she can look at a bill and tell which printing plant it came from."

"Yup. She's so smart you wouldn't believe. I personally don't think you stand a chance with her but hey, talk to Mum."

"I think I will."

Daffy could only take a minute of this, and after a valiant struggle she dashed out with a muttered "back in a minute." She rushed upstairs to her room, closed the door and lay on the bed with a pillow in her mouth, her legs kicking the air, dying of laughter.

* * *

Jane came downstairs that evening to an appealing aroma of moussaka. She stopped before the full-length mirror between the front windows. The others were in the kitchen: she could hear George's voice, then Michael's, higher-pitched, then laughter.

She stared at herself in the mirror, calculating how long before she could decently go back upstairs to bed, and try to sleep and hope that tomorrow would be an improvement over today. She scowled at her reflection and turned away.

Standing next to the stove, David waved a wooden spoon at Daffy. "I'll get you," he said, "you wait."

He was wearing his cooking gear, a blue-and-white striped apron and chef's cap, Christmas gifts Jane had never used, discovered in the linen closet. Now he turned to the oven. "What's he do, this Frenchman?"

"He's a Quebecer." George sat at the kitchen table, Mike perched on the table next to him. Mike's face tightened as Jane appeared in the doorway.

Daffy amplified George's answer. "He's a research scientist in the Counterfeit division of the RCMP. In Ottawa."

Holding an earthenware casserole with the oven mitts, David turned, gaped at Daffy then at Jane, and dropped it. It cracked open, exposing neat layers of eggplant, meat and béchamel sauce.

"Oh, David!" Jane stared aghast at the casserole.

He stared at her. "You," he cleared his throat, "you phoned the RCMP? To find out about counterfeit money?"

She bent over the casserole. "I used to worry, you see. About what to look for."

"Why the RCMP? Why not the Secret Service?"

She glanced at him and then straightened up, going to the sink. "Oh, I couldn't feel comfortable calling them, David. Have you seen the way they drag people out of rooms when there's a crisis? I don't care for that. And I thought, well, the dear old RCMP. It's like home, isn't it? And we aren't growing Canadian money, so I didn't feel, you know, insincere about talking to them."

George rubbed Mike's back. "She called them when we were in Ottawa that time, remember, Mikey?—," Mike nodded, and George continued, "—and sweet-talked her way through to Yves."

Mike jumped off the table and went to crouch over the casserole. He sampled a fingerful.

"Stop that, Michael." Jane helped David take the larger pieces of casserole dish over to the sink. "It was years ago, George, I hardly think he could remember."

"Yes, I do. This is good, Dave." Mike tried another fingerful.

Daffy joined him and reached for a taste. "Mm. Can't waste it. Think of all the starving refugees." She made herself comfortable.

George watched, amused. "They were on the phone for an hour and a half, David, on and on."

Jane looked at the casserole. "It *is* a frightful waste. . . ."

"I think we've got all the pieces," said David. He looked at her and sketched an elaborate bow, and she laughed.

"Go on with you."

"Oh Yves," cooed Daffy, "tell me more about intaglio."

"What rubbish."

"Oh Yves, Yves," piped up Mike in a horrible falsetto, "I love your body."

George roared with laughter. "Told you he remembered."

Amid the general laughter, Mike looked cautiously at Jane. She bent over him, laughing, her eyes laughing, too. Light as thistledown, her fingers touched his hair and cheek. "You. . . ." She sat down on the floor. "Spoons, George. Just ignore them, David. He was charming and very forthcoming and I felt a lot happier after that. Daffy, stop picking at it."

George joined the circle on the floor and passed round the spoons, and they all dug into David's moussaka while Jane told him all about her chat with the RCMP and Mike gazed at her, dazed with adoration.

Chapter 11

Actions and Reactions

Bannerman & Co. had handled the affairs of the Carruthers family for more than two hundred years. They had been executors of the estate of the fourteenth Earl of Craggan; they had handled his wife's affairs and his daughters', and such legal matters as arose from the stewardship of the fifteenth earl, mad Angus Carruthers. The firm had grown in those two centuries, in a temperate, measured way. Today, in addition to property and family matters, it had branched carefully into issues surrounding branding and reputation. The acquisition of a sports organization had led to further clients in that line of business, and the partners were currently dipping a cautious toe into the waters of media management.

By today's standards, the firm was relatively small but it remained independent. Tara Saunders was the Office Manager, a woman in her fifties with the requisite levels of competence and good nature required of one on the blunt end of panics, late filings, court re-shufflings and unexpected depositions. She supervised the secretarial pool and the office boy, assisted the Accounts manager during end-of-quarter billing, and handled the mail.

This morning she sorted letters into the pigeonholes for partners and associates, gave the office boy letters for accounting, IT and business management and, having poured herself a cup of coffee, turned to her own mail. Two letters held circulars for office supplies, while the third, with a Canadian stamp, had a hand-written address and contained a sealed envelope and a note. "Hi Tara, could you please mail this letter? There should be a reply and I told her to write to Michael Smith in care of you, so could you send it to me, please? Thanks, Tara—Mike."

She turned over the sealed envelope to find the name "Ms. Ariadne Wu, Wu & Associates" printed neatly on it, followed by an address in Vancouver. In the bottom left corner, bold black and underlined, she read: "Private & Confidential."

"What's that scamp up to?" She read the note again, amused. Tara had met the Frisbys several times, first at Jane's wedding, which she'd attended with Sir Joseph before he retired. She knew why she'd been invited: because the earl thought it wise for his family to cultivate a relationship with the person likely to be their first point of contact at Bannerman & Co. She'd met the Frisbys several times since. They made a point of calling in when they were in London because Tara was their conduit to the world. They did not care to give out their Canadian address: "It's such a small island, Tara, and we really aren't set up for visitors" was how Jane had put it. Tara wondered sometimes how small it could be, but it was none of her business if the Frisbys were reclusive.

A lawyer walked by, reading *The Times*. "Morning Marcus," she called, "you're due in court at eleven, don't forget."

She dropped Michael's envelope in her Out tray. The office boy collected it with the other letters in mid-afternoon, metered them and took them along to the post office at the end of the street.

Two weeks later the morning post held a letter for Michael Smith, care of herself. She was puzzled by the name and the return address, "Wu & Associates, Realtors," until she remembered Mike's earlier letter. Later that day, she inserted the letter in one of the firm's manila envelopes, addressed it to Michael on the island, put it in her Out tray and thought no more about it.

* * *

Maggie Kendrick closed the suitcase and carried it across the sitting room, hesitating before the two piles on opposite sides of the entrance hall. "Rubbish," she muttered, deposited it on the rubbish pile and returned to the sofa. She hoisted another suitcase onto the seat, sat down, opened it and appraised the contents. "More letters." She picked up a bulging manila envelope at random and peered inside, pulling out a clutch of letters on lightweight air letter paper. She riffled through them quickly, and through another handful, and again, until the envelope was empty. "All from John," she muttered, then lifted her head. "John?" she called, and then louder, "John!" She sat a moment, then sighed, rose and crossed the dining room, opening the glass doors that gave onto the patio. "John?"

"Down here!"

No sign of him. It was a large garden, with flower beds round the borders, and rose beds cut into the grass. From the patio, she could see down the hillside to Carrick Roads, the wide channel of the River Fal. She shook her head impatiently. "Do you want to keep the letters you wrote to your mother?" she called.

"Come and look at this, Mag." He sounded excited.

She walked across the grass toward the shed at the foot of the garden.

"Maggie? You won't believe this."

She found him staring at an evergreen tree, six or seven feet high and with two curious branches on top. "The estate agent will be here in half an hour. Have you done any clearing out or not?"

"I've made a start. Look at this." He made sure she was watching, then faced the tree. "Boo!" Then after a pause, "Yah! Boo!"

Maggie watched obediently, eyebrows lifting, a middle-aged woman well-used to her husband's ways who found this behavior curious even for him. He'd always been close to his mother but her death had not incapacitated him. Or so Maggie had thought.

"Yes, dear? I asked whether you wanted—"

"Dammit," he muttered and seized a shovel propped against the shed wall. "Watch this." He bashed it against the stone base of the shed, producing a hard ringing sound. The tree contracted. Maggie, who had been watching the shovel, stepped backward.

"What happened?"

"You see? You see?"

"What did I see, John? What's going on?"

"Look, look." He swung the shovel against a piece of corrugated tin lying against the shed. The tree actually leaned back, away from the noise.

Maggie gave a small shriek, which, she was horrified to see, made it shrink even more. "It's alive!"

"Of course it's alive."

The tree returned to the upright position, its branches spreading, giving every appearance of engulfing John.

"It's a man-eater! Look out!"

"It is *not* a man-eater."

"Then what is it?"

"Damned if I know." He stepped closer, ignoring his wife's warnings, and examined a branch of the tree. "What's old Mum been up to, I wonder?" He reached for a branch to his left and stepped on something, stooped....

"What is it? What are you doing?"

"Good lord, Mag. There's lots of them."

"Lots? What lots?"

He extended his arm in her direction. In the palm of his hand lay a nut, a sort of Brazil nut.

Chapter 12

Christmas Preparations

David was back, scarcely a month after he'd left. He arrived unannounced, having traveled standby to Miami then across the continent via one puddle-jumper after another. He hadn't wanted to call, email or Skype. "Must have caught a touch of Jane's paranoia," he said apologetically, but Jane assured him that he had merely taken sensible precautions.

"There's a tree growing on your street in Falmouth. At least one," he amended. "If there are more they'll have found them by now."

"Who will?" Jane topped up his tea. They were sitting round the kitchen table with tea and cake mid-afternoon. David had been on the go for thirty-six hours.

"The police."

He had decided to take a look round the SBP experimental farm, he told them. "Since we know the tree can seed out, it occurred to me that Falmouth might already have a cottage industry in money production. Alternatively, I thought I might be able to find a tree to transplant, or take cuttings for my own use." He saw Mike's expression. "I wasn't trying to cut out my franchisor, I promise."

But the experimental farm was closed. "That wouldn't have stopped me looking round, but there were guards at the entrance and close-circuit TV cameras, so I thought it best to tiptoe away." He glanced at George. "I did wonder whether Pedro and the crowd in Dusseldorf have been found out."

He drank some tea and ate a mouthful of cake.

"So that's why you tried the street," said George.

David nodded. "I had some idea of posing as a collector of exotic plants. I was going to wander up and down the street peering in peoples' gardens. But when I turned in and drove along, I saw a sale sign and two police cars outside one of the houses. So I drove to the end, past your place, and parked and strolled back."

He'd joined a cluster of homeowners on the pavement near the house and had posed as a house buyer, directed to that address by an estate agent.

"Apparently the old lady who owned the house had died, and it was her son who found the tree. It was number seventeen," he replied in answer to Jane's query.

"Dear old Mrs. Kendrick, remember her, George?"

David was unable to learn much more, except that everyone on the street had received a visit from the police and had their gardens searched. The consensus among the gossipers was that the old lady had been growing something hallucinogenic, like cannabis.

"I didn't hear any mention of money, but what with that and SBP, I really thought you should know as soon as possible."

He finished his tea while the Frisbys evaluated this news. Jane was concerned about the family's vulnerability with a basement full of nuts, and wanted to process them immediately. George worried about shortening the curing time. Normally Jane would have deferred to him, as she did on everything to do with the trees. But now she waved this away. "Suppose we did them tomorrow. That's less that two weeks early. Surely two weeks wouldn't make much difference? You'll stay for Christmas, David?"

David declined. He had to be back in the UK by the twenty-second at the latest. The family looked at him curiously and he elaborated.

"As a matter of fact, you inspired me to take the initiative with my own family." He'd discovered, when he first returned home, that his grandmother had been asking after him, so he'd driven to Wiltshire to visit the old lady. She lived alone in a ramshackle house on acreage, and by the end of his visit they'd agreed that David would take over the back half of the house and look after the overgrown gardens. "I think we were both slightly shocked at this proposal. I know I was. It hadn't been on my mind when I went to see her, but I'm certain she was pleased. It was so simple, only I'd never have thought of it, much less asked, if I hadn't stayed here." The Frisbys looked doubtfully at one another and he went on, "We're a rather passive family. Everyone has their own space and tries not to invade anyone else's. You're not like that. You're . . . you interact."

"I like your way better," said Mike, and George laughed.

"Anyway," David wrapped up his story. "I wanted to be just a bit proactive for a change, so I drove home and invited my parents for Christmas. Gran had agreed. They nearly fell over." He looked almost pleased with himself. "I wouldn't go so far as to say they're thrilled, but they're certainly coming, so I want to be back in good time to get the house ready and cook dinner."

That gave them a week, and George conceded that processing the nuts a week early should have no ill effects on the quality. Jane immediately revised her menus, sending Daffy and Mike over to Sidney for groceries while David unpacked then toured the farm with George. It was as though he'd never been away.

The car returned just before six as the men were going in, and David stopped to help Daffy with the bags of groceries. George was tapping the barometer as they entered. "Nippy out there this evening."

"It won't freeze, though, will it, Dad?"

"Never has."

He disappeared into the den to make his Blue Book entries. David and Daffy unpacked the groceries then got out of Jane's way.

"What's on your mind, young Daff?"

She was preoccupied. "Hm?"

He peered at her. "What's hiding behind the mask?"

She smiled. "I'm glad you're back, David," she said sweetly as she climbed the stairs.

"I'm glad to be back."

"I don't use makeup as a mask," she added loftily. "I use it to express my mood." She'd been very Goth all week because the markets were making her—and everyone else—nervous.

She'd nearly reached the top of the stairs when she stopped. Turned. Saw David standing outside the den door looking up at her. She clumped thoughtfully downstairs and pulled him away from the door.

"What are you doing tomorrow?" she asked softly.

* * *

David stared at the seedlings scattered throughout the clearing.

"What do you think?" Daffy wanted his approval. "Twenty are for you."

He said nothing, unwilling to be the bearer of bad news.

"They're well protected, David. They'll be okay." She knelt in front of a group of seedlings and removed a stray branch covering two of them. She saw David rubbing his chin and looking dubious. "It never freezes here."

"It never freezes at sea level. We're two hundred feet up, Daff. And you'd get wind chill as well."

She pointed out the mulch heaped protectively over each seedling, but David shook his head doubtfully. "It's a tropical plant, remember."

Daffy looked away. After all her work. . . . He went on talking as she blinked away tears.

David circled the clearing, studying the trees from all angles. He halted near Daffy. "Here's what I'd do. Concentrate on these ones, do you see? They're in a slight depression." The area encompassed perhaps half of the seedlings. "Either wrap each one individually or—Daffy?" She was looking away from him. "Are you listening?"

A sob escaped Daffy's lips despite her best efforts.

"Look, it's not the end of the world." He approached the still-kneeling figure and squeezed her shoulder gingerly. He looked uncomfortable. "Cheer up, young Daff."

"Oh, shut *up*, David!" Daffy scrambled to her feet, produced a Kleenex and blew her nose. "Sorry. It's just . . . this wouldn't have happened to Mike or Mum. Just me."

Angus suddenly made an appearance, followed by Mike, right on cue, red-faced and weighed down by a loaded backpack. "Hi, Dave!" He stared at David, then peered at Daffy. What was going on? He decided he didn't want to know. "So anyway, I was thinking we should add some frost protection." He struggled out of the backpack.

"You see?" Daffy looked wryly at David, who moved away.

"I'll leave you to it, then. George wanted a hand. . . ." He nodded to Mike and headed off down the hill. Daffy looked ready to cry again.

"I found some burlap sacks in the barn. And I thought we could spread 'em over the seedlings and cut little holes just enough to let the heads through. Then totally cover them with leaves and stuff." He was wrestling with the sacks jammed into the backpack, as tightly wrapped as a money-tree kernel. Daffy took hold of the backpack and pulled as he tugged them free. "Then we should just put big branches over them, Daff. So they don't even show. Just in case anyone comes."

He produced two pairs of scissors and they sat on the ground and began to cut open the sacks along their sides. Daffy looked at him.

"I love you, Mikey."

"Yeah. You okay?"

"Yeah."

*   *   *

Jane stood at the kitchen sink in her dressing gown, sipping her tea and looking out at the south field. In the past month, she had cooked lunch or dinner for a hundred and fifty bodies, not counting family or the late lunch for the twenty-three ladies of the Women's Auxiliary and their quilting bee. She had helped out at three charity craft fairs, one of which she had organized, and had agreed to chair a fundraising committee next year. Today she had one more luncheon, for twelve, and that was it for Christmas.

Daffy retrieved the mail from under the fruit bowl and sat down at the table where George, Mike and David were already eating breakfast. She flipped through the stack of letters. "Some for you, Mum, one . . . two for Dad, a bunch for both. Here's one for you, Mike, looks like Tara's writing. One for—," she paused, then added, "for David."

Jane turned.

"I thought no one knew you were here," said George.

"No one does. What the hell is this?" The envelope was large and gold-lined. He pulled out the card and opened it.

Mike snickered.

"Mike?" said George, astonished.

"The ones with gold envelopes cost way more."

David was touched. "Do they? In that case, I'll keep the envelope as well."

Jane picked up her cup and saucer, gave Mike an approving look and returned to the sink.

"Oh Mikey, that's so cute."

"You should have seen your faces."

"That's a nice gesture, son, I'm proud of you."

Mike opened his own card from Tara. "Dear Mike, you've probably received your Michael Smith letter by now— Happy Christmas, Tara." He stared at this unwelcome reminder. He had indeed received the reply from Ariadne Wu. He had no idea what to do about it.

*   *   *

David put a finger on the ribbon and pressed. "What did she say?" He sat on the floor of Mike's room, helping him wrap presents. "May I see her letter?"

"Yeah, later. It's hidden away." Focused on the business of present-wrapping, Mike said nothing more until the job was done and the bow added. He admired the box, put it on one side and reached for another gift. "She said I sounded like a serious person with a serious offer and to make an appointment with her secretary."

"Ariadne Wu."

"She lives next to the Parkers. She loves money."

David remembered the expensive home with the boat and seaplane. "Isn't she already loaded?"

Mike frowned. "You can't have too much money."

"All right. When are you meeting?"

"The thing is, Mum hates her. She'd kill me if she knew what I'd done."

"Then why—"

"I didn't know! I didn't find out till after I'd sent my letter." He took a piece of scotch tape from David and applied it to one side of the box. He did the same on the other side. "She practically wants to take over the island."

He'd heard his parents talking about how the realtor wanted to sell off the Rock. "She wants to turf Mrs. Bagnold."

David looked askance. "That can't be right."

Mike unrolled more wrapping paper. "Cut," he instructed, and as David cut, he added, "Yeah. Mum said. She's getting pressured to join the committee that votes on it."

"So don't do anything. She doesn't know who you are. Just let it drop."

But this didn't sit well with Mike. Ariadne Wu was a prequalified prospect and he wanted to negotiate.

They discussed it as they wrapped another present. Mike had been thrown by the "make an appointment" instruction but suddenly decided to bike over to her place during Christmas. He voiced this idea to David. "That would give me the advantage of surprise, see?"

David nodded, and glanced at the bookcase. Napoleon Hill, Donald Trump, Sun Tzu. Mike had not entirely read the books, he'd said; he was working his way through them a bit at a time. "Think you can handle her? She must have a lot of experience negotiating."

"Mum said she's like a bulldozer." He applied scotch tape, leaned back to admire the wrapping, then added, "But I'm like a butterfly."

Their eyes met. "Sting like a bee," they said together. Fist bump.

*   *   *

Mike took down the pictures of the eighth Earl and Mona Lisa, unlocked the padlock on the retractable wall and pushed it open. A sea of nuts lay deep and dark over the floor to the far wall. He clambered over the pile selecting a nut here, another there, dropping them in a bowl. He came upstairs to the kitchen and joined Daffy and David.

David reached for a nut and Mike looked doubtfully at Daffy. "Shouldn't we wait?"

"Dad just wants to know if they're ready," said Daffy. "And this way we can skip the Christmas pets."

"And the Cratchits," agreed Mike.

David cracked the nut and twisted the kernel, unfurling it carefully, revealing a hundred dollar bill. Mike and Daffy pored over it. "Looks fine."

"It's incredible." David's head was filled with bushels of hundred-pound notes and yachts and villas and Lamborghinis.

"It's a dud," said Daffy prosaically, pointing to the numeral in the bottom left corner. Part of a zero was missing.

Angus whined and Mike gave him a pat. "Maybe later."

They put the bill on one side to show George, while David cracked another nut.

"What was that about Christmas pets?"

Daffy explained as he loosened and unfurled the note. "Dad says if we gave people trees they'd lose interest after a couple of days, like they do with pets." She nodded at David's look of amused skepticism. "Exactly. But you try telling him that. And then he goes on about screaming and shouting and traffic noise. He won't take any risks with them."

"What sort of risks?" David unfurled the bill, another hundred. They all scrutinized it.

"We need a used one to compare the color," said Daffy, and looked enquiringly at David, who shook his head.

"Credit cards only." The reverse of the bill stated, "In God We rust." He gave it to Mike and took another.

"I think we should give trees to inner-city families," Daffy went on. "I bet they'd be fine. And I'm going to prove it one day."

David glanced at her curiously then returned his gaze to the kernel.

"Daff," said Mike, "we only allow one grower per country, remember?" He wasn't sure what to think about his sister.

She didn't sound right and she didn't look right. She didn't even have any makeup on, not so you could notice. Her hair was red, but her eyes weren't all black like they were normally.

"You know what, Mike? The monetary system's like a house of cards. No kidding. It's going to collapse one of these days no matter what we do. But if some of those families had trees, they could get ahead a little bit before that happens."

Mike was aghast. "For crying out loud!"

"Look, Pollyanna," said David. "wouldn't it be more con- structive to try and reinstate the gold standard?"

"The gold standard is passé, David."

"Maybe. But it's better than what we've got now, isn't it?"

"Plus we could still grow our own," added Mike.

"Michael! David wouldn't do that, would you, David?"

David was spared the need to reply by George's arrival. He came stamping in from the barn, and wasn't at all put out by their having started without him. "Now then," he said, pulling out his wallet and sitting down at the table. "Let's compare. He turned over the corner on a used hundred and put it next to the other bills. It was a needed precaution because they were indistinguishable one from the other. "Excellent!"

They opened the rest of the nuts, putting the flawed ones on one side. Jane arrived as the light began to fade.

"Never cleared up so fast in all my life," she said, after she'd sat down with a cup of tea. She looked at the bills. "What's the verdict?"

"We're all set for tomorrow," said George.

They had fruit cake and tea, and planned the day. Mike fed Angus two of the dud bills.

Jane smiled. "Ah, the annual ritual. We usually do this on Christmas Eve, David, in front of the fire."

Mike and Daffy exchanged a look as she went on, "I always like to think of the Cratchits."

"No!"

"Give it a rest, love," suggested George kindly.

"The who?" David asked.

"The Cratchits, David. Be quiet, you two. You know, Scrooge?"

Daffy closed her eyes, while Mike got up, stood behind his mother and feigned banging his head on the counter as she continued.

"I like to imagine them, huddled round a lump of coal, sipping their mulled wine and cracking nuts." Her voice was soft, almost dreamy. "That little crutch propped against the wall. That piping childish voice—"

David snorted with suppressed laughter.

"What?"

Mike met Daffy's eyes and together, in piping childish voices, they said, "Look, father, here's a hundred-pound note."

There was a beat of silence.

"Well done, my boy," said David bluffly, "that'll pay for the other leg."

They screamed with laughter, while George watched in amusement and Angus skittered out into the hall and hid in his basket.

"I think you're all horrible," said Jane.

Chapter 13

Dog's Dinner

"How many?" Halloran studied a glossy photo of nuts lying on the ground under the Falmouth money tree. He dropped the picture onto a pile and studied the next.

"A hundred and fourteen," said Gumble.

Jaio McCaffrey found a close-up of a one-pound note in the stack of photos.

"Some were spoiled," said Hicks. "Most were perfect."

Jaio looked up. "Spoiled how?"

Missing numbers, letters or other parts of the image, he explained.

Halloran kept returning to a picture of the whole tree. "At least we know what we're looking for." He studied the branched head. "It's responsive to sound, huh? Would a gunshot kill it?"

"Dunno, sir. The Brits are still studying it," said Gumble.

"They find any others?"

"Not so far." Gumble looked over at Hicks.

"We think SBP has something to do with this," said Hicks. "The German pharmaceutical?"

Halloran remembered the incidents map. "The monkey in the Boston lab?"

The agents nodded and filled him in. They had seen the deserted SBP experimental farm outside Falmouth. On the flight home they had reviewed the company's history and annual reports. "They used to fund these expeditions to the Amazon. What if that's where they found the tree?" They had not said anything to the British.

"We need Professor Pringle," said Jaio.

"No," said Halloran flatly. "He won't keep his mouth shut." He considered the information. "The British will have to be told. And the Germans." He issued instructions. The agents were to return to Boston and question the management this time, as well as the two lab technicians who had witnessed the monkey eating the bill.

This discussion was interrupted by a call from Brinks, with an incident to report. "A dog attacked a guard with a sack of money. Apparently the dog actually tried to eat the money, although we're still investig—"

"Where? Where did this happen?"

"Vancouver, British Columbia."

* * *

The east Vancouver streets had been bright with Christmas lights in the late afternoon. Pedestrians thronged the streets, weaving around panhandlers, druggies (the needle exchange was nearby) and Salvation Army volunteers with donation globes. A Brinks truck pulled up and parked near a bank, and two guards emerged. One went to the rear and carefully brought out a Doberman on its leash. The other guard had already reached the bank's doors, and continued inside.

The Doberman wanted to do its business, and the guard cursed under his breath. They were already running late because of the damned dog. Either it had some kind of intestinal problem or it was constipated: he didn't care. The fact was, it had tried on several earlier occasions to eliminate, without result. Now it wanted to try again, so he waited at the curb while the animal squatted. He fumbled for a baggie, cursing again. But there was no output and he walked the dog toward the bank. Through the glass he could see his partner approaching with two bags, so he stood to one side and held the door.

The laden guard came past. The dog suddenly yelped and leaped at the bags. The guard tried to quicken his pace toward the truck. The dog yelped again, and made a serious attack on the bags while its handler vainly tried to pull it off. Several pedestrians stopped to watch.

The besieged guard broke free and sprinted for the truck door, and the dog leaped, sank its teeth into a bag and wrenched it free. The neck opened and bills fell out and began to scatter.

Pedestrians swooped down on the bills while the dog snapped at them randomly then grabbed the bag and dragged it down the street. More bills flew out and scattered over the sidewalk, galvanizing druggies and panhandlers.

The dog stopped, shoved its muzzle inside the sack and gorged. The guard grabbed its leash and it swallowed, snapped at him and took off with the bag in tow, guards and pedestrians streaming after it like the tail of a comet.

Chapter 14

Processing

"More egg, David?" Jane hovered with a saucepan of scrambled eggs. David, his mouth full, shook his head.

"Another piece of toast?" Mike's look was solicitous, hand poised over the loaf of bread, ready to insert another slice into the toaster.

"Leave me alone." David swallowed a mouthful of egg and sausage. "I cannot believe it's as bad as you two make out."

George buttered a piece of toast. "Lot of fuss about nothing. Right, Daff?"

Daffy was absorbed in the news, checking the English press for word of the Falmouth tree. "Right," she said absently. She switched to US news; nothing exciting there. Canada: ditto.

Jane sat down and Daffy was about to turn off the tablet when a headline caught her eye: "A Dog's Christmas Dinner." She clicked on it and her jaw dropped. "Holy—"

She read silently and rapidly, oblivious to questions.

Jane leaned over and looked. She saw the headline, and a picture of a dog, muzzle inside a canvas sack, and a man in a uniform with a Brinks logo on his shoulder.

"Oh my God."

Mike dodged round his mother's chair and looked at the tablet. "It's a dog eating a bunch of money!"

Jane had gone quite white. She got to her feet, staring blindly around, seeing nothing. George went to her.

Daffy looked up. "It happened yesterday, in Vancouver. It has to be one of the donations."

"Help me look," said Jane.

David got to his feet. "Look for what?"

"To see if everything's all right." She had completely lost her poise. "George, we'll have to burn the nuts." She stared in the direction of the basement door. "We've got to burn the nuts, George."

"Mum." Mike tugged her arm to get her attention. "It won't take as long with Dave helping."

Jane tried to think. "The stove would take too long. We'd have to get them up out of the basement to burn them." She stared unseeing at David.

Daffy had been looking for other references to the incident. George took the tablet and read the story.

"We don't even know if anyone's picked up on this, Jane," said David. "Right, Daff?"

"There's just the one story, Mum."

George finished reading. "It's not just that. I'm confident the Essence will work. If it does, this sort of thing," he waved the tablet, "won't happen again."

They waited. Jane made up her mind.

"Right. Angus, outside with you."

*   *   *

Standing ankle-deep in money nuts, David faced a machine. It was small, perhaps eighteen inches wide and waist high. It was basically a bucket on a piston engine, with a funnel emanating from one side. Its purpose was to inhale nuts at one end and spit out kernels at the other.

George pressed a button and the machine came to life with a putt-putt-putt. He motioned, and David dumped a shovelful of nuts in the bucket on top. They trickled down a funnel and George pressed another button. A hammering device, linked by flywheels and belts to the engine, began to smash nuts, rat-tat-tat. The shells flew out the funnel on the side. The kernels began to fall out at the bottom, into a laundry basket. Putt-putt-putt, rat-tat-tat: the machine had a noise level out of all proportion to its size.

As David shoveled nuts into the bucket, George used a stick to stir the contents, preventing them from clogging the entrance to the funnel. At appropriate moments, he topped up the fuel and applied oil to moving parts. A two-inch rubber hose took the fumes to a vent in the wall near the ceiling.

The nuts were deepest at the eastern end of the basement, under the loading chute. This was nothing more than a recess in the basement wall, with a gap in the ceiling and a trapdoor. Above it were the wooden trays holding the bed of shrubs at the side of the house. The nuts flowed around a cast-iron wood-burning stove against the south wall. The level declined toward the middle of the room where David worked. At the other end of the basement a dust sheet covered various items of furniture.

When the laundry basket was full of kernels, Mike replaced it with an empty one from a stack next to the wall, and carried the full basket over to Jane and Daffy, putting it on an upended basket in front of them. Sitting on folding chairs near the steam room, they reached for kernels.

Their job consisted of brushing off any remaining shell, giving each kernel a hard twist to loosen its folds, and tossing it into the steam room. Normally Mike would have returned to help George, but now he helped Jane and Daffy, so the work went faster.

In an hour, they had enough for the next stage, so Mike took over from George, stirring the bucket as David shoveled in more nuts. George and Daffy huddled over the Essence. They were debating whether to add it to the steam process or wait until the drying stage. Daffy shouted in George's ear:

"Let's do both, Dad. How could it hurt?"

George stared at the wall unseeing, then came to a decision. "Right!" He dampened a rag with the liquid, then hung it on a hook inside the steam room, not far from the steam head. Closing the door, he checked the controls on the outside. The steam generator was a small box mounted on the wall. He set the temperature, pressed a button and steam flowed through a connecting pipe into the sealed room.

Jane, meanwhile, was shoveling nuts into the center of the room, closer to David. When George returned, she and Daffy resumed brushing off kernels, dropping them into another laundry basket for the next steam room session.

The steam room could be vented by pushing a lever next to the generator, and after allowing ten minutes for the steam to clear, Jane opened the door. All over the bench and floor, the notes lay more or less opened and flat. She and Mike filled baskets and took them to the two dryers. Daffy had soaked more rags in Essence, and she wrung them out and tossed one into each dryer along with the damp notes.

Now the dryers added their muted hum to the noise level, as the Frisbys and David carried on with their work, stress pushing them to depart from the customary schedule and finish in one day a process that would normally be spread out over a week. They broke briefly in the morning and afternoon, and had a longer break at lunch. "We normally have turkey sandwiches," said Daffy as she built a ham and cheese roll. "This is weird."

At six pm they came upstairs for dinner. Most of the nuts were processed and they had had enough. "We're shell-shocked," said David, but the others were too tired to enjoy the joke.

They each carried baskets of dried notes ready for sorting. Mike led the way, stopping in the hallway opposite the dining room door. He put down his basket, found a flawed twenty and opened the back door.

"Angus!" he called and crouched down, offering the bill.

George waited, with a sense of pleased anticipation.

Angus came bounding up, tail wagging, and sniffed at Mike's hand. He licked it and wriggled past him to find Jane. He nosed at Mike's basket while the family watched in fascination. Snuffle, snuffle. Snuffle. Zero interest. He came over to Jane and got up on his hind legs, wanting a pat. She put down her basket, which he ignored, and made a great fuss over him, saying all the while, "Oh George, oh George."

"Dad, you're brilliant!"

Angus looked at all the humans clogging up his bedroom and hopped into his basket.

"Legitimate at last," said David, "what a relief."

"You have no idea," Jane got to her feet. She turned to George and embraced him. "Oh, darling, thank you. Thank you."

"Knew we could fix it if we kept trying," was all he would say, looking happier than he had for weeks.

*   *   *

By nine the last nut had been shelled and steamed, and George was filling the dryers for the last time. Daffy added another load of shells to the flames of the wood stove. They were both working in tee shirts.

Upstairs, the dining room table was covered with bills. Jane, David and Mike sorted them rapidly, discarding the obvious duds. The rest went into a basket in the middle of the table. When it was filled Mike placed it against the wall with other checked baskets. Jane upended another batch onto the table.

The floor was calf-deep in dud bills. "Time for a clean up, darling," she said, and Mike gathered up armfuls of bills into a garbage bag and dragged it downstairs for burning. He returned with two more baskets of fresh notes. The work continued.

Mike was the quickest of the three, taking a bill, studying each side and then discarding it or dropping it in the basket. They'd taken turns checking David's output, pointing out the deficiencies he'd missed. "Don't worry about it," said Mike. "It's just practice." After a couple of hours he'd been promoted to Trusted Checker, along with the other two.

George entered with two more baskets. "That's the lot." He put them with the rest, swept the duds into a bag and returned downstairs. The others took a breather. They had finished the primary sort and were relaxing before beginning the next stage.

Jane gazed at the piles of bills on the table and sighed. "People think life would be so easy if money grew on trees. Honestly, they have no idea."

"It must be very trying for you," said David, straightening and stretching his back.

"You're making fun of me. But I forgive you. You've been such a help."

Mike nodded through a mouthful of sandwich.

"I want to compliment you on your decision not to use starch," said David. He added, as Jane laughed, "Starch is vastly overrated in money laundering."

"Very vastly," said Mike.

By one in the morning, the job was largely finished. The stove had done its work and Daffy was vacuuming throughout the basement. George had dismantled the machine and cleaned its working parts. It was now stowed in the recessed loading chute, along with a stack of nested laundry baskets.

Upstairs, the piles of bills on the dining room table were dwindling. Mike took a fresh stack and gave the top bill a close inspection on one side. He passed it to David, who inspected the other side. Jane gave both sides a sweeping look through a magnifying glass and dropped the approved bills in a basket. The floor was littered with duds, which George removed.

Downstairs, he and Daffy did a final check: the steam room, inside, behind and under the dryers, throughout the basement. The inspection team completed its work, and David carried down a basket full of approved bills, bundled into twenties and hundreds. The area carpet in the front of the basement was rolled back and Jane opened the floor safe. Mike sat on the carpet and added the new bundles of bills to the safe, riffling pleasurably through each bundle as he did so, his hands agile and quick. The remaining basket went in the loading chute along with all the others.

George removed the dust sheet from the furniture at the far end of the basement. Underneath were a bookcase on casters, two area rugs, the pictures, a standard lamp and two armchairs. They rolled the bookcase over, fitting it against the gap. A matching baseboard was slotted into place, concealing its castors. They rolled out the larger carpet, arranged the armchairs and standard lamp at right-angles to the bookcase, facing the stove, hung the eighth Earl and Mona Lisa on either side of the bookcase, and stood back to admire the tableau.

"Very nice," said George. "Now we have our library back."

"I've been looking for that," said Daffy, reaching for a book.

*   *   *

David left midmorning. George was driving him over to Sidney where he would catch an Island Airways flight to Vancouver Airport then a flight home to London. Carryall over his shoulder, he stood with Jane and Mike in the hall, while Daffy watched from the bottom stair. Jane gave him a peck on the cheek. "I can't begin to thank you for all your help, my dear. Take care, have a lovely Christmas and we'll see you in the spring."

"I hope all goes well here," said David. He feinted a spar at Mike, who hugged him. He lifted one hand, "'Bye, Daff," and turned away, going out the side door.

"'Bye, David," said Daffy.

Chapter 15

Sleuthing

Gumble sat on the floor in a Brinks office, waving twenties and hundreds under the nose of a dog.

"This isn't what I signed up for, Hicks."

The agents had arrived at Vancouver airport late at night, to be met by Inspector Bob Kohl of the RCMP Counterfeit section. Briefed by Yves Simard, Kohl had gone through both sacks of bills and divided them into Canadian and American, putting them in separate offices. A Brinks employee had volunteered her dog for the cause. The Chihuahua, bad-tempered at being dragged from its warm bed in the dark of night, had displayed no interest in the Canadian bills, lifting its leg on the nearest of them.

"I pulled out the ones, fives and tens from the US bills," said Kohl during the drive to the Brinks office. "The dog wasn't interested." He was a big man in his late thirties, slightly younger than the two Americans, and fascinated to be working the case with them. "I'd say we're looking at about a hundred thousand in twenties and hundreds."

Gumble and Hicks had continued working through the night, and now Gumble picked up another handful of bills. The dog was losing interest.

"Come on, Teacup, pay attention." The Chihuahua pricked its ears; the routine continued and eventually it lay down, bored.

Hicks put a plate of bills in front of it: Teacup yawned.

Gumble yawned.

At seven, Kohl returned along with the western vice-president for Brinks in Canada. Brad Leung was bright, young and ambitious. He arrived with coffee and Danish, and the men sat down at the table. Hicks gave Teacup a treat. Leung held out a newspaper.

"Write-up on the incident."

Hicks took the paper and began to read the story.

"Lot of money lost to pedestrians," said Leung. "I talked to head office. Sorry, but we're not responsible. I'm telling the bank that."

Gumble and Kohl said nothing; it was not their problem.

Hicks sipped his coffee. "We can figure out how much tainted money we got here, but that won't tell us how much the dog ate."

"Your guys in Washington will figure that out," Leung said brightly. "We pumped its stomach and sent them the bottle."

Hicks put down the Danish with a grimace. "Thanks for sharing."

Leung was happy to give them the details. As soon as he had heard from the driver of the truck, back in his vehicle with a wounded partner and a sated dog in the rear, he had made some rapid phone calls. He had never heard of a dog eating money, but proving it wasn't the company's fault would probably require an analysis of the bills. He called his head office and the RCMP and soon after that found himself on the phone with Ottawa and thereafter, he had no idea why or how, Washington DC. Strings were pulled and when he found no veterinarian clinic open and able to pump a dog's stomach, the guards were instructed to drive like hell for the nearest hospital.

There, they were met by a reception committee consisting of a doctor and two nurses with a gurney. They displayed a deplorable lack of interest in the guard's bitten hand and enquired after the dog. The hapless animal was sedated, loaded on the gurney and wheeled off to an emergency room. Some time later it was wheeled back, accompanied by a nurse and a large bottle filled with disagreeable contents that certainly included bills: Ben Franklin stared out on one side. A waiting RCMP officer produced a padded shipping container, loaded the bottle and took off for the airport and a flight to Washington. The dog lay there, head lolling over the side of the gurney. The injured guard asked if he could have a tetanus shot.

*   *   *

Halloran held a print-out of US dollar deposits made at the Royal Bank, Main and Hastings, in the past three days. He ran his eye down the list: retail food chains, restaurants, coffee shops, convenience stores, hotels. . . .

Earlier he'd paid a visit to the lab, cleared of everyone except Jaio McCaffrey and Yves Simard, who had flown in last night. The two scientists were bent over a long metal tray on a counter, in which pieces of currency blended with lumpy gray-green substances. Halloran hadn't lingered.

At noon, Hicks phoned with a Teacup total. "Damned animal didn't get excited until the bottom of the pile," he said. Halloran was testy from too little sleep and told him to ship the bills back by courier. A little later the scientists arrived with a stomach contents total, and were invited to stay while Halloran reviewed the newspaper article faxed by Gumble then passed it across the desk.

"So we can eliminate deposits under three thousand," he said.

Jaio studied the article. With a glance at Yves, she said, "It would take a substantial quantity inside that sack to produce that kind of reaction."

"So—how high can we go? Five thousand?"

"That's safe enough. You could probably go higher."

Halloran picked up the phone, and Yves added, with a grimace, "It may have been many small deposits."

The Deputy Director was already dialing. "We have to start somewhere." He picked up the deposit list. "Gumble? Only depositors of five thousand or more . . . that's right, forget them for now." He ran his eye down the list. "There's only a handful. . . ."

*   *   *

Kohl, Gumble and Hicks pulled into a Safeway parking lot, entered the store and asked for the manager. They explained their business and he led them through the store to a swing door at the rear and up some stairs. They emerged into a glass-fronted office overlooking the entire store.

"We're a Safeway, for goodness sake. We just don't get cash purchases of five thousand dollars. Five thousand US dollars? I don't think so."

He produced a bank deposit book from a desk drawer and Gumble flipped back to a deposit two days ago. Cash for that day had been $55,000. He looked back through earlier entries while Hicks, Kohl and the manager looked out at the deserted store.

"Good view up here," said the agent. "Get a lot of shop-lifters?"

They had undercover staff, said the manager, working near the doors. His eyes came to rest on a large, empty bin near the entrance, with a sign easily readable from their vantage point: "Food Bank Donations (canned and dry goods only)." He paused in mid-sentence.

Gumble said, "Can you remember anything unusual—"

The manager snapped his fingers. "The food bank." He turned. "We donate two-day-old bread and other perishables, you know?" Hicks nodded. "They pick them up by truck every morning. But we got a purchase order from them, too—here." He strode over to the same desk and brought out a clip full of invoices. He flipped through them and pulled out an invoice for five hundred turkeys and five thousand pounds of potatoes at cost. It was addressed to the EastVan Food Bank, and was marked "PAID."

Chapter 16

Foreign and Domestic

The dog incident appeared to be closed: nothing further had shown up in the media. Daffy continued searching for news about SBP or the Falmouth tree. She had been looking every day since David's departure and every day she had drawn a blank. No news, no stories anywhere. It was as though he'd made the whole thing up. But looking for news was a distraction: it stopped her from thinking about him.

"Did I do the right thing, Mum?" Self-doubt was not normally a problem for Daffy, but these days, second-guessing herself was killing her. "I wanted to throw my arms around him, but I thought that might scare him off."

Jane covered Daffy's hand with her own. "It's early days yet, darling."

"What do you mean?"

"You know—absence makes the heart grow fonder. These few months away may make him realize what he feels for you." She added, "If he feels anything, Daff."

"I'm pretty sure he does." She looked at her mother. "Is that how it was for you, Mum?"

Jane smiled. "Dad never left me alone. He pestered me nonstop for months." She turned away. "I was awful to him."

"I knew I should have done something. I shouldn't have just let him go."

"Love can be terrifying, Daffy." Incomprehension was not something she often saw on Daffy's face. "For people who haven't known love, it can seem as terrifying as a tidal wave, darling."

Daffy tried to wrap her mind around that. "What should I do?"

"Follow your instincts."

Now as Daffy hunted for news, she debated whether to phone David and decided against it. She'd done the right thing when he left. Leave it be, at least for now. *Maybe he'll call,* she thought.

She left the top-level news sources, the *Wall Street Journal*, *Times*, *Telegraph* and *Guardian*, and *Spiegel*, and drilled down to the local level. She started in Falmouth, searching the local papers front to back, looking for pictures or references to SBP or the tree. She did the same with the local Dusseldorf papers, where it was easier and quicker than Falmouth because, unable to read German, she was not distracted by stories of playground incidents or local fairs. For yet another day, she found no pictures of the money tree, and while numerous references to SBP occurred in the Dusseldorf papers, they seemed innocuous.

She finished by turning to her normal sources: the advisors and bloggers of the financial world. Markets continued weak and her favorite blogger wrote again of the general underlying unease in financial markets.

Pushing herself away from the computer, she walked over to the bed and planted herself cross-legged on it. Something was wrong, seriously wrong, Daffy was sure of it.

She closed her eyes and let her mind run free, along all the fiber-optic arteries of the Internet, into newspaper offices and Fed boardrooms, into banks and businesses, into restaurants, bodegas and coffee shops.

Jane's voice penetrated her concentration but she ignored it. What was going on? What was wrong with the picture?

"Daffy." Her mother's voice persisted, distant but distracting.

"What?"

She knew Mum wouldn't answer. Jane refused to conduct conversations through closed doors. Daffy unwrapped her legs, stood up and opened her door. Jane was putting laundry away in the linen cupboard.

"Thank you, dear," she said drily.

"I'm really, really busy, Mum."

"Yes, dear, so am I and I want the house looking like a new pin before the Parkers come." The Parkers came for dinner every year between Christmas and New Year's. "Who's doing vacuuming this week?"

"Daffy is."

Wearing one of his Christmas presents, a hoodie and sweatpants, Mike stood in the doorway to his bedroom, dodging, weaving and jabbing at an imaginary punching bag and muttering inaudibly.

"I'd like it done today, Daffy."

"Mum, what's more important—"

"Today, dear. Michael, make sure you clean *all* the bathrooms, and give the powder room a really good going over." She closed the linen closet and smiled as she passed Daffy.

"'Kay, Mum," Mike jabbed a double left in Daffy's direction and muttered some more.

"What're you doing?" Daffy was unhappy and right now she begrudged anyone else's happiness. Mike seemed to be enjoying himself and she glowered resentfully at him.

"Practicing my negotiating skills."

She turned back to her room, then paused. "Fine. What'll you charge to do the vacuuming?" Her mind was already off on its fiber-optic travels.

"Fifteen." Left jab.

"Oh, come on, Mike. It was ten last time."

"Twenty." Mutter, jab.

"Michael!"

"Twenty-five." Dodge, duck, jab.

She lunged at him. He squeaked and bolted into his room, slamming the door. She thumped it.

"Thirty!"

"Take a breath, Daffy." Jane's voice came up from downstairs. "You're always talking about trends, dear. Do you see one here?"

Daffy made herself breathe. "Okay, Michael," she said distinctly.

"I don't touch the vacuum till I see the color of your money!"

She restrained herself from kicking the door and fetched her wallet instead, sliding two twenties under the door. "You owe me ten," she said unnecessarily.

* * *

Jane opened the heating bill and her lips tightened. "God help us if we ever have a really cold winter."

"Hm?" George stood at the den window staring out at the north field.

"It's time we bit the bullet, George. The windows need double-glazing and this is as good a time as any to do it." From January until March, with no nuts on the trees or in the basement, the Frisbys were able to behave like other families and undertake activities proscribed during the other nine months. Reducing the heating bill was top on Jane's list. She glanced over as George came back to his desk. "See what the deal is, will you darling? On the Hydro website?" BC Hydro offered advice, deals and discounts to homeowners who upgraded their homes to reduce their heating bills, and Jane was relieved to see George plunge into a welter of details with a fair semblance of good humor.

She opened another bill and added it to the pile. The whole family had been at outs since David's departure. Daffy was miserable, George morose, even she herself missed him, and not just for his help in the kitchen.

Michael came in with a bag of salt and vinegar chips, and flung himself onto the sofa. He was the only cheerful member of the family.

Jane lifted her head. "All done?"

He nodded at her, his mouth full.

"Don't eat those anywhere else, darling."

"No way," he said around the chips.

Mike had good reason for his mood: everything was going his way, for a change. Christmas had been great, his ROI on presents even better than usual. That was mainly because the two presents he got for his mother had cost a total of one dollar plus tax. Better still, she'd been thrilled with them, having asked for a yellow Sharpie (the dollar plus tax) weeks ago. The mincer she'd mentioned back in the summer, describing it in detail from childhood memories. Neither Dad nor Daffy had any interest in giving her a used, cast-iron, antique kitchen appliance, but Mike had been ready to devote the whole day to finding one on the family's annual Victoria shopping day outing. It hadn't been necessary. By the greatest good fortune, he'd picked up a mahogany box one day in the recycling gazebo, and inside was what looked like a meat grinder. Daffy had found the identical item online with a description that matched what Mum had wanted. So Christmas had been a big success, and now he was preparing to add another franchise to his stable. He'd discovered Ariadne Wu would be back on the island in a couple of days, and he was ready to surprise her with a visit. Today's windfall was the icing on the cake. Two hours for thirty bucks, more than he earned from Mrs. Bagnold. He ate his chips and thought about having another chocolate After Eight session. Too bad Dave wasn't here to help him.

George and Jane were discussing building contractors when Daffy came in. She flopped into the armchair, waiting for a break in the conversation, and glowered at Mike. He smirked.

"I've been thinking. . . ." she shifted and turned, draping her legs over the arm of the chair and facing her parents.

"What is it, Daffy?" George sounded impatient. "We're busy."

"I think we're in danger. I think we're in danger of being disappeared."

"Has there been something more in the news?" Jane's voice was sharp. She had begun to relax after the dog incident.

"No. And that's scary because there should have been." She looked from one parent to the other. "Someone should have called the local paper in Falmouth, don't you think? Isn't that what would happen here? But there's been nothing. And I think it's because it's being shut down at the highest level. Because they're scared."

She could see her father was skeptical.

"Dad, think about it. If word gets out that you can grow your own money, the bottom will fall out of the markets." She hugged her knees. "I never thought about it before, but they're scared. They're scared of the tree. And people who have a lot of power, especially when they're scared of losing it, are going to get ugly." She glanced over at Mike. "Remember me saying I wanted to give the tree to inner city people?"

Mike nodded. George intervened.

"Daffy, we've talked about that. It's impractical."

Daffy's voice rose. "It doesn't matter!" She took a breath. "What matters is making them think it's practical. The Feds."

Jane shook her head. "I don't understand."

"How many trees are out there?" No one answered. "We know of one here and one in Falmouth. How many others are there? We don't know and it doesn't matter. We have to assume there are lots. And maybe there are."

It was George's turn to shake his head. "I doubt it. They're too delicate."

Daffy shook her head and started to say something, then changed her mind. "Dad, it doesn't matter. We have to forget about franchising the tree. We have to spread the word about how to grow money. If people find a tree, they need to know what it can do and how to take care of it."

Jane understood. "So that there's no point in getting rid of us, is that what you mean?"

"That's exactly what I mean, Mum."

*   *   *

Jane knocked on the door.

"Go away."

"I'm not going away, Michael. I want to talk to you."

"You just want to gloat."

"I most certainly do not." She waited. "May I come in?"

Silence.

She opened the door. Mike lay in a straight line in the exact center of the bed. She sat down on the side.

"I never liked your franchise idea, Michael, but I know how much it meant to you." He continued to stare straight ahead. "This—what Daffy is proposing—goes against everything she's been telling us for years. I don't blame you for being upset."

Head on the pillow, Mike stared between his feet, debating which member of the family to stop hating first. The notion that it might be his mother was so novel that he was momentarily distracted from mourning his franchises.

"The thing is, you're really needed downstairs."

"Oh, *please.*" That felt good.

She studied him. "Do you believe what Daffy said? About how our safety lies in making the Feds believe there are lots of trees out there?"

Mike considered this. Eventually, reluctantly, he nodded.

"Then they need your help. They're thrashing about, the pair of them, talking about websites and YouTube videos and infomercials. When I left they'd decided to write a how-to book and sell it for a thousand dollars."

Mike's interest level recorded an upward blip.

"Or it may have been ten thousand. I don't know." She stood up. He lay unmoving. She walked to the door. "I'm fairly sure Donald Trump wouldn't take a market reversal lying down." She left. The door closed with a soft click.

Dinner was nearly over when Mike finally joined the family. He appeared at the table wearing a red hard-hat and carrying a clipboard.

"Hello, son. No hats at the—ahem!" George fielded a look from Jane and added, "Good to see you. Have some dinner."

"I have an announcement."

"Would you like us to adjourn to the dining room, darling?"

He was okay with them staying put, he said, as long as they listened.

"We're listening," said Jane.

Mike consulted his clipboard. "This book, it'll cover everything?" His glance fell somewhere between George and Daffy.

"It's going to be great, Mike." Daffy was enthusiastic and went on at length. They were going to allow for buyers in all countries and regions, and provide nutrient variations for every climate zone.

Mike listened politely. At the first opportunity, he said, "Will it tell people how to grow money?" He looked at each of them in turn, and this time George answered.

"Yes, it will. Right from when the tree is first planted, including the starter recipe, spring nutrient cycles, common diseases and treatment. Then harvest, curing and processing."

Mike made a note. "Will it be ready by tomorrow?"

"Tomorrow?" Daffy looked offended. "Of course not."

"This news could break at any time, right?"

She nodded reluctantly.

"I'm asking you to have the book ready in no more than forty-eight hours. We'll go with e-book format at first, but I want to roll out with a print edition as soon as possible."

A print edition. *A print edition.* Daffy looked at George, who put his knife and fork neatly together on the plate. "We'd better get at it, Daffy." He stood up.

She followed him out. "Let's work in the den. Mum, can I use your laptop?"

"Go ahead, darling." Jane passed Mike the rice. "That went well, I thought."

Digging into Chicken Divan, Mike said, "I want Ken to build us a website. So I have to tell him we're growing money."

Jane thought, *in for a penny, in for a pound.* "Let's ask him to dinner."

That night, after she'd brushed her teeth, she said, "Michael thought I would gloat over the loss of his franchises."

Writing pad resting on his drawn up knees, George adjusted the pillows against the headboard. "What did you expect? He's hurting." He looked up at her. "Do you remember what you were like at his age?"

Jane glanced at the Northumberland painting on the wall near her dresser, and went to the window. "I was as hard as nails." She parted the curtains and knelt on the window seat looking out at the cove.

"He isn't. And we don't want him to get that way, do we?"

Tiny wavelets formed a moonlit path through the cove. Was it possible, she wondered, that despite all his talk of soakers and soakees, Michael was not in fact the callous child his mother had been? Her spirits lifted. Perhaps after all he was beginning to take after his father.

George finished jotting down points for the next chapter. "Come to bed, love." And as Jane came over, he went on, "I know you love Michael. But I don't think you approve of him, maybe because he's so like you." She got into bed and he leaned over and kissed her. "That's why he delights me." He turned over and fell asleep.

Chapter 17

Dead End

No one took money more seriously than the Germans, and Halloran sighed as he listened to the low, urgent voice of the German Federal Reserve Bank chairman. This was his second call. The first had come after Halloran had alerted his counterparts in the UK and Germany about the possible involvement of SBP. Rumors of the kind the Fed chairman had heard were sufficient to impel him to call Halloran directly for confirmation a few hours later.

"Do you know that other currencies are involved, Jack? Have you heard of Euros being grown?"

"No, Helmut, I haven't. Trouble is, I can see no reason why they wouldn't be." He explained that the tree was known to have produced both British and US currencies, and possibly Brazilian as well.

That silenced the chairman and he rang off. Within twenty-four hours, every bank in every German city had walked a dog through its vaults. Every bill in every currency in every bank had received a canine sniff. He had called again today, to inform Halloran that nothing untoward had happened.

"Our people have so far made no progress with Schmidt Brothers. What goes in Vancouver?"

Nothing went in Vancouver: the investigation was stalled. The agents had interviewed the food-bank operator, gone away and had a huddle with Washington and Ottawa, then returned and interviewed her again. Her responses remained the same: "We never saw the donor, it was left in the drop box. That's the third time. They always give us twenty-five thousand in American money." She eyed the agents reprovingly. "It comes in handy, especially at Christmas time." In response to Kohl's question, she said the other donations had come in February or March and sometime in the spring or summer.

Now the agents were making the rounds of Vancouver charities, to see if others had received donations.

Halloran briefed the chairman. "Believe me," he concluded, "as soon as we get a break, you'll know about it."

Chapter 18

Going Public

A report of arrests at SBP appeared on page three of a German newspaper. Short on details, the report mentioned the CEO, two research staffers and a Brazilian botanist as the persons detained.

Preoccupied with the manual, Daffy spent only half an hour checking her news sources and none checking German papers. She had been up late writing the section on loud sounds, music and pleasant voices, so the German news escaped her attention.

Ken arrived in the afternoon, invited for dinner by Mike. He was on his own again, his parents having returned to Los Angeles. He brought his small laptop, and after Mike introduced him to Jane, he sat down at the kitchen table in his preferred mode, one knee up with his phone resting on it. He brought out the laptop and positioned it near his left hand.

The kitchen was filled with baking smells. A glossy dark brown ginger cake cooled on the counter next to a rack of cookies and Jane was putting the finishing touches on a strawberry and rhubarb pie.

Mike consulted his clipboard. "Can you build me a web-site with a shopping cart?"

"Sure, no problem."

"What would you charge?"

"Dunno. What are you selling?"

"An e-book."

"Simple," Ken dismissed it. "Let's say dinner is my fee."

Mike hesitated: he would have preferred to pay. You knew where you were if you had to pay. He glanced at Jane. "Sounds more than fair to me," she said, and brought over a plate with cookies and slices of ginger cake. The men helped themselves.

"Got a domain name?" Ken swallowed a mouthful of cake. "Know what you want to say?"

"Yeah." Mike took a breath. Ten years of keeping a secret. This was harder than expected. He took another breath, watching as Ken answered a text, tapping away on his knee. He looked down at the table. The silence lengthened.

Brushing egg white on pie crust, Jane understood her son's difficulty. "We grow money, Ken," she said briskly, thinking, *It isn't easy, even for me.* "American money, as a matter of fact. We want to sell a book on how to grow your own."

"Cool," said Ken, and answered another text. He looked at Mike curiously. "What do you want to say?"

Mike handed over a flash drive and the cryptographer inserted it in his laptop and studied the file. "The money tree dot com?" He typed rapidly for a minute or two, his right arm snaked around his knee to reach the keyboard, then swiveled the laptop. Mike saw his website in a pleasing green. "Perfect!"

They spent a minute tweaking the look then discussed payment methods. Mike could have PayPal, the major credit cards and Bitcoin, which had the lowest processing fees and no chargebacks, as well as being anonymous.

"You mean, no one will know who buys our book?"

"That's right."

"Will we know?"

"Nope."

"That's what I want," said Mike, and they talked about the disclaimers he would add, explaining these details up front to prospective buyers. "Is there any way to disguise where the website is? We don't want the Feds shutting it down." Ken said he could set it up with a floating address so no one would easily be able to establish a location. They finalized the remaining details, and Ken promised to have the code ready to upload tomorrow.

Dinner was a quiet affair, George and Daffy so preoccupied with the book that beyond an initial greeting they had little to say to their guest. After dinner, George went for a walk before returning to work. Daffy visited the north grove. "You're going to be famous, Meshach," she said. "You too, John A." A faint rustle greeted this announcement.

Mike showed them the website that evening after Ken had left to bike home. They hated everything about it. They were unusually candid, starting with the picture, which showed a cartoon tree—"it's not even an evergreen!"—with dollar bills hanging from its branches.

"That's awful, Mike. It's so tacky."

"We want a photo there, son. We've put one in the book of the trees at harvest time, and we'd like to use it on the cover and right on the homepage there."

Mike was patient. The photo was nice but wouldn't work as a small picture, he explained, or as a brand. The cartoon was instantly identifiable at any size as a money tree.

They hated the text. The content was all wrong, they said, and they disliked the way it went on and on down the page, all money and greed.

"It's meant to excite people to buy," said Mike.

"Excite?" George was offended. "It doesn't speak to our audience."

"What's our audience, Dad?"

"People who love trees."

Jane laughed, and dropped a kiss on the top of George's head. "Oh, darling, I do love you."

"Dad. Our audience is people who love money."

"Actually," said Daffy, "it's people who love freedom." No one paid any attention to that, however.

At the bottom of the page was the price. If George and Daffy hated everything else, the price incensed them.

"I'm offended, Michael. Fifteen years of my life have gone into this book and you want to give it away?"

"Nine ninety-five? What's the matter with you?" Daffy stared at her brother. "This is because of the franchises, isn't it? This is payback."

Mike waited patiently until they fell silent. He stood his ground. "This isn't for people who have a money tree, people who might spend a thousand dollars on a manual. This is for people who *want* a money tree, like they want a winning lottery ticket. This is for people who want to get rich quick. To them, ten bucks is nothing if it gives them everything they need to know once they find a tree."

"But it isn't a get-rich-quick type of thing, Mike." George drummed his fingers on the table. "You know that."

"That's why I go into so much detail before they buy, Dad. That's why I mention all this stuff about nutrient cycles, and pruning, and harvesting and processing. If they do decide to spend ten bucks, they can't say they weren't warned."

George studied him, and forgot about his trees. "Tell me something. Who are the soakees?"

Mike returned his look unafraid. You never needed to worry about Dad not loving you, no matter what you did. "All those guys out there, the ones who want to win the lottery."

George looked quizzical. "They're getting the benefit of my expertise and years of labor for only nine-ninety-five. How can they be soakees?"

Taken aback, Mike couldn't think of a response.

"I guess we're the soakees, Mike, aren't we?"

"No! Dad! Listen, lots of people are going to buy this book once we get the word out. Thousands of people, maybe even hundreds of thousands. You're—we're going to make lots of money probably."

George smiled at his son. "Sounds like a win-win situation to me, what do you think?"

Mike frowned, turned on his heel and left.

* * *

The news had finally broken, and SBP dominated the headlines:

Multinational pharma growing money? Senior executives at SBP in Dusseldorf are being questioned . . .
Test tube money tree? The pharmaceutical firm SBP has developed a plant that purportedly grows currency . . .
SBP offices closed worldwide as money tree investigation widens . . .

Daffy's favorite blogger cautioned against ascribing too much to SBP:

This is a company that hasn't had an original product in fifty years, a company that exemplifies the worst characteristics of family-run businesses, a company that cut its research budget and doubled its marketing budget ten years ago. Its people are poorly paid by industry standards. If indeed SBP has acquired some sort of money-growing plant, it's likely they stumbled over it on one of their tropical expeditions.

She mentioned this assessment at breakfast. George agreed. "Dieter wasn't a bad sort," he said of the older Schmidt brother, now deceased. "No rocket scientist, you understand, but he was reasonably competent. Werner, on the other hand—," he shook his head, and buttered a piece of toast. "Unpleasant fellow. Smarmy. Always promoting family members. I never cared for him."

"That's what my guy said." Her guy had gone on to say that the money tree represented a staggering threat to the financial system. The markets bore this out. "The Dow dropped a thousand. Gold's up, the euro's way down. Some spokesperson for the German government said the tree only grows ones, so there's no need to worry." She paused. "Oh, right."

Jane brought the meeting to order, wanting a rundown on everyone's activities. "We have the Parkers coming tonight, don't forget." The website would go up later today, Mike said. He wanted to create a short video of Daffy explaining how the money tree would affect the global financial system, and what people could do about it.

"When should we call the network?" asked Jane.

"Soon," Daffy said, and glanced at her tablet to find that the pound and euro were both dropping like stones. She looked up. "Today. We should call today."

They debated how to proceed, and decided Jane should make the call, with the others listening in. They tried to anticipate reactions and questions, and Jane made notes. Later in the morning, she called the network, blocking caller ID.

"We want them to use their economist, Mum, don't forget."

George called through from the TV room. "I thought a horticulturalist. The guy who does the farm and garden show?"

"Maybe we can have both, dear," said Jane pacifically, as she waited on hold. When the News Director came on the line, she read from her notes. "I want to give you an exclusive on a story with national and international interest."

"Yes?" The voice was polite.

"But I must have your promise that if you choose not to follow it you will not leak it to anyone else."

"Uh—okay."

"That won't do." Jane was decisive. "My family may be in danger over this. I'm not going to risk my children's lives on a tepid, half-hearted, marginally—"

"I promise. I do promise."

"Not to say anything?"

"Yes."

"To anyone."

"Not to anyone. Please tell me your story."

Jane turned to look at the others, and got thumbs up from all. They listened intently, phones to their ears, as the conversation resumed.

"Very well," said Jane. "We grow money." She felt more comfortable saying it for the second time.

"Oh?" The News Director sounded doubtful.

"Have you seen today's news?" Jane heard faintly the sound of tapping. "Have you heard the European news about Schmidt Brothers Pharmaceutical growing money?"

"So you grow money? Like them?"

"Not like them. In fact, my husband, who is a horticulturalist, doesn't think they've managed to grow anything at all. He used to work for them."

"Where are you? And—could you tell me your name?"

"Jane Frisby. My husband's name is George. We live on Ledyard Island. We have forty money trees."

"'Kay, Jane. Yes, we'd like this exclusive." A pause, then, "We'd like to interview you at home with your husband and family." Another pause. "I'd like to make it tomorrow morning? Say ten o'clock?"

"Tell them to get Will McIver," whispered Daffy.

"Yes. My daughter suggested Will McIver for the interview?"

"Yes, I was planning on McIver."

Jane ignored a muffled exclamation from the next room as the News Director finalized the details and she provided the farm's location.

"Mrs. Frisby—Jane—tell me something." He paused. "I don't want to lose this story, it's easily the biggest one of the year for us. But I'd like to ask you what McIver will certainly ask you."

"Yes?"

"Do you not think that what you're doing is criminal?"

Jane spoke aloud the words she had said to herself through the years: "There's no law against growing money."

She disconnected feeling it was a rather feeble response.

*   *   *

"Hiya, Mr. Frisby." Kneeling next to the tractor, Terry Parker looked up at George with a grin.

"Hi, Terry. Call me George. Your dad around?"

"Underneath," Vern's voice came from under the tractor engine, and a moment later he rolled out and stood up, wiping his hands on a rag. "Try her now," he said, and while Terry climbed onto the tractor and started it, he talked to George.

"Aren't we coming to dinner tonight?" He cocked an ear, listening to the engine, exchanged a glance with Terry and nodded. The engine died. "She'll do."

"You are," agreed George. "I wanted to have a word first."

Terry paused after gathering up the tools. "I won't be coming tonight. Say hi to Daffy for me?"

George promised and watched absently as he took the toolbox back to the barn. Vern glanced back to see that Terry had gone. "He's off to his girlfriend's for a couple days."

George nodded.

"Daffy won't mind, will she?"

"Shouldn't think so. I think she's taken with David— remember him? Our guest?"

"Oh sure, nice guy." He chewed on a straw as they walked slowly toward the farmhouse and George's car. "I never really thought that'd work out, you know? With her and Terry."

George agreed. "Not really suited, are they?" He halted. "Look Vern, I've got something on my conscience. Something I've wanted to tell you for a long, long time, and I feel bad for keeping it a secret."

Vern looked uncomfortable. "Oh yeah?" He wasn't crazy about personal secrets. "Look, don't worry about it." If George had a drinking or gambling problem, Vern really didn't need to know.

George turned to face him squarely. "We grow money, Vern."

"What, you mean like Dad? Texada Timewarp or Purple Star or something?"

"US dollars."

"What?"

"We grow dollars. Have done for ten years." He could see the other's incomprehension. "I just didn't want to spring it on you this evening. You've heard about the financial markets going haywire?"

Vern hadn't heard anything.

"We've got a TV crew coming over tomorrow to tape an interview. Daffy says we have to go public so that if we disappear, people will know why."

"What the hell are you talking about?"

Vern was getting angry, and George was getting angry because Vern didn't get it. He started over.

"I've got forty money trees, Vern. I grow twenties and hundreds on them. The apples—they're just a cover, I guess, and that makes me sound like a criminal and maybe I am." His anger disappeared and he looked sorrowfully at Vern. "I hope we can still be friends."

*   *   *

Dinner was subdued. Vern was reserved. He'd told Marge and Ron on the way over in the truck and they had hardly had time to absorb the news. Ron was the first to recover.

"The government's not going to like you," he said, sitting with a scotch on the rocks in one of the armchairs. He had on a pale green shirt and seasonal suspenders of red and white Christmas trees on a dark green background. Mike was immensely taken with them.

George sighed. "You may be right, Ron."

"I *am* right." He savored his drink. "Why the rush to go public? What do you expect to gain?"

"We know the tree is cropping up in different places. We want the public to be aware of it and to hunt for it. In fact, you might want to take a good look all over your farm, Vern." He sat on the loveseat next to Marge. "We've put up a website with a how-to manual for people who want to know how to care for it if they do find one."

Marge looked at him uncertainly. "Will they all grow US dollars?"

George explained how the money tree worked and then added that the Frisby trees were probably influenced by the proximity of the US border. "David suggested that aboriginal influence could be confusing the signal as well." He drank his rye and water. "All we know is, we get a large amount of spoilage every year."

He poured Ron a second drink, and Vern also. Mike topped up wine glasses.

"Still doesn't tell me what you hope to gain," said Ron. "Unless you're trying to pull off a hyperinflation?" He noticed Daffy's stare. "No need to look surprised, missy. I read a lot. And maybe because I grow something that's only semi-legal, stuff about government power interests me. And they are going to come down on you like a ton of bricks."

"That's why we're doing this," said Daffy. "And I wasn't surprised, Mr. Parker. It's just that no one could ever want to create a hyperinflation. It's too horrible. But I realized that we have to be prepared to risk that, if we want to achieve a change. If the public thinks there are lots of money trees out there, it'll destroy their faith in fiat currencies. That would normally cause a hyperinflation because people will try to get rid of their paper money in favor of tangible things like gold and silver."

Ron watched her narrowly. "So you're thinking if they return to the gold standard, that'll fix things?"

Daffy shook her head. "No."

"Good for you, because even if they did, it wouldn't be for more than five minutes."

"Oh, Ron." Marge was both stressed and distressed and her wine glass made a sharp tap as she put it on the coffee table. "Don't be so cynical."

Jane intervened. "Marge, I wonder if you'd help me with the vegetables?" She smiled at the others. "Dinner in about five minutes."

After the two women had left, Ron looked inquiringly at Daffy, who said, "We've had a monopoly in currency creation for so long, no one even knows whether a gold standard would be a good thing anymore. But that's not what we're aiming for."

"What then?"

She smiled. It had come to her in the middle of the night, a plan so simple and so obvious that she lay there in bed staring at it as though it were tangible, a Christmas ornament suspended from the ceiling. "It's really simple. All they have to do is remove the monopoly. That's all. If they do that, if they allow competing currencies, the money tree won't know what to grow."

Vern began to perk up during the rack of lamb. "So anyway, George, how much do you make here?"

"Vern, please. It's none of our business." Marge shot Jane a look of apology which Jane waved off.

Vern ignored his wife. "Must be more than your apple income, I'm betting."

"We average around a million," said George. "Isn't that right, Jane?"

"Thereabouts," agreed Jane. "Mind you," she spoke to Marge, "we give a lot away. And we have to set aside a large chunk for taxes, and interest and penalties."

George and Daffy gazed at her with open mouths, and Mike's face took on a look of horror.

"No need to look at me like that, Michael. Of course we have to pay tax. Did you really think we wouldn't?" In answer to George's inquiry she said, "It's in the safety deposit box in Vancouver." She paused, then added, "I just haven't worked out how to give it to them."

Ron threw his head back and laughed. He raised his glass to Jane, and Marge looked happy for the first time that evening.

"Good for you, Jane." She thought of the farm accounts and all the little places where one could, and did, hide a bit of income. "That's very . . . commendable," she said. "Very Canadian, if you don't mind me saying so."

"Well I'm damned," said George.

"There's one good thing, anyway," added Marge cheerfully. "At least you're not growing Canadian dollars."

"Yeah, but there's a tree that is," said Mike, enjoying a bit of payback.

Ron had a quiet word with him as they were leaving. "Is that why you wanted to know about Ariadne Wu?"

Mike nodded.

"God, there's someone who'd love that tree."

He nodded to Daffy. "Remove the monopoly, huh? Very neat." He held out his hand, and Daffy took it. "Good luck to you, missy."

Chapter 19

Clarence Pringle

"Can you hear me now?" The reporter leaned forward, pulling a pad toward him.

"Yes. Better." The signal was weak but clear. "Can you hear me?"

"Yeah. Okay, Professor Pringle, your wife says you have something on this money tree thing in Europe?"

"It's not just in Europe."

"Oh?"

"That's why I'm here. Because the Secret Service sent me down here last November."

"The US Secret Service sent you to Brazil in November?" The reporter searched for the notes of his conversation with Pringle's wife. She'd called yesterday because, she said, her husband, in the depths of the Amazon river basin, couldn't get a decent signal for his phone and was traveling to higher ground. The reporter found the details he wanted. Pringle was an associate research professor at George Washington University, currently on extended leave in the Amazon.

He finished reading his notes and asked his caller to continue.

"They asked a lot of questions about tropical plants," said Pringle. "What they really wanted to know about was the money tree."

"Go on."

"There have been rumors for years. I told him about them."

"Him?"

"The Deputy Director. Halloran."

He paused, and the reporter wondered if the signal was lost. But Pringle had only been drinking some water. He continued and his voice was clearer:

"I asked the Deputy Director if he'd ever seen a note grown from a money tree, and he produced a torn hundred-dollar bill."

The reporter sat up. "One of ours? An American bill?"

"Yes."

"A hundred-dollar American bill?"

"Yes."

"How did he know it came from a money tree?"

"That's what I asked him. He said they did a forensic analysis, and the bill was grown, not manufactured."

"We're talking about a US hundred-dollar bill?"

"Yes. I examined it closely and could not distinguish it from the real thing. It's a pity it was torn."

"Why was it torn, do you know?"

"He said a dog ate it. I tried to learn more, but he wouldn't share anything further. That's when he asked me to lead this expedition."

"Expedition where, to do what?"

"To look for the money tree in the Amazon. He said they wanted an American to find the tree, and he proposed that it be named *Juniperus pringle.*"

"And you agreed?"

Pringle demurred. "I told him it might be a Cupressus. But yes, I agreed. It's hard enough these days to get funding for research so when he offered this expedition, all expenses paid, certainly I agreed." He added, "If this remarkable species existed, I wanted to find it."

"Guess someone got there before you, Professor," commiserated the reporter.

Chapter 20

Celebrity Status

Daffy checked the news as soon as she awoke. By that time, the markets had already recorded the worst percentage drop in history.

"US $100 bill grown not manufactured." The story in the *Washington Post* concluded with a statement by a US Treasury spokesman that money-tree dollars could be easily distinguished from real money because animals liked them.

As soon as breakfast was over, Daffy and Mike went down to the north grove.

"This is a money tree." She spoke into the smartphone camera, held by Mike. "See the two branches?" She pointed to the head of the tree, and the camera angled upward to show the grove and the tops of the trees. "That tells you." She draped a branch over her hand and Mike brought the phone in for a close-up. "It's kind of a mixture of a cypress and a juniper. This is Meshach," she said, and the camera returned to her face. "He's the strongest one. Sounds don't bother him as much. We used to camp out here in the grove because we couldn't have sleepovers, and I always talked to Meshach." She smiled. "I probably sound like a fruit loop. So anyway, I'm going to say this one more time. You can grow money without buying the manual. But you'll get a bigger crop if you follow my dad's nutrient plan. And I have to say *this* again, too: if our plan works, and your government drops its monopoly on money, your tree may not produce any money at all. Because it'll be too confused. See?"

She smiled again and walked toward the entrance. "Back up, Mike," she muttered and the camera maintained the same distance as Mike backed out. She resumed speaking into the phone: "So we're going out of the grove now. It's not that we don't want you to buy our manual, but there's no refund, remember. So make sure you really want it. It's great to grow money. But it's even better to have good money, money that holds its value. That's what we want."

She stopped.

"And . . . cut," said Mike, lowering the phone.

The website was ready. Ken had offered to upload it, and Mike would send him the video, to be added right near the top of the page.

"Did you tell Dad about the seedlings?" He reviewed the video as they walked up through the apple orchard.

"No," said Daffy. She half-turned to him. "No, not yet. I will, but after the interview. Okay?"

Mike nodded.

*   *   *

"What about Gresham's Law?" Will McIver studied the girl across the table. He had no doubt she knew all about Gresham's Law.

"I've thought about that," answered Daffy. "I'm not sure, but I don't think it'll matter."

McIver, in his early 60s, casually dressed in slacks and turtleneck sweater, looked directly into the camera, positioned in the kitchen. Jane leaned on the counter out of the picture, watching the proceedings. "For viewers who may not know, Gresham's Law says bad money drives out good." His gaze returned to Daffy. "You're too young to remember, but we had an example right here in Canada in the early sixties."

Daffy nodded. "You mean when paper dollars and silver dollars were both circulating."

"For a short time," agreed McIver. "But people quickly realized they could pay with paper and put the silver in a drawer for safe-keeping, and many of them did. The bad money—paper—drove the silver money out of circulation." He looked at the camera again. "Now Daphne, here, is proposing that the government monopoly on money-creation be lifted, to permit competing currencies. And my question to her is," he smiled at Daffy, "how will that work? Won't Gresham's Law come into play again?"

Daffy rested her chin on her hand. "I think it would more likely just give people options," she said, then added. "They could choose which one to use, or use more than one. And it would keep all the issuers honest." She showed a flash of anger. "And force governments to choose between spending alternatives and stick to a budget, instead of just loading future generations with debt."

McIver was an economist who hosted a popular weekly financial markets show. He'd interviewed many people during his career, but never a family quite like this. George Frisby was no low-grade crook working on a basement Ricoh. He was an educated man with a degree from McGill and a stint at Kew in England. He radiated intellect and enthusiasm and McIver knew he would engage the TV audience. The trees were both beautiful and sinister, and he'd seen that the cameraman grasped their import, angling his shots to show light and darkness on the branches, while the sound man followed McIver and his subject around during the interview. As for the girl, she was precocious and brilliant, with a smile like a sunburst after a storm. He couldn't fault her grasp of economics. He wasn't sure he wanted to, although this would wreak havoc with markets that were already desperately vulnerable. But he himself had been openly advocating a return to a modified gold standard as a means of shoring up the declining values of global currencies.

"Why do you say the gold standard is passé, Daphne? Is there something better than gold out there? Platinum, maybe?"

"I don't know. Nobody knows. When you have a monopoly . . . progress stops, doesn't it?" She hesitated. "That's partly why the Internet is so interesting. Because it's unregulated. Look at Bitcoin. Who could have predicted that? It's brilliant."

McIver's eyebrows went up. "Bitcoin has nothing backing it," he said.

"I used to think that, too. But it's versatile and private and convenient. And people value those things. And the code that governs the creation of new Bitcoins seems to be airtight."

"But it doesn't even exist in the real world."

"Look. Money is whatever people want to use to fill the exchange function, right? People have used sea shells and cigarettes and beads as money, as well as gold. Anything that holds value. Bitcoin will probably get taken over by the government. They could buy up all the Bitcoins in existence without thinking twice. And even if the government leaves it alone, the code might be hacked by crooks. But there are risks with everything. Right now it looks like a plausible alternative to fiat currencies."

McIver wrapped up the interview soon after, realizing he would never be able to fit what he had into an hour, the time allocated by the network. "I'd like to have you on my show, Daphne. Will you come sometime?"

Daffy lit up, which was all the answer he needed. While the assistant and crew packed up their equipment he said his goodbyes to the family in the field near the helicopter.

"You'll see this tonight, George. The network won't dare delay it any longer than that, in view of the market turmoil." He hesitated, then said, "Take care. You must know the government will be paying you a visit."

The rotors began to turn and he climbed in the helicopter. "I'll want a follow-up," he yelled, and George raised a hand.

*   *   *

George wanted Jane to take the children and leave, but she refused to consider it. He tried to persuade her to let the children leave, but she was firm. "We have to stay together," she said.

They gathered round the TV that evening at six, hoping for some mention of the McIver show. They weren't disappointed. The news anchor looked gravely at them.

"Severe losses in the world's financial markets today. That's our lead story and it has a unique BC angle. I'm Leslie Chen."

After the logo and theme she came back on: "Markets in Tokyo, Toronto, New York, London and Frankfurt experienced their fifth straight day of declines, with indexes falling to new lows and gold rising to nearly $2500 an ounce. The rumors of a tree that can grow money, started in Germany, spreading to the UK and the USA, have ripped through the global financial world. And we now know the rumors are true. BC resident George Frisby has a money tree. In fact, he has forty of them, as Will McIver discovered today. Will?"

The Frisbys sat up as the farm came on the screen, with McIver in the foreground, standing in front of the house. "Thanks, Leslie. I'm here at the Ledyard Island home of George and Jane Frisby and their children Daphne and Michael. They're a most unusual family," (the greenhouse showed in the background, with George and Daffy inside and Mike and Jane loitering outside the door), "because they grow money." The picture changed to show George in the grove. "These are money trees," he said into the camera, and held out a branch. The camera zoomed in. "*Pseudojuniperus lucre*, that's what I call the species."

"Anything you want to know about growing money," McIver continued, "you can learn from George. He's been doing it for more than ten years. His wife Jane is a professional caterer—and mother."

A close up of Jane. "We live such an isolated life. I worry, you know, that they might be growing up warped and maladjusted—," George shushed Daffy, "—but I don't know,

I think they're probably not that different from other children."

McIver appeared. "Though they live on a Canadian island, the Frisbys grow US dollars. George has theories about that, which we'll hear later. But he also knows of trees elsewhere in Canada that do grow Canadian money."

He held up one of the Canadian dollar bills. "This is a one-dollar bill from a tree that has not been—to use George's term—programmed. Notice the plastic strip down the left. That's organic plastic, folks, produced by the money tree. And this is Angus."

A close-up of Angus, looking anxious to please. McIver dropped to one knee next to him. He held out a ten-dollar bill. "Here you are, Angus." Angus looked at him, then at the bill, sniffed in a perfunctory way and regarded the economist politely. "No interest in your standard, assembly-line ten-dollar bill, huh?" He put it away and drew out the one. "How about this?" Angus cocked his head, spotted the bill, lunged and took it between his jaws. Three chews and a swallow.

The picture showed George and McIver from behind, walking through the orchard toward the grove. McIver's voiceover continued. "George Frisby says with the proper additives, a money tree can be made to grow any denomination you want, and to have no appeal for dogs or other animals." They reached the grove. "We're going to learn all about how to grow money tonight. Because the Frisbys have a plan to deliver the global banking system from itself, and they want you to know about it."

The picture returned to Leslie Chen. "Thank you, Will," she said. "Will McIver's full interview will air at seven tonight, immediately following the news hour."

They went through to the kitchen for dinner.

"Warped and maladjusted?" Daffy banged the cutlery onto the table. "How could you?"

"It's a free country," said Mike.

George was pleased with himself. He'd got his name in. "*Juniperus pringle*, my eye," he said. He looked along the table at Jane then at his two children, then out at the darkness. "I'm sure McIver's right. We can probably expect the government tomorrow."

"But we controlled the story, Dad." Daffy helped herself to vegetables and passed the bowl. "That's what you're supposed to do and we did."

"Plus we get a whole hour free advertising in prime time." Mike was pleased at the low-cost way the campaign was developing.

Vern called during dinner. He'd seen the news, he told George, and could hardly wait for seven o'clock. He was in the middle of a sentence when the phone went dead, and the lights went out. They heard loud banging at the front door.

Chapter 21

The Raid

Gumble and Hicks were eating lunch with Bob Kohl when his phone rang. "Hi, Yves," he said.

"Hi, Yves," said Hicks solemnly.

Gumble's phone rang. It was Halloran. "Yes, sir?"

"I want Hicks to hear this as well," said Halloran.

Gumble motioned to his partner and they listened on each side of the smartphone. "Okay, sir."

"We've found them. Got a tip from a film editor at one of the Canadian networks. There's a broadcast going out tonight. The Canadians are trying to suppress it, but you two and Kohl will be leading a taskforce to pick up the grower and burn the trees. Now, listen up."

*   *   *

Halloran finished issuing instructions and rang off. He scowled at the e-book, "The Money Tree, *Pseudojuniperus lucre*," open on his computer screen. Paying for it had turned out to be a major pain in the neck because the website only accepted Bitcoins. Halloran knew the FBI had acquired thousands of Bitcoins after arresting the owner of a black-market website, but when he called a colleague at the Bureau he learned they were unable to use them because the owner refused to divulge the private key. Halloran interrupted a lecture on brain wallets to ask if his colleague knew anyone else who had Bitcoins. This query was overheard by Jaio McCaffrey, who had come in to report on the satellite photos.

"You want the manual, Jack? I've already bought it."

Halloran rang off and looked at her.

"You've got Bitcoins?"

"Sure, why not?"

She had been over the satellite photos of Ledyard Island. "These are the trees. Two groves of them, here and here."

They'd discussed the trees and the island, and after she'd returned to her desk she sent him a copy of the manual. He'd read it and watched the video of the girl.

"Goddamned teenagers'll run the world one of these days," he said.

*   *   *

Gumble and Hicks stood in the entrance to the south grove. They had arrived three hours ago, in daylight, and had taken photos of the trees in both groves to send to Washington. The Falmouth tree was not nearly as luxuriant as these trees. Hicks felt astonishment that they could be so beautiful and yet so deadly. He expressed this thought to Gumble, who merely grunted, "Not for long."

They had returned to their landing point, a beach on the eastern coast of the island, to find Kohl and a ragtag team of officers and agents, augmented by sailors from a nearby naval base. The group had dispersed to cover the whole island, looking for other money trees. They'd had to hurry, to complete the job in daylight, and had found none. There had been no incidents with islanders. Now it was six-twenty and they heard the helicopter in the distance. That was the signal for Bob Kohl and his team to enter the house, and as they watched, a flare went up and all the lights in the house went out. They would no longer be able to use their cell phones; all communication to and from the island had been cut.

Gumble and Hicks stepped backward, out of the grove. Gumble turned to two men standing nearby with flame-throwing equipment.

"Now."

They moved into the entrance and sprayed the trees with fire. The flames seem momentarily smothered by the luxuriant growth, then suddenly the trees were torches. The heads folded and blackened, the trunks twisted ... and they were gone. Only ashes remained.

The helicopter had landed by the time the agents reached the north grove. Again the trees were torched, and a squad of sailors removed the seedlings and saplings from the greenhouse. These would be taken over to the mainland and flown to Ottawa and Washington for analysis.

Hicks sent the team down to the boats in the cove. He and Gumble entered the house.

Numerous LED stick lights on tripods threw a cold bluish-white light. They could hear the tramp of boots upstairs and irregular thumps, as of books being dumped on the floor. An officer indicated a room to their right, the living room, where they found Kohl talking to the family. "Ma'am, we can get a court order." He spoke to a striking-looking woman, presumably the wife. The agents recognized the Frisby girl from the video. Her face was tear-stained and she stood near the window with a man who had his arm around her. A boy sat on the sofa, holding on to a terrier.

"Then you don't need my help." Her voice was flat.

The click of nails sounded on the hardwood floor and a police officer appeared in the entrance with a dog.

Kohl saw the agents, and turned away from the family. "We're nearly done here."

"What was that about?" asked Gumble, and Kohl explained the Frisbys had a safety deposit box in Vancouver. "Come on downstairs," he said and waved the handler and his dog to a door under the stairs. He turned back to the living room. "These are agents Gumble and Hicks from the Secret Service. They've been looking for you for quite a while. Mr. and Mrs. Frisby, please come with us."

The agents followed Kohl and the Frisbys down to the basement. Books and what looked like plastic laundry baskets were strewn all over the floor. A policeman knelt over the circular floor safe.

Kohl addressed the couple. "We can blast this open but you might prefer to give us the combination."

Good-looking woman, thought Hicks. Her lips tightened and she hesitated, then gave them the combination. The policeman opened the safe and began to bring out stacks of bills, mostly twenties and hundreds, Hicks noted. He glanced at his partner, who looked even more morose than usual. Kohl waited until the safe was empty then waved the dog cop over. The dog snuffled once or twice at the bills in a perfunctory way, and Gumble and Hicks exchanged looks.

They had read the Frisby manual on the flight over. If the grower really had succeeded in masking the smell, law enforcement had a serious problem.

Kohl instructed the kneeling policeman to bring the money with him and the others returned upstairs.

"Mr. Frisby, you're coming with us."

Frisby turned away and embraced his wife. The two kids watched silently from the living-room entrance and Hicks saw the woman join them, then he closed the door and followed the others to the helicopter. Depending on what they learned from Frisby, tomorrow the island would be burned to the shoreline.

Chapter 22

Quarantine

"Get the binoculars, Michael." From the front door, Jane stared out at the cove and the ship beyond it. Gleaming white in the morning mist, with a bold red diagonal stripe down the hull, it was an 80-foot US Coast Guard cutter. Two or three inflatables buzzed around it like satellites.

Mike handed her the binoculars and she focused on the ship then either side of it. Beyond the cutter, barely visible in the mist, she could make out numerous craft, from small boats and dinghies to yachts larger than the *Calypso Sue*.

"We should go up to the peak," said Daffy. "What are they doing?"

Jane finished her survey and handed the binoculars to Mike. "Keeping an eye on us, I suppose. And keeping others out."

"I meant the others. Wonder what they want."

Jane shook her head and went off to the kitchen. The house was a shambles. Last night, they had watched silently through the living-room window as George climbed into the helicopter. Their eyes followed its rise, and not until it had disappeared and the sound had faded away did they stir. They had made a start on cleaning up the mess, groping in the mudroom cupboard for the big flashlights, then starting in the kitchen by returning all the frozen items to the freezer.

The barn floor was strewn with the contents of the outside freezer and Daffy's boxes of books. Mike's After Eight boxes had been opened and the contents tipped out. With a thankful cry he got down on the barn floor and began to gather them up, while Daffy held the flashlight for Jane as she primed and started the emergency generator. It sputtered to life, to her relief, and moments later the lights came on. They restored the contents of the freezer, and Jane returned to the house.

The den was littered with the contents of both desks, and the TV room was a mess. She had already seen the basement and she couldn't face going upstairs.

They had no phone, no television and no Internet. They tried all the laptops and Daffy's tablet, but there was no Internet access. Later they lit a fire in the living room and Jane and Mike played Snap while Angus watched and Daffy stared at the flames. "Where's Dad?" she asked out loud at one point, voicing the question on all their minds.

"I'm sure he's fine," said Jane, and Mike glanced at her but said nothing. She brought down blankets and they slept in the living room that night, Daffy and Mike next to each other by the fire. He woke with a cry in the night, and Jane saw Daffy's hand go out to him and heard her whisper, "He'll be okay, Mikey. Honest." Mike's hand came out and joined his sister's, and they slept like that until daybreak.

* * *

Daffy followed Mike along the narrow trail. They were climbing the south flank of Signal Hill, a path marked by gnarled roots, boulders, occasional detours round fallen trees and, in the steepest places, wooden steps cut into the slope. The summit was boulder-strewn and bare except for scrubby shrubs and patches of foot-high dry grass. They emerged from the trail to find several other islanders, including Ken Yamata, surveying the surrounding waters. Two picnic tables occupied the center of the summit area and Mike clambered onto a tabletop to give himself a view, and put the binoculars to his eyes. Daffy stood on the bench of the same table.

The morning mist was clearing, dissipated by weak sunlight. US Coast Guard cutters marked off the four cardinal points of the compass, with assorted RCMP patrol craft at the intermediate points. They formed a cordon around the island, beyond which lay a flotilla of small craft, most of them motionless in the water.

"Wow!" Mike turned round on the table, sweeping the entire circumference. He spotted the *Chinook*, the RCMP high-speed catamaran. A regular sight in the waters of the Inside Passage that stretches from Puget Sound in Washington State to the Alaska Panhandle, the catamaran was patrolling the cordon. It traveled round the southwestern point, circled the cutter at the southern end, then continued on round and up the eastern side.

Daffy jumped off the bench and joined Ken. An islander glanced around, saw her and nudged his companion, who also turned and looked. They exchanged an inaudible comment and Daffy felt uncomfortable.

Like the Frisbys, Ken had had to resort to his emergency generator. He had seen no lights in the harbor or the store while biking round to the summit trail, and suspected the entire island was without power. "No Internet, either," he added. "Bummer." He took another look at the flotillas of boats. "I don't get this. What are they doing? What do they want?"

"I think it's our fault," said Daffy. She told Ken about the ransacking of the house. "They burned our trees," she said miserably and tried to keep her voice matter-of-fact. "They took Dad away and we have no idea where he went or when he'll be back."

"That can't be because of the website. Jeez, we only published it midday yesterday." He glanced over at Mike, who had jumped down off the picnic table and was making his way over.

"Could they shut down the whole Internet?" asked Daffy.

"No way. Too many access points. They might be able to shut it down for a small area, like this island. But the whole Internet? Uh uh. That's why you always get social media input from places like China or the Middle East during uprisings. They can't block all the feeds." As Mike joined them, he asked, "Did you do some kind of online promo yesterday?"

Mike shook his head. "It was the TV show."

Ken knew nothing about the McIver interview, so they filled him in. "Somebody from the network must have told the police," said Daffy, "because they never even had a chance to run the full interview."

"Maybe. Or maybe they did run it on the mainland. Either way I'm betting somebody uploaded that interview and it went viral." He glanced at her. "You guys are celebs."

Later, after they'd left Ken and returned down the path to the island road, Daffy asked, "Should we check on the seedlings?"

"I think we should stay away from them," said Mike. "Let's see what Mum says."

*   *   *

Vern's truck was in the driveway when Jane returned from the creek. The *Calypso Sue* was a shambles, like the house, but as far as she could see, nothing was missing or broken, except for the cabin door. "If we don't lock it, it won't get broken," George had said, but Jane had insisted on installing a lock, and when she saw the door, hanging off its hinges, she sat on the cabin step and her eyes filled with tears. "Be safe," she whispered to George, wherever he was. Mattresses and cushions lay every which way, lockers had been emptied, their contents strewn over table and floorboards. Jane repaired the door as best she could and closed it, returning up the bank and across the road to the house.

She found Vern at the entrance to the north grove. "I never even got to see them," he remarked gloomily. "George must be pretty upset." The grove lay like a black cavity, the adjacent evergreens scorched and blackened on their tips, and fine gray ash covered the ground where the money trees had stood for ten years. Jane steeled herself to look at it, and felt guilty when she wasn't overcome with grief. She felt an emptiness, like the grove itself; nothing more.

When Vern discovered what had happened the previous night, he urged Jane to bring the kids to stay. Touched by his concern, she smiled but shook her head. "We want to be here when George comes home."

He checked the generator and made sure she had enough gas for it. "You need more, come and help yourself," he said, adding, "It's the people without their own generators I'm worried about."

Jane stared at him. "I'd assumed it was just us," she said, distressed to hear that the entire island was powerless. "Do people blame us?" When Vern looked away she added, softly, "Oh dear."

"Just a few. They'll get over it."

He reassured her about Doris Bagley and the other elderly islanders. "Helga and Marge are organizing things and I've got some guys digging a pit near the church parking lot. We're going to cook a side of beef tonight."

About to climb into his truck, he looked out at the cove and the cordon. "Dad said it's just a knee-jerk reaction by the government, trying to contain the problem while they figure out what to do." He shook his head. "Me, I think it's like a giant grow-op raid and I'll tell you, there are a couple islanders who are pretty steamed about it." He climbed into the truck and shut the door. "You should see their backyards," he finished. "Weed as high as an elephant's eye." He laughed and waved as he drove off.

Daffy and Mike returned soon after, and Jane's mood lightened when she heard about the seedlings. "Dad will be thrilled," she said, putting an arm around Daffy's shoulders. "That was very enterprising of you, darling."

"Yes but do you think it's safe to check on them?"

"The government could be watching from a satellite or a drone, or something," added Mike.

Or, Jane reflected, they could have found and destroyed them last night. "Let's wait a day or two and see what happens."

* * *

"That's the girl from the television."

Jane and Daffy had left two large desserts in the annex and returned to the car in the small parking lot. About to open the door, Jane glanced over to see the Eastens, neighbors of Morgan Lee, standing near their car. In their late eighties and white-haired, they stared at her.

"Hello," said Jane, smiling. "I'm so sorry about the power."

The old man wore an overcoat and carried a cane. His wife wore a padded jacket over a woolen twinset and a wool skirt. He took tighter hold of her arm, as if to steady himself, and stared at Jane through watery eyes. "You're the reason our pension doesn't buy much any more."

Daffy stepped forward, shaking off Jane's hand. "Mr. and Mrs. Easten?" Her hands were gripped together. "I'm so so sorry about your pension, but it wasn't us." She twisted her hands in distress. "We're just the catalyst." She gazed at them earnestly. "This trouble in the markets, it's been going on for years, long before we started growing money. Please, please believe me."

The Eastens stared at her, and Jane put an arm around her shoulders.

The elderly wife spoke. "We only wanted it to see us out. That's all we wanted." She turned, carefully helping her husband to turn, and they walked slowly toward the marine supply store.

The Frisbys watched them. "I hear that a lot from my shut-ins," said Jane at last. "They just want their money to see them out."

They returned to the car. "My heart hurts," said Daffy.

"Look, darling. Whenever change happens, some people are always going to be vulnerable. If you believe the change is for the better, you must stick to your guns. But try to help the vulnerable ones if you can."

*   *   *

Jane sat in the dark in the living room, looking out at the cove. She had pulled an armchair around to face the north field and she sat with her knees drawn up looking through the bare apple trees toward the cove.

It was after eleven, the house was quiet, children in bed. Daffy had discovered several much-loved childhood books while clearing up the mess in the barn. "They're like a security blanket," she had said to Jane, and had taken them upstairs.

The Coast Guard cutter was ablaze with lights and strobing searchlights. She glimpsed another boat in the cordon, also lit up, and heard an occasional sharp whistle and once a megaphone warning-off of a vessel that had presumably drifted too close.

The living room was impersonal, better than the den, where she found she could not sit for long without missing George. When she heard the crunch of wheels on gravel, she wondered fleetingly if he was back. She straightened, listening, and heard another vehicle and still others. Doors slammed. She heard voices, louder than conversational, and laughs. Were they drunk? Momentary silence, then the crunch of feet on gravel. They were coming along the north side of the barn to the front door. Daffy's bedroom window was on the north side.

She sprang up, relieved that she hadn't yet undressed, took up the sweater draped over the loveseat and put it on as she ran to the side door. Angus sat up. "Stay!" She brushed the yard light switch and opened the side door. Like moths, the intruders turned into the yard. They stopped, swaying, beyond the range of the light, pointing their own lights at her. Several held flashlights, others had kerosene lamps.

"Yes? Who is it?" She was relieved that her voice sounded strong, and shielded her eyes, trying to discern faces, to find anyone she knew. "What is it you want?"

They carried bottles, she saw, and one of them lifted his to his lips and drank. "You tell her, Gar," he said. "Your idea."

The men shifted their feet. A flashlight dipped momentarily and she was able to see a figure step forward. Then the beam was raised once more. She heard a shuffle of feet again, and a low, shared laugh.

"GiveFeds . . ." the man was almost too drunk to articulate. He got it out on the second try: "Give Feds what they want." Murmurs of agreement from the others. He elaborated with drunken doggedness: "Yeah. Give 'em what they want. Go away."

Interpreting this, Jane said, "I think they'll go away when they're good and ready. I don't know what else I can give them." She looked from one face to another, still unable to make them out. "They burned our trees, ransacked our house and took my husband away."

Had they know this? She was unable to tell. They seemed to confer wordlessly; one lifted a bottle and took a swig.

"Quit that, Eric," said Gar. He swayed and looked at Jane. "We lost lotta money. Hard-earned. Your fault. S'all I have to say."

"I'm so sorry. But it really isn't our fault, truly it isn't." She recalled one of Daffy's phrases. "We were just the catalyst. But the system was already in a bad way." Her gaze went around the group. "Now, please—go home."

The men stirred, turning at random, and two of them staggered and their lanterns swung together and broke. Flaming kerosene ran across the hardpan of the yard.

"Burn it down," said the man called Eric. "That'll do it."

Jane could hardly believe her ears. Frantic images filled her mind of the children and Angus. Then rage overtook fear, and the blood of four hundred years of fighting for your own coursed through her veins.

"Stop it!" She walked forward and the group fell back. "Shame on you," she said. "Shame on you." She tried to think. "We're neighbors, have you forgotten? We're—we're tied to one another." Her voice rose in protest. "We can't behave like this." She stopped, then in a calmer voice she added, "We have to pull together."

They swayed in front of her, and heads turned seeking guidance or consensus. Gar's head dropped. He staggered slightly, righted himself and tugged at the sleeve next to him. Alone and in pairs, the men turned away, crossing the yard, rounding the corner of the barn, their feet crunching in the gravel along the wall.

Car doors slammed, engines started. One by one the cars reversed out of the driveway and drove off along the Island road.

Jane let out her breath and backed toward the house, making sure no one was still there to attack her. Then she went inside and locked the door.

*   *   *

"I must admit I was quite—annoyed with you, Jane." Helga Johnston sipped her coffee, sitting at the kitchen counter.

Jane was ladling sauce onto pasta, making a mammoth vegetable lasagna for tonight's harbor dinner. "Because we're growing money? You're not the only one."

"Oh no. I mean, that's hilarious, of course, although Stuart says I'm being idiotic to say so but it *is* funny when you stop to think. No, I was annoyed because you didn't tell me. Or anyone else, Marge said."

Jane was beginning to appreciate that secrets, unless shared, were not at all conducive to good relations. She sighed and looked up. "We wanted to tell people. We just didn't see how we could."

"Hm." Helga digested this. "Is that what stopped you joining the Channel Dredging committee?" And when Jane confirmed that it was, she said, "Will you join now that your secret's out? Ariadne talked to everyone at dinner last night. I swear she's winning people over."

"How many turned up?"

At least half the island population, Helga estimated. Many had been either drunk or high by the time it broke up, at nine. Her mind was still on Ariadne Wu. "She's a strange woman. I happened to be chatting with Cam when she came roaring into the harbor. You know he's selling all his food at cost, don't you?"

Jane nodded. She thought well of Cam for doing it, although it was also a good way to shift stale inventory, and he did have a habit of leaving items on the shelves beyond their best-before dates.

"Anyway, she barged into the store wanting to know why nothing worked. Apparently she'd flown over just before the lights went out and when she saw the Coast Guard parked off her living room she became convinced we were being annexed by the Americans."

Jane stopped filling the lasagna dish and laughed.

"I don't know," Helga said. "Anyway, Cam and I explained that we thought it was because you were growing money, and she stared and stared. I don't think she got the concept at all. Then she picked out a few canned goods and when she discovered Cam was selling at wholesale she wanted to buy up the store." Helga sniffed and sipped her coffee. "Probably so she could double the prices. Rancid woman."

Helga wanted to see where the trees had been, so Jane gave her the tour, starting with the south grove, which looked every bit as ugly and depressing as the north. The grey squirrel chattered at them from a branch of the Garry oak. "I used to feed him bits of money," said Jane. Then she had to explain how money-growing worked in this particular neck of the woods, and how much spoilage they had.

Helga was fascinated and said she was going home to look for a tree on their property. She was unable to persuade Jane to come to dinner.

"Better for everyone if we're not there," said Jane.

"Hm. We're going on with this until they lift the embargo. Or whatever you call it. Salmon tonight. Swimming as we speak."

*   *   *

"There you go, Mike." Cam Shockley took the clippers off the grinder. "Anything else?"

"Nope." Holding the clippers in one hand, Mike took the hoe and edger in the other. "Thanks," he remembered.

"You're welcome." Back at the till, Cam opened a notebook. "Call it three-fifty. I'm adding it to the account, tell the old lady." Doris Bagnold settled up once a month, generally on Fridays after visiting her late husband.

Mike nodded, and Cam wanted to know if he was taking the scooter back. Since the beginning of the quarantine, someone had brought it in each night to be charged on the store generator. No one had yet picked it up this morning. Mike had brought the tools over on his bike, but balancing the hoe and edger had been awkward and he decided to leave the bike for later and go back on the scooter.

He unplugged it from the outlet on the far side of the store, put the clippers in the basket and balanced the longer tools across the handlebars. He glanced out at the harbor as he backed up. Local craft dotted the waters beyond the entrance, many with fishing rods out. The cordon was much farther out at the south end than up at the cove.

He heard a high-pitched whine and his eyes brightened as a Jet Ski emerged into the harbor from the narrow channel between the Rock and the island. His schoolmate,

Cory, was riding it, and he turned sharply before reaching the far rank of berthed boats. After him came another Jet Ski ridden by an older boy, who tore round in a tighter circle and chased after Cory back into the channel.

Mike cruised the few hundred yards to Mrs. Bagnold's blue house, left the scooter at the garden gate and jogged the short distance to the causeway entrance, just in time to watch Cory's return trip. Waves arced up from the rear of the Jet Ski, Cory yelled at him and a few minutes later pulled up and stopped. Mike helped him pull the Jet Ski onto the mud bank.

Cory glanced up the causeway. "You working for the Old Bag?"

"Yeah. She's not so bad."

"Rather be doing this."

"Yeah. Christmas present?"

"Yeah."

The other boy joined them. "I got to go."

"This is Mike," said Cory.

"Yeah."

Mike had been thinking. "You guys ever try that at low tide?" The channel at low tide was a narrow ribbon of water through steep mud-laden banks.

They stared at him.

"Like snowboarding, only on mud."

They got it. They exchanged a look. They liked it.

"Come and watch," said Cory. "We'll try tonight."

Mike said he'd see. He returned to the scooter as the other two launched their Jet Skis and headed for the harbor. He carried the tools through to the back shed before returning to drive the scooter up the path and into the house. Sharpening tools had not been on the original list drawn up by Mike and signed by both parties. Mrs. Bagnold had asked him to get the job done because little else needed doing at this time of year: no grass to cut, or leaves to rake, no bulbs to plant.

Mike regarded the break as his due. The contract had been tough to fulfill, week after week, in the allotted two hours and he had grown resentful of Mrs. Bagnold, forgetting that he himself had drawn it up and had failed to allow any time for delays or larger loads. No wonder she'd been so quick to sign it. *She should have said something*, he thought resentfully; *I'm only a kid*. To fall back on this excuse in a situation of his own creating was a cop-out, but he shut his mind to that. He skirted, too, the thought that Mrs. Bagnold was a soaker because if so, what did that make him? It didn't bear thinking about.

He buzzed the scooter through to the back of the house where the old lady spent most of her time, at the small round table in the kitchen. Here she ate her meals and wrote her letters, did jigsaw puzzles on bright days, and watched TV on the screen that sat on the open cabinet against the opposite wall.

"All done?" A chocolate box was open on the table in front of her.

"Yes, ma'am." He glanced at his watch: another fifteen minutes before he could leave. He decided to make a start on tidying up the shed so that he didn't have to waste time trying to find things.

"Come here, Michael."

He reached the table and, about to sit down, he stopped and stared. The chocolate box was filled with coins, silver coins. Mrs. Bagnold was poking through them with a finger that trembled only slightly. "Have a seat," she said.

She found a dollar and transferred it to the table, where several others lay. "I haven't looked at these for years. Tommy said we should hold on to our silver, after the government started making coins out of tin."

"It was copper and zinc, Mrs. Bagnold. And nickel."

"Was it?"

Mike leaned across the table, peering at the contents of the box. Dollars, half-dollars and quarters were mixed up together, some black with age. He picked out one of the black coins, dated 1898, a fifty-cent piece with a stern young Queen Victoria on the front.

"Look at this." The old lady dropped a coin on the table in front of him. Dated 1908 it showed George V and on the reverse, the single word, "Newfoundland."

"Tommy brought those with him when he moved out west."

"That's before Newfoundland joined Confederation," said Mike. "Wow. He must have been really really old."

Mike had learned from Permastone Parker that Mrs. Bagnold used to teach school on the island, and that she had been strict. "She still calls me Ronald, and I'll tell ya, kid, I still jump." Now a smile altered the severe cast of her face, and laugh lines wrinkled the corners of her eyes.

"I'm really really old, dear. Tommy was only eighty-three when he died." She went on reminiscently. "I remember, oh, years ago, when silver suddenly became valuable. It was in 1980. We hadn't been retired long and it seemed like such a windfall when it rose to fifty dollars an ounce. We turned the house upside down collecting all the silver coins we could find." She smiled ruefully. "Unfortunately, it didn't last long enough for us to sell them. So, we just put them all in this box and saved them for a rainy day." She folded her hands and looked at Mike. "I've run out of cash, my dear, and I can't get to the bank because of this quarantine. Would you mind if I paid you with silver?"

"I like silver," Mike assured her. And because there were no more secrets, he unbent enough to add, "I've got lots at home."

"You have?" Mrs. Bagnold regarded him benignly. "You're a sensible boy, Michael." She pushed the coins in front of her over to Mike. "There. I think that's ten." And as he opened his mouth, she forestalled him. "I know it's probably worth a little more than ten dollars now, but it pleases me to put this old silver to good use."

Mike knew he should say something. If silver dollars were still worth sixteen dollars, then he was looking at a cool one-sixty. For two hours' work. He looked at Mrs. Bagnold. She was continuing her reminiscences. He pocketed the dollars.

"Such turbulent times, back then. Interest rates were at 18 percent. And that poor young family in the valley had to renew their mortgage and they just couldn't afford it. So sad. The bank repossessed the farm. Oh, such a lot of that went on back then."

* * *

"I know I've always wanted you to be more like your father, Michael," said Jane. The two of them were eating tuna melts, with an extra one for Mike keeping warm on the stove.

"I like being me."

"Yes, dear." Jane was intent on delivering the message. "I just—you do?" She regarded him curiously. He nodded. "How marvelous," she said.

Mike ate another mouthful. It was, in fact, a pretty great time to be Mike Frisby and he was glad he had the franchise. He pushed away thoughts of his father and Mrs. Bagnold. He had not mentioned the windfall to his mother.

The side door slammed and Daffy came in. "Honestly, Ken's hopeless. He doesn't even know how to cook hotdogs." She saw the tuna melt and looked over at the table, where two pairs of eyes regarded her. "What?"

"Do you?" They spoke together.

"I don't have to." She pointed at the stove. "Is this for me?"

"No." Unison again.

Daffy carried bread and cheese and butter and pickles over to the table. She went back for milk.

"We're nearly out of milk, darling."

Daffy poured a glass of water, good-humoredly delivered Mike's second tuna melt, sat down and began to build a sandwich.

"How's Ken?"

She shrugged. "We're both suffering from social media withdrawal." Sandwich complete, she lifted it to take a bite, then put it down again. Her face contorted.

"Darling!"

Daffy shook her head. "I'm okay, Mum. I'm sticking to my guns." She wiped her eyes. "I just don't like not being liked. You know?"

"Ken doesn't like you?"

"Not him. Other people."

"It's okay," said Mike. "You get used to it."

*   *   *

"Twenty pounds of potatoes, Raaj. The golds, please." Jane watched as Raaj Dhasi filled a box with Yukon Gold potatoes, adding two extra for the box weight. He carried it round and Jane unlocked the trunk of the car. She chatted with him as he returned to stand behind the counter. The Dhasis were managing, he said, running short of a few things but not seriously inconvenienced. "One thing's for sure, Mrs. Frisby. No shortage of fruit and veg." He sounded cheerful.

Earlier, she had paid Ken Yamata a visit, to invite him to stay during the quarantine. Busy working with pencil and pieces of torn up cardboard boxes, he had declined. There were pieces all over the living room floor and she had left him to it, driving back through the Dhasi fields and stopping at the vegetable stand.

"I'll take four pounds of leeks." Leek and potato soup would fill the corners nicely. She paused at the winter squash, but the family's favorite squash recipe called for both egg and milk. Instead, she bought an assortment of vegetables for stew and stir fry and vegetable cottage pie.

She held out a US twenty dollar bill. It was the only paper money she had, discovered in a corner of one of the workbench drawers. Raaj took it, hesitated, and held it up to the light.

"Looks good to me," he said cheerfully.

"It is," said Jane. "That's the trouble."

He laughed and reached over with her change. "We'll be there tomorrow night, father and me. You don't have to worry, Mrs. Frisby. We'll look out for you."

Another car pulled in but Jane ignored it, staring at the East Indian. "I have no idea what you're talking about, Raaj."

"Jane!"

Marge came up and enveloped her in a hug. "You should have come to us. What are friends for?"

Jane wasn't sure what she meant. "I'm fine—we're all fine, Marge."

"Vern and Ron will be around tonight. The Dhasis will come tomorrow, and Morgan and Stuart Johnston will do the next night. You won't see them, they'll park in the road." She patted Jane's arm. "Don't bother arguing, Jane. Some things cannot be allowed to happen."

Jane drove home feeling less isolated. A long time afterward, she learned that Navi, Raaj's younger brother, had overheard an exchange between two customers, women whose husbands had evidently been up to no good, thought Navi. He told his father, who drove to the Parkers and told Vern, who gathered his friends for an impromptu meeting.

Chapter 23

At War

At three in the morning, Halloran entered the make-shift command center on the floor below his office. It was filled in the daytime with staffers taking calls from agents on the west coast. Now, in the middle of the night, the only people there were Jaio McCaffrey and her team, each of them bent over a stereoscope. They were reviewing satellite pictures of the west coast, looking for money trees. She looked up and saw Halloran, rose stiffly to her feet and joined him.

As a key element in the war to eradicate the tree, the Canadians had agreed to burn the island. But they insisted on proof first, proof that there were no other money trees anywhere. Otherwise, this action would be tantamount to closing the barn door after the horse, or in this case, tree, had departed.

Halloran smiled. "Buy you a cup of coffee?"

Jaio nodded. She had been up for forty-eight hours straight, peering into a stereoscope for most of that time, and she was glad of the break.

They sat at one of the empty desks, drinking their coffee in silence. Halloran was the first to speak.

"Are we winning?"

Jaio sighed. "I don't know." She sipped her coffee. "It's slow work, you see. There are several blue-green species in that region. Cedar, cypress, spruce. And juniper." She was silent for a while. "And it's such a big area, Jack."

He glanced over at the wall map showing sightings. They'd found a number of trees in the San Juan islands, and environmentalists were up in arms about the burnings. Three more trees had been found in Washington State, south of Bellingham, and Jaio and her team were poring over Oregon.

In the morning, teams of federal employees would go back into the woods in Washington, Oregon and northern California, with Gumble and Hicks coordinating the effort on the ground, using the DC team's findings.

There had been some thought that sound might be a weapon in the war against the trees. One expert had proposed blanketing the west coast with a series of sonic booms. However, tests in Ottawa had proved that while loud noise might be lethal to seedlings, saplings or grown trees could tolerate the same decibel levels as humans.

"What do I tell the Secretary?" Halloran had a meeting with the Treasury secretary in three hours.

Jaio shrugged tiredly. "I don't know." She glanced up at the clock, then let herself relax and leaned back.

"You know, Jack, part of me isn't sorry this tree came along." She saw his frown and went on. "Don't get me wrong. I'm proud of what I do. And I'm proud that our dollar is the world's benchmark currency." She shook her head. "But I don't like what's been going on in Congress. Maybe it's my Scots blood but it offends me that we can't stick to a budget."

Halloran turned sideways in his chair, stretched out his legs and put his hands behind his head. "That why you bought Bitcoin?"

"No. Not really. I just like trying new things."

"It's gone up a lot. Good investment."

"That's not why I bought it. But I find it interesting that the creator of Bitcoin was so concerned about limiting the issue. Like the Frisbys."

Halloran opened an eye and glanced over at her. "What?"

"Didn't you read his introduction? The girl wouldn't let him roll out with trees because of hyperinflation. She's paranoid about it."

Jaio got to her feet and picked up both mugs. "The government could take a leaf out of their book, Jack." She took the mugs over to the sink on one wall. "Check back with me in a couple of hours."

Chapter 24

Coming Together

That night, David arrived. Jane had been out to check on Vern and Ron, sitting in their truck on the roadside north of the driveway. She had locked the front door and was crossing the hall when David appeared in a wet suit and incongruous-looking brown shoes. Her near-shriek of surprise and pleasure brought Mike and Daffy out of their rooms and they tumbled downstairs as he hugged her.

"My dear boy," she touched his hair. "How on earth—are you frozen?"

"Dave!" Mike threw his arms around the wet-suited figure.

"Hi, Mike." he looked across the hall, and seeing his expression, Jane realized why he had come. "Oh, Daff. I'm sorry—"

Daffy hurled herself into David's arms. "Oh, David!" She kissed him.

"Daff." His arms went round her.

"David." Between kisses.

"Sweet Daff."

Mike looked doubtfully at his mother, who was about to say a few words on the subject of love when they heard the side door click shut. There stood Ariadne Wu. Jane was speechless. Mike regretted his polka-dot pajamas.

"You are Michael—Smith?"

"Frisby." Mike walked toward her and held out his hand. "Nice to meet you."

"Michael?"

"It's okay, Mum. We had a business proposition."

"I was to have a money-tree franchise," said Ariadne.

David dragged his eyes away from Daffy and turned. "Ariadne gave me a meal when I swam ashore. She can't get round by boat, so we came over the ridge. She wants to talk to Mike."

He had swum from Sidney, a distance of about five miles. He held out a small black plastic carrier that he'd tied to his back. "Got me undies," he said. "Could I borrow some of George's things? Where is George?"

While Jane and Daffy took him upstairs, filled him in on their news and found him some warm clothes, Mike sat down with Ariadne at the kitchen table. He discovered she had heard nothing about the Frisbys or the money tree beyond a few bare details provided by Cam Shockley and Helga Johnston. He reached across the table for Daffy's tablet and turned it on. "We have a website," he said, and showed her the prototype. She read the entire page and listened to the video of Daffy, by which time Jane and Daffy had returned. They stood quietly in the entrance to the breakfast nook, behind Mike.

Ariadne considered him. "So if I can find a tree, I can have it?"

"That's right."

"For no franchise fee?"

Mike nodded.

She thought for a moment. "David said there are trees in the San Juans and Oregon."

"No kidding?" Mike was fascinated.

Ariadne frowned. "I wanted twenty trees, like you said."

"Why?"

"Why?" She looked at him as though he were mad.

"Where do you want to grow them?"

She stared silently at him, ignoring the others. "In China," she said. "My relatives are poor farmers. I want them to have trees."

Mike considered. "I can supply you with twenty trees."

"You can?" She seemed pleased. "That's very good."

"But I'm charging you for one manual per tree."

"Wat?" Her gaze took in Jane and Daffy. They disappeared from view. "I only need one manual. Why would you charge me twenty times? Is it even in Chinese?"

Mike allowed these questions to percolate. Then he said, "You're right. You don't need twenty manuals. It's not in Chinese either, so how about I don't charge you for the manual. It's free."

She seemed pleased. She nodded. "Let's get those trees."

"You can have twenty trees for twenty-five dollars each."

She frowned. "Too much. For a tree that may not even grow money?"

Mike agreed that it was a risk. The haggling resumed.

Eventually she settled on one tree and one manual for $9.95 total. Then came the shipping and handling fees. She wanted the manual on a disk, and she wanted to fly the tree to China. For that, Mike explained, it would have to be packaged with care, and insulated from the noise and any change in temperature.

They eventually agreed on $14.95, all in.

"You can invoice my office," she said. "Where is the tree?"

"Cash in advance," said Mike. "You'll have the tree tomorrow, by lunch time."

Slowly she produced a money clip, and a ten appeared on the table between them, followed by a five. Mike, mentally reviewing his resources, made no move.

"I'll have to owe you the nickel," he said. "May I bring it tomorrow with the tree?"

Ariadne inclined her head. Mike picked up the bills, folded them and put them in the breast pocket of his pajamas, Ariadne watching. He patted the pocket and stood up. She did the same. They shook hands, concluding the deal, and he escorted her to the door. She declined David's offer to return part way with her, and set out, crossing the south field and climbing through the trees on the western slope to the ridge.

David sparred with Mike. "Nice work, partner."

*   *   *

They lit a fire in the living room and gathered round David, avid for news of the outside world.

"What's gold up to?"

"About three thousand dollars."

"And climbing, I bet," said Daffy.

"How about silver?" Mike wanted to know.

David nodded, appreciating the question. "Silver's gone up a lot because some countries are talking about restoring silver coinage. I'm not sure what the price is, but one economist said it had gone up proportionately more than gold."

He responded to Daffy's comment. "It's not climbing, Daff. Not now. At least, not officially. Everything's halted. All the markets are closed. The G20 countries have been meeting all week and everyone else is banging on the door wanting to be in on it, but the fact of the matter is, no one seems to know what to do."

Daffy was about to explain what had to be done, but he continued. "I meant, no one wants to be the one to propose it. Most economists seem to agree currencies have to be devalued, and I guess if they all did it at once, the net effect would be a wash out. I don't know. But no one wants to be the first to propose it, because it's political death. And no one wants to talk about the elephant in the room. Competing money. Giving up control."

"They have to do that."

"I know it, Daff, and you know it. And I think the authorities are beginning to recognize they don't have much option."

"David, tell us everything," said Jane. "Why did you come?"

"I had to. As soon as I heard about the embargo. It cleaned me out getting here. Vancouver's completely jammed, you know. No flights in or out."

"Start at the front, Dave." Mike craved an orderly presentation.

David had heard the news as soon as he got up. "It probably came on in the middle of the night, when they broadcast it here."

"So the interview did go on? Just not here. We've been completely cut off."

"Yeah, no one knows why, but I talked to a guy on the plane over, and we agreed it was probably the government overreacting. Also, Daffy was pretty potent." He gave her a one-armed hug. "The new cult queen, you are."

He'd booked a flight to Calgary, and from there managed to get a seat on a company plane flying to Kitimat, on the northwest coast of BC. "An executive and two engineers," he said, who made no objection when he said he had urgent family business. From Kitimat, he'd caught the ferry to Port Hardy, and rented a car to drive the length of Vancouver Island. The lower end of the island was almost impassable. It had taken him a full day to drive from the north side of Sidney to the south, because of the jammed traffic, but he'd managed to pull off the island highway and on to a side street that gave him access to the shore. He had donned his wetsuit, waited until night, then climbed down into the water and swum across.

"So you knew about the quarantine before you left England?"

"Absolutely." He hesitated. "I don't know what might have happened if they hadn't had an audience. Someone said there's talk of burning the entire island." He added quickly, "That's probably just a crazy rumor. There have been a lot of rumors."

Private boats had been drawn to the area when a craft in the strait had uploaded a picture of the flaming north grove.

"Who could say what it was? It showed flames in the dark. But the GPS on the phone proved where he was and the picture went viral. He came down until he was stopped by the cordon. Then he blogged, and others joined him." The media had been interviewing boat occupants for the last three days. "Some people want trees. Some are there for the fun. A lot came for support, to make sure nothing bad happens." He looked at Jane. "You won a lot of people over with that stuff on taxes. I mean, George was likeable and educated and obviously not a nutter. And Daffy's the poster girl for competing currencies. But I think parents really related to you when you said you'd put aside money for taxes and interest and penalties. That's what made you seem like a normal family facing a lot of trouble. That and the warped comment," he added, and Daffy groaned.

Jane sat up. "They absolutely cleaned us out, David. They took all our money—"

"Including all the apple money," said Mike resentfully.

"And all the tax money. They wanted me to sign a form and I wouldn't." She paused. "I didn't do anything to stop them," she added quietly.

"What could you have done, Mum?" Daffy sat up. "I was the one who wanted to be a terrorist and I didn't do a thing. . . . There were so many of them. And they burned our trees."

Jane spoke briskly. "I can't reimburse you for all your expenses, David, I'm so sorry."

"Don't talk such nonsense," he said, and put an arm around Daffy. "Of course I had to come. Several people on the plane were reading your manual," he added. "I don't think you're exactly going to be penniless when this is over."

"I don't see why they had to take George, I really don't."

David had been thinking about that. "They've got plenty of economists telling them what to do. What they don't have, or didn't, was reliable information on the money tree. No one wanted to believe it could actually grow money, and reading it in a book isn't the same as talking to the grower."

They talked and talked, hearing about David's Christmas, updating him on everything that had happened since his last visit. "Daffy said we should tell everyone, just because it would make us safer." Jane made no mention of her night-time visitors.

Daffy spoke up. "I think we should dig up the seedlings and re-pot them, and give them away when the quarantine ends."

Jane looked out the window at the Coast Guard cutter, lights ablaze. "When will that be?"

"You know," said David, "a chap on the plane said he knew someone in Devon who had dug up a tree and taken it home. I think that's going to be the key. If the government realizes they can't eradicate the tree, they'll have to do what Daffy said and remove the monopoly."

They decided to go up to the clearing at first light, see if the seedlings had survived, and bring down a plant for Ariadne and some for George. "Those must go in the mudroom," said Jane. "I'm not having the greenhouse overrun by hordes of tourists."

"They're not tourists, Mum."

"Whatever. We'll use the fruit stand, and see if we can use Vern's and the Dhasis' as well." They would serve as focal points for the invasion, she explained. "It might reduce the damage."

*   *   *

Jane stood at the open linen closet, taking out sheets and towels. Daffy's face fell.

"Mum," she began.

"No, Daffy."

"But Mum—"

Jane closed the closet. "I wouldn't be comfortable about it, and I don't think Michael would either. As for your father, you know he'd have a fit." She walked along the hall, watched sadly by Daffy, and joined David in the guest room.

She put the towels in the bathroom and waited while he finished putting the fitted bottom sheet on the bed. Then she shook out the top sheet.

David picked up a blanket. "I feel as if I'd won the jackpot," he said and stared unseeing at the wall. He looked at Jane as she straightened up. "She's the loveliest person I've ever met."

Jane smiled. *Like father, like daughter.*

*   *   *

Mike sat cross-legged on the floor contemplating the ten silver dollars from Mrs. Bagnold. They lay in two stacks of five coins each on the window seat before him. He frowned and rearranged them into five groups of two. No change. He tried three groups: three, three and four. Nothing. There was no good feeling to be had from these coins.

Money did not make you safe. It did not compensate for losing Dad. And he didn't like the way this particular money made him feel. He hadn't stolen it but he felt as if he had.

Mrs. Bagnold wasn't a soaker after all, but he didn't want her to be a soakee either.

He reached a decision and pushed the stacks together into one jumbled heap of coins.

*   *   *

Jane was in the barn, putting primer on a long strip of plywood, when the van pulled in. A tall man got out, and a woman. Angus dashed over to make their acquaintance, and Jane turned, holding the paintbrush over the can. She smiled and the woman, whose face seemed familiar, looked away. Jane regarded the man.

"What can I do for you?"

"Ma'am." He, too, looked away and she knew instantly what this was about. He turned back to face her, with an effort. "My name's Eric Watts." He grimaced and his voice cracked. "I was here the other night."

Jane looked at him. "What were you thinking?" She had not spoken of that night to anyone and she was suddenly shaken by a gust of pent-up anger. "You—"

She put down the paint brush and walked over to confront him. "What were you thinking?" She caught herself before saying something worse.

Watts had the russet skin of one who works outdoors and his hands, clasped before him, showed nicks and cuts. He wore slacks and a sweater over shirt and tie. "I got no excuse, Mrs. Frisby. If it helps any, I haven't been able to sleep since that night."

Jane regarded him silently. "So," she said at last. "You drank far too much and did a very stupid thing. Is that it?"

He nodded miserably.

She stared out at the cove unseeing. Eventually, she sighed. "I suppose we've all done that at one time or another. I know I have."

"I doubt you ever said you'd burn someone's house down." He turned away, pulling out a handkerchief.

"No," she conceded, "but I've done things I'd give a great deal to undo."

Eric blew his nose violently. Jane's glance fell on the woman and she smiled. "Haven't we met?"

"The Hospice—"

"Sheila!" Jane's voice betrayed relief at the prospect of a change of subject. "I do apologize."

As chair of an umbrella charity that assisted various organizations and activities pertaining to the sick, Jane generally met all the volunteers at least once through the year. She'd visited the Sidney Hospice a number of times. "I hope you had a lovely Christmas?"

Eric gestured at the paint can. "Mind if I finish that for you, ma'am?"

"That's not necessary."

"Let him do it, please," said Sheila. "He's not good at talking."

So Eric took over the painting, after removing his sweater and rolling up his sleeves. When he finished the first board, he primed the second and third. "The house is a mess," said Jane, explaining that she wouldn't invite them in. But she brought out coffee and had a cup with Sheila while Eric went around to the yard and began to split logs for the kindling basket.

They were a couple in their thirties, Jane learned as she and Sheila walked down through the orchard, and they lived at the harbor. Eric worked for a construction company in Sidney and they had two children. Sheila had not worked while the children were very young, but now she was taking a legal secretarial course and would shortly be looking for a job. "We don't live high on the hog, but it's so hard to save." She still had difficulty facing Jane. "When the markets went down these last few weeks, it looked like all our savings were for nothing. It just makes you mad."

She looked out at the cove. "This is nice up here, isn't it? Except for those boats." They talked about the quarantine and when they returned up through the orchard to the house, the woodpile was tidy and the kindling box was full. *Should I thank him,* Jane wondered. She nodded instead. He nodded back, and after saying goodbye, Sheila joined him and they drove away.

*   *   *

David dug out another seedling and transferred it to a plastic pot. Mike had left hours ago to deliver Ariadne's tree. Daffy sat on a rock gazing out at the cordon.

"Mind lending a hand, Daff?" They had decided to move all the seedlings, not just the few for George. "I want to get those shepherd's pies done."

She looked over at him. "I'm glad you're a good cook, David. It's so important."

"Cooking's easy. I'll teach you."

Daffy got back to work, carefully removing the heaped mulch from around a seedling to expose the burlap sacking underneath. She ripped a wider hole in the burlap and used her trowel to dig up the plant. "Honestly, when I think of all the work it took to bring these up here."

"Good thing you did, though."

Later they stopped for lunch, sitting on a rock looking out at the cordon.

"Daff, what do you think about kids? I know it's a bit soon, but I was thinking several. Simon, Belinda, Megan and—"

"David. We can't start a family until we fix the tax code."

"What?"

"We have to fix the tax code. That's the next job. It's awful. It's unfair and wasteful and inefficient."

"Maybe we could do both."

Daffy shook her head. "Mum always says, one thing at a time."

"But there are two of us, Daff. You can take the lead on the tax code. I'll take the lead on the family."

She looked at him doubtfully. He nodded and saw the smile of distilled sweetness that transformed her face. His throat tightened. "Ah, Daff." He bent his head and kissed her.

"Oh, David, I'm going to love you so much you just can't believe."

* * *

Mike skidded on the gravel and pedaled along the driveway to the garage.

"Hullo, darling. Come and hold Angus, will you?"

He propped his bike against the wall. In the space normally occupied by the car, currently parked on the hillside where David and Daffy could load seedlings, a white board, perhaps two feet deep by six long was propped against some cardboard boxes of books. It was wrapped in newspaper except for brown paper stencil letter cutouts. Mike held Angus as

Jane shook a can of spray paint. The stenciled letters changed from white to green. "Money Trees."

"Nice."

"We'll dismantle the fruit stand and move it to the cove."

"What about the harbor end?"

She pointed to the other plywood boards. "One for the Parkers, one for the Dhasis."

They got to their feet. "I thought you were helping to move the trees," said Jane.

Mike leaned against the wall and took out a silver dollar. He flipped it. The coin felt good. Solid and heavy and good. "Mrs. Bagnold paid me." Angus whined, sensing his satisfaction.

"In silver?" She smiled and turned back to the sign to remove the stencil. "I thought she paid you on Saturdays."

"Yeah. She gave me ten dollars."

Jane peeled the stencil away. "Can you move this one carefully over to the wall."

Mike put his coin away and propped the finished sign against the wall, then brought over the second one and helped his mother position the stencil.

Jane shook the spray can. She stopped. "Ten dollars? In silver?"

"Yeah." Mike spoke casually, holding Angus. He felt his mother's eye on him and glanced up. "It was too much."

"Did you tell her that?"

"Yeah. Sort of." He pulled a face. "So anyway, I went back today. You going to spray that thing?"

Jane recollected the spray can, gave Mike a look, then shook and sprayed a green "Money Trees" on the second board. "What happened?" She turned back to him.

"We negotiated. I kept one."

Jane stared at him, unable to believe what she was hearing. "She gave you ten silver dollars and you gave her nine back?"

He flipped the coin again. "Probably worth at least twenty bucks. It's a win-win situation, Mum." He looked at his mother. She wasn't smiling but she looked sort of lit up anyway. He moved the second board away.

"I'd be fascinated to hear how that conversation went," she said, while they taped the third board. So Mike told her all about how he'd explained hyperinflation to Mrs. Bagnold, and told her how much her coins were probably worth, and how she could use just one of them or even just a quarter, to buy stuff, and they'd last quite a while. Jane listened and asked questions and when he finished she looked at him silently.

"I'm proud to know you, Michael Frisby," she said at last.

He stepped back. "You are?"

She nodded.

"Because of the coins?"

"And because you took the time to explain how she could use them."

He saw approval in her gaze, and acceptance. His lips trembled and he stumbled toward her.

Jane put her arms around him. "My lovely boy," she whispered, head bent over his.

They drove the tractor down to the point after the signs were finished. Mike stood on the hitch, his arms round Jane's waist, and Angus trotted behind.

"Family's good to have, isn't it, Mum?" he said.

"It's the best security in the world, darling."

Chapter 25

The G20

Halloran was in his office when Gumble called.

"Sir, you'll want to see this."

"What is it?"

"One of our people in northern California. She's found a bunch of trees."

"Define bunch." Halloran was testy from lack of sleep.

"At least twenty. They're well established. I'm sending more people up from Sacramento."

When Halloran reached the command center, he found the focus had shifted to southern Oregon. The agent's expression told him this was serious. "What?"

The agent gestured to a fifty-inch wall screen, on which appeared film of a forested area. "This is south of Grants Pass."

In amongst the pines and firs, Halloran saw money tree after money tree. None of them were as large or luxuriant as the Frisbys' trees, but there were plenty of them. Halloran sighed.

"It gets worse," said the agent. He pulled up another film. "This is from Agent Gumble in the Sacramento Valley." The picture showed evergreen trees along the side of a road, with cultivated fields beyond. The picture zoomed: a money tree. Panned to the left and zoomed again.

"What?" Halloran couldn't see anything except two evergreens.

"On the ground, sir."

He looked at the ground between the trees. There was a hole, perhaps two feet in diameter. His eyes met the agent's.

"We found a lot of them, sir," said the agent. "Holes, I mean."

*   *   *

The meeting with the Secretary was unhappy. None of the G20 countries cared to admit defeat, and no one wanted to be the first to suggest lifting the monopoly on money creation. Halloran got to his feet. About to leave, he turned back to the Secretary. "Do we continue defending the dollar? I've got a report of a counterfeiting ring in St Louis. I'm wondering whether—"

"Of course! That's your job, Halloran." The Secretary smiled briefly. "You'll probably be glad to get back to chasing real counterfeiters." He sensed a stillness in the other man and looked up. "I meant . . . chasing *traditional* counterfeiters, Halloran. You'll be glad to be doing that, I'm sure."

*   *   *

Back in his office, Halloran took a call from Yves Simard.

"The British and Germans have been interrogating Frisby. It seems SBP is not a factor, Jack. They had a single tree, quite a sickly one at that. In Dusseldorf. It's been put out of its misery."

Halloran grunted. The entire staff of SBP's Boston facility had been interviewed, and no one had known anything about growing money. The hundred-dollar bet had undoubtedly been paid with a Frisby bill, one of those still in the system. "Any more trees in the UK?"

"Those three, but there are rumors of more. They're still looking. Frisby lived on the same street as the woman who had the Falmouth tree." Yves paused, then added, "The UK authorities want to charge him with unlawful importation of a foreign plant."

"What's that, a misdemeanor?" Halloran was sour.

"I have no idea." He paused, then went on: "Our people are charging him with improperly importing plants with novel traits."

There was a dangerous silence. "Are you kidding me?"

"I know."

"Plants with—?"

"Novel traits."

There was a lengthy silence. Halloran heaved a sigh. "It certainly fits that bill. Any jail time?"

"Just fines, I'm afraid."

"For God's sake!"

"We should send him to the chair?"

"Damn right," said Halloran.

"Well." The Gallic shrug was almost audible. "You know. We Canadians are soft on crime."

"Damn right," said Halloran.

Chapter 26

The Invasion

Jane's cell phone woke her and she shot out of bed. It was David, stationed at the fruit stand. "It's over. Come on down."

The cordon was visible from her bedroom window in the dawn light. It was not yet moving but movement showed on all its boats. David disconnected to call the Parkers and Dhasis, and Jane was about to turn away when she heard the buzz of a small plane. Beyond the western ridge, Ariadne's plane rose into the dawn sky and headed north.

Jane threw open bedroom doors and woke the children, and her phone rang. She took a call then turned it off and dashed downstairs to put the coffee on, relieved that she had insisted on an early night. They'd had a hunch today might be the day, and before going to bed they had distributed all the seedlings, and David had stayed all night at the fruit stand.

Last night, they'd joined the other islanders for dinner at the harbor, and had been made welcome. Mooring the runabout at the wharf steps, they'd been greeted by the Parkers, Johnstons and Dhasis. Morgan Lee had offered a smile and an elbow, and Jane had laughed and been escorted along the wharf, with David and Daffy behind her.

"You come with me, kid," said Ron to Mike, and took him over to Vern's fire pit, where two spits were rotating, and trestle tables from the annex held cold salmon, hot casseroles, vegetables and preserves.

The harbor was strung with lights between the pylons, and a makeshift group consisting of the church organist, three-fourths of a string quartet, a guitar and a trumpet played jazz and light classics and rock and roll all evening. Jane agreed to serve on the Channel Dredging committee and Daffy and David talked about money with a group of brokers and investors. The evening closed with "Smoke Gets in Your Eyes," and as the trumpet soared, pure and clear, into the night sky, a flare went up beyond the cordon, and then another. That had not happened before, and the islanders agreed it might portend a change in their circumstances.

This morning, Mike gulped his breakfast and dashed down to the stand, followed soon after by Jane. Vern arrived, dropped his father off and took Daffy and David. Ron checked to see that the doors of the house were locked, then carried a wicker rocker to the corner of the verandah. From there he could monitor the yard as well as the front. He pulled out a jackknife and began to whittle a piece of kindling, feeling no pain.

Down at the cove, Jane and Mike watched as a large luxury motor yacht nosed its way past numerous small craft. It dropped anchor and a small inflatable materialized from the rear and roared toward the shore. Out stepped a large Asian male in a white suit. He surveyed the sign. "Wonderful! I'll take your entire stock."

"May I ask where you're from?" Jane handed him a money tree.

"Singapore, madam."

Perfect, thought Mike.

"How much for all of them?"

"One per boat," said Jane, adding, "You're welcome to look for more on the hillside." She couldn't see the suit doing that, but he could send a minion if he wanted.

A middle-aged couple ran up, took a tree with thanks, and dashed off again. "Tofino," they called back, in answer to Jane's question.

"What a waste," she murmured to Mike. Tofino was on the west coast of Vancouver Island.

"North Dakota," said a lanky individual wearing a leather belt with a large gold buckle in the shape of a Stetson. He saw Mike's skepticism and added, "Flew out to Portland, hired a boat." He handed over a card. "Tell your dad I'd be glad to talk to him about a consulting job." He nodded to Jane and walked back to his boat.

"Did you see his belt, Mum?"

Another man loped up, bearded and deep-voiced. "Which one are you," he asked Mike, "warped or maladjusted?" He roared with laughter, and Jane bent over and crooned to his tree. "Don't worry, little MB," she soothed.

The drooping fronds rose and the bearded man gaped at his tree and at Jane. She straightened and looked severe. "Did you read the book?"

Other people had gathered.

"Yes, ma'am. What did you call it?"

"MB. Meshach's Baby." She addressed all of them. "You really must be careful not to make too much noise, especially while they're small."

Several people nodded and the bearded man, handling his tree like a Ming vase, tiptoed back to his boat whispering hoarsely, "Say, little guy, you and me are gonna be good friends."

"Guadalajara," said a Mexican couple. "Gracias."

"Burlington," said another couple.

"Ontario?" Jane handed them a tree.

"Vermont." No one wanted to chat.

After twenty trees, they called a halt, telling boaters they were free to explore the property. They wanted to give the sailboats an equal opportunity.

"It's not fair," the first sailor began as she ran up, a girl of Daffy's age. She broke into a grin as Jane gave her a tree, and dashed off.

"Damned motorboats," said the second sailor, a man from San Diego.

Two Koreans left with a tree, and several more North Americans, along with people from Panama, Bermuda, Honduras and Brazil.

*   *   *

"Ooh, Daffy! Can I have your autograph?"

Raaj Dhasi laughed as Daffy signed her name for one of the boaters. The Dhasis had erected a small stand in the middle of the central valley road. Raaj and Navi had built a barrier on either side of it, to discourage invaders from plundering the fields. Assorted Dhasi relatives were patrolling the fields, just to be safe. Daffy gave away money trees and answered questions.

"Do you think we should switch to Bitcoin?" The speaker was a young American.

"Do you?"

"I don't know, that's why I'm asking. Have you used it?"

"No," said Daffy. "Except for the website. But I'm going to try it."

"Yeah. Maybe for small stuff, do you think?"

"See how you like it," agreed Daffy, and added, "I'd like to see a digital currency that's actually back by something." She handed a tree to a Danish couple.

"Want to buy some veggies?" said Raaj. "Prevent scurvy." The Dhasis were having a bumper sales day.

The young American was still hovering. "What's happened with the dollar?" asked Daffy.

"They said it's going to be backed by gold. They have to work out the details. And Congress is supposed to pass legislation today. That's what they said, anyway."

"For what? To lift the monopoly?"

He nodded.

"Wow," said Daffy. "That's amazing."

"Good luck with Bitcoin," said the American and took his tree.

"Same to you," Daffy called after him.

*   *   *

Once their forty trees were given away, Mike dashed off on his bike to see the action down at the harbor. Jane joined Ron on the verandah and they drank coffee and watched people scavenging all over the hillside on the west, and around the burnt grove area on the east.

A group of invaders headed for the side door and Jane ran to deal with them, while Ron watched an approaching orange search and rescue helicopter. It set down fifty feet away, in the field, and George emerged and waved to the pilot as it rose and left.

"Hiya, George," called Ron. "Good to see you back."

"What's going on? Where is everyone?" George walked up to the verandah.

"Jane's out back." Ron stood up, looking downfield. "Hey! Stop that!"

George turned to see two young men, bearded, in shorts and sandals, galloping down to the cove carrying a six-foot balsam fir. He felt an unreasoning anger and started after them. "Bring that back!"

They reached their boat and began to load the tree. One of them looked up, hearing George's voice, and bellowed back. "Why are you so mean?"

George stopped. "Why are you so stupid?"

The invader elevated a finger and they tumbled into the boat with their prize and maneuvered out of the cove. George calmed down and saw the funny side and began to laugh, then turned to see Jane coming around the side of the house. They met in the field. "Hello, love," he kissed her. "Did you see those two idiots?"

"Are you all right? Did they torture you or anything like that?"

"They kept me away from my family, if that's what you mean. They had the manual but they refused to believe what it said. I had to repeat everything twice." He put an arm around her and they walked up to the verandah. "There are bad things coming, Jane. I'm not sure what," he added in response to her look. "I'm out on bail, effectively, and not allowed to leave the country."

Jane was phlegmatic. "Whatever it is, darling, we'll face it together."

They reached the verandah and he greeted Ron and pulled over another chair. "What's the fruit stand doing down there?"

Jane told him about Daffy's hundred seedlings. "There are six in the mudroom for you, darling," she said. "And if I see one more person trying to break in I'll get out the rolling pin and start doing some damage."

George was elated to hear about the seedlings. "Good for Daffy! You know, they wanted me to stay there and work with their people. 'After you burned down my trees?' I said. 'I don't think so.'"

"Attaboy," said Ron.

*   *   *

They were in the kitchen eating lunch when the others returned. Ron left with Vern, while David busied himself chasing off gawkers and novice botanists. George gathered both children in a hug, and heard all their news.

"Before I forget," he said when they were seated round the table, "Yves sent his regards."

"My Yves?" said Jane. "You met him?"

Daffy clapped her hands in delight.

"I not only met him, I actually spent quite a bit of time with him. Do you know, Jane, he's a world authority on counterfeiting? You picked a good one there, love."

"He never remembered me, George. You're pulling my leg."

George assured her he was not. "I didn't want to embarrass him in front of his colleagues but I told him privately how much he'd helped you, and a couple of days later he took me to one side and said he remembered the conversation because you had a pleasant voice. He promised to look us up the next time he's out this way."

Mike suddenly remembered the website. He used Daffy's tablet and logged on to his Bitcoin account. Jane heard a small gasp. "One million dollars. . . ." he breathed reverently.

Daffy extended an arm and he handed over the tablet. She studied the screen. "Mikey," a gentle admonition. She handed it back and he looked again and drew a ragged breath. Jane laughed.

"*Ten* million dollars," he said hoarsely.

"We get half, Dad and I."

He rose from the table, his eyes glued to the screen. "Fifteen percent is what you get."

David heard that as he came in. "I think he's fixated on that amount."

"That's what authors get."

Daffy followed him. "I'll bet Stephen King gets more than fifteen percent."

"I'm going to create a foundation for pre-teens."

"Fine. You can do that with your share."

"Pre-teens are the most abused, overworked and under-appreciated people on the planet."

"Great to see you, George."

George looked puzzled.

Mike could be heard clumping up the stairs. "You're talking to the president of the Pre-Teen Foundation."

"Give me that tablet."

"I thought you were in England," said George to David. "Isn't that my sweater?"

*   *   *

Later on they compared notes and tallied up the countries. "Twelve," Jane announced. She sat at her desk in the den with George, back in his rightful place opposite her.

"Did you count Denmark?"

"Don't forget Ariadne," said David. "She took off at dawn."

"Ariadne Wu?" George raised an eyebrow.

Jane recalculated. "Thirteen countries."

"I negotiated with her, Dad."

"I don't think she knew what hit her," said Jane, regarding Mike with pride.

George looked from his son to his wife and back to Mike again. He reached out an arm. "Did you grow while I was gone? You look at least an inch taller."

*   *   *

Daffy's favorite blogger was euphoric.

... It's difficult to see what form such a system might take but if the bureaucrats can keep their regulatory hands off it for a while, we may end up with a more streamlined financial system, with lower fees and more innovative products and services, and massive job creation potential. The coming days and weeks are going to be difficult as we all adjust to less spending power, but we're all in the same boat.... A dollar backed in some fashion by precious metals should serve as an adequate stopgap currency.... Borrowers, investors, savers and consumers will be looking

for different features and benefits.... As new issuers arise,
they may choose to apply to join the federal reserve system....

Congress was debating lifting the restrictions on money
creation. Two senators had come out firmly in favor of
competing currencies, and a vote was expect late that
evening.

Daffy had been invited to appear on the Will McIver show,
airing immediately after the Prime Minister's address to the
nation, and David had flown to Vancouver with her in the
helicopter. The Frisbys sat in the TV room listening to the
speech. The Prime Minister had announced that the Canadian dollar would be backed by precious metals in some
complicated ratio determined by the G20 finance ministers.
An amendment to the legal tender laws was to be tabled next
week in the House of Commons, removing the government
monopoly on currency creation. And a Royal Commission
was to be set up to examine potential new currencies.

"She won't like that," said George.

Jane was comfortable with Royal Commissions. "Imagine
if it had been the CRTC."

"Mum. That's TV."

The Prime Minister wound up, the Canadian flag disappeared and moments later, Will McIver appeared with
several guests. Daffy had opted for green hair, in honor of
the new currency era, and she was easy to spot amid the
treasury boffins, bankers and analysts. After these guests
had expressed varying degrees of approval with the speech,
McIver invited Daffy to give her opinion.

"Why do we need a Royal Commission?" She looked at
the other guests, at McIver and at the camera. "What have

Canadians got against competition? That's what I want to know."

The Frisbys could see a speech coming. "Steady on, Daff," said Jane.

Daffy seemed to gather herself. "All I have to say is, if Satoshi Nakamoto had had to get approval from a Royal Commission, we'd still be waiting for Bitcoin."

The banker said something about unbridled competition.

"What does that even mean?" Daffy glared at him.

*   *   *

"Forgot to mention," said George later. They were back in the den, and he was putting his bookcase in order. "They analyzed the DNA and it's official. No more pseudo. It's *Juniperus lucre.*"

"Well done, darling," Jane was dealing with a backlog of emails. She smiled across the two desks. "Dancing with the Stars tonight."

"Excellent. . . ."

THE END

Acknowledgments

I'm grateful to Christopher Weber and the late Jerome F. Smith for their research and writing on the subject of money and banking. I was fortunate to serve as editor to both for several years. Mr. Smith's *The Reinstitution of Money* described the origins of money, and its key characteristics. And Christopher Weber is a brilliant and independent mind in the field of money and investments, someone who weighs both Fed statistics and Main Street activity before making his recommendations. His newsletter is available at www.weberglobal.net/.

I want to thank editor Barbara Pulling for her review of an earlier draft. She liked many elements and quite decisively did not like others, and thereby played a significant role in shaping this story.

Many thanks to readers Ruth Binney (who also served as botanical guru), Laurence French, Sheila Martin and Connie Flanagan. Thanks also to Chris Weber for reviewing the economics and Jeremy Bonney at Coindesk (www.coindesk.com) for reviewing the Bitcoin discussion in Chapter 9. Needless to say, any errors or omissions are my own.

As always, a thank you to my sister for her encouragement.

About the Author

Helen Yeomans was born in England and raised in Canada. She worked in book publishing in Toronto and London, then launched her own firm, providing editing and later writing services to corporate clients worldwide. She began writing fiction more than 20 years ago. *The Money Tree* is her third novel.

For more information, visit www.helenyeomans.com.

*   *   *

Please consider expressing your opinion of this book on Amazon (www.amazon.com) or GoodReads (www.goodreads.com), or by email to comments@helenyeomans.com.

CPSIA information can be obtained at www.ICGtesting.com
Printed in the USA
LVOW10s1820021213

363586LV00003B/11/P